TETHERED TO OTHER STARS

TETHERED TO OTHER ☆ STARS

ELISA STONE LEAHY

Quill Tree Books
An Imprint of HarperCollinsPublishers

Quill Tree Books is an imprint of HarperCollins Publishers.
Tethered to Other Stars
Copyright © 2023 by Elisabeth Leahy
All rights reserved. Printed in the United States of America.
No part of this book may be used or reproduced in any manner
whatsoever without written permission except in the case of
brief quotations embodied in critical articles and reviews. For
information address HarperCollins Children's Books, a division of
HarperCollins Publishers, 195 Broadway, New York, NY 10007.
www.harpercollinschildrens.com
Library of Congress Control Number: 2023933186
ISBN 978-0-06-325548-7
23 24 25 26 27 LBC 5 4 3 2 1
First Edition

For Edith Espinal, who should never have had to seek sanctuary
to keep her family together.

And for Graciela, Mateo, and Rosali.
My Sunshine, my Warrior, and mi Bella Estrella.

Matthew, you'll have to wait until the next one.

ONE

WENDY AND TOM sat on the plastic-wrapped sofa in the middle of the sidewalk and stared up at the crooked house.

"Papá knows houses." Tom's voice was confident, as usual. "He would know if it wasn't okay."

"You think it's *supposed* to sag in like that?" Wendy's voice was skeptical, as usual.

She eyed the dip in the roof, the angled redbrick walls, pockmarked where the mortar had chipped away. "The whole thing is practically curling up to die. I'm *so* sure that's a design choice."

On the rickety front porch, their dad was attempting to peel the city notices from the filthy door. Their mom stood back warily, a box of cleaning supplies clutched tightly in her arms, watching as the paper came off in thin, reluctant strips.

"Papá better be gentle with that," Wendy muttered. "This place looks like it's held up by thoughts and prayers."

1

Tom snorted. "Nah, it's just old," he said. "Remember what Papá said? Like a hundred and fifty years old. He checked out the foundation and all that stuff, though. And he said they just redid the roof last year."

Wendy squinted at the house. In some places the walls seemed to bend, like objects did when you looked at them through a concave lens. But refraction, while valuable in a telescope, was 100 percent not something you wanted in the walls where you lived.

"Yeah, he told us how old it was, like, five times," she said. "I just didn't think it would have *actual wrinkles*."

Tom let out a laugh and Wendy's mouth tipped into an almost smile. It had been a long time since she'd heard her older brother laugh. Too long.

Papá scraped off the last paper notice and dug a key from his pocket. He turned to wave it at them, looking pleased, and Wendy felt a sudden pang of homesickness.

The strips of white-and-red paper hanging limply from his hand reminded her of the intricate tissue paper banners that Mamá and the other women had hung from the streetlamps last July fourth. Wendy remembered sitting outside their apartment building, the steamy pavement warming her flip-flops as her best friend, Alicia, braided her hair and Don Leo scowled at them from across the street.

"*My* dad is 'señor.' *Your* dad is 'señor.' So why does grumpy Leo get to be a *Don*?" Alicia had whispered as she finished weaving the red ribbon into Wendy's braid. "Remember when your brother made his girlfriend watch that movie and we spied on them? *The Godfather*? It was all *Don* this and *Don* that, and he was a *mob boss!*" She widened her eyes dramatically. "Just saying."

Wendy had snorted with laughter and pulled her friend out of sight of the supposed mob boss. They'd giggled behind the Dumpster, hiding from Don Leo while the mouthwatering scent of tamales and Peruvian anticuchos flavored the bright summer night. Tom sat on the front stoop with his girlfriend, Gina, strumming his guitar. More neighbors found their way out to the street, unfolding their chairs under the fluttering paper banners. One of them joined in with the music from Tom's guitar, banging out a rhythm on a wooden box. Then someone started dancing and soon everyone was in the road, their feet a blur of movement. Alicia grabbed Wendy's hand and marched her in a dramatic tango down the block until they collapsed on the curb to share a giant bowl of syrupy shaved ice. They squealed together when Don Leo caught them staring at him. But he smiled through the crowd, his cane swaying as it dangled from his arm, his trembling hand on Tía Ceci's shoulder as they danced across the pavement. The Fourth of July firecrackers popped like stars in the darkening sky over their little street, a whole galaxy of cultures dancing in celebration of this country.

It felt like light-years ago.

"I wish we were still in Melborn." Wendy's voice was just loud enough for Tom to hear.

He nodded, his eyes on their parents as Papá struggled with the rusty lock. "Yeah . . . well, *they* don't."

Wendy bit her lip. Melborn had been their home for half her life, ever since they had moved from South Carolina to the Midwest when she was six. But over the past year, everything had changed. The tension crept in slowly, suffocating their whole apartment block. Kids stopped playing outside. Grown-ups peeked out the window before rushing to their cars for work. Neighbors stopped sharing gossip on the stoop. Entire families faded away.

"Besides, Melborn sucked for middle school, kid."

Wendy looked at him, narrowing her eyes. "You did fine in middle school."

"Sure, but I'm Torpedo Tom, track star."

He grinned, stretching his arms out over the back of the couch. Even with the plastic crinkling every time he moved, he actually looked cool. Wendy wrinkled her nose. She'd been "Torpedo Tom's sister" all last year at Melborn Middle. It was probably good that she wouldn't have to start seventh grade at a place where everyone was part of her big brother's fan club. She couldn't compete with his movie star looks. At least her grades were better than his.

"Besides," he added, reading her mind, "you're too brainy for Melborn. Genius Academy is way more your thing." She dug her elbow at him, and he yelped.

"That's not what it's called! Anyway, I don't know anyone there." Wendy heard the whine in her voice and hated it. She kicked the ragged toe of her blue Converse sneaker against a crack in the uneven sidewalk. "Probably wouldn't know anyone back home either. Who knows if anyone's even left in Melborn," she muttered at the ground.

Tom's smile faded instantly. Wendy kept her eyes on the cracked cement. Neither of them had mentioned the raids for months, not since Papá sat them down and told them they were moving. He hadn't said why and they hadn't asked. There were some things they all knew to avoid. The universe was full of asteroids and black holes and other things that could demolish the entire planet. But thinking about them wouldn't help. So her family stuck to their own safe orbit. According to Papá, that meant blending in. And what better place than Rooville—their new, All-American neighborhood in Columbus, Ohio.

Wendy made herself look up. The houses next to theirs were much nicer than the cramped apartments back home. Good thing Papá's construction business was doing so well. Buying a house in Rooville, even a run-down one no one wanted, must have been expensive. The lawns were all neatly mowed, and she saw a cat curled up on a windowsill next door. A sleek black SUV drove by. She watched it turn the corner and noticed the tip of a church steeple peeking over the sloping roof of the crooked house. Shiny cars, pets, and a little white church. She'd bet no one here had ever disappeared in the middle of the night. Like Don Leo. And Gina. And Alicia.

5

Wendy clenched her teeth and blinked hard. She felt Tom's hand press down on her shoulder, just for a moment. Then he sprang up and turned to the truck.

"I'm taking in a load and then I call dibs on rooms! No more of you messing with my stuff, Chiquitín!"

Yeah, at least they had that. For the first time in Wendy's life, she wouldn't have to share space with a big brother who called her *little one*. She grabbed an armload of bins and followed him up the worn front steps.

TWO

WENDY BLINKED AS her eyes adjusted to the gloom inside. Ahead of her, Mamá glanced from the cracked floorboards to the ceiling and immediately scurried aside with a gasp of, "¡Ay, Diosito lindo!" Wendy followed her gaze up and took a quick step back. The grimy chandelier appeared to be hanging by spiderwebs. Its cable had partly ripped out of the white tiles, leaving it dangling dangerously low.

Papá touched Mamá's arm gently with his rough hands and murmured something in Spanish. Wendy didn't bother asking what it meant. Her parents would only say, "You are American. You speak English." And Alicia wasn't here to whisper translations anymore.

But then Papá looked at Wendy and Tom and said in English, "These things may be broken, but they are *our* broken things. And that means we can fix them."

He looked so hopeful that Wendy had to smile back, even though the expression felt rusty and cobwebby, like

7

the house. Then Mamá clapped her hands together, the sound ringing through the empty room. Her small frame seemed to grow as she glared at the dusty walls. Wendy recognized the look and set the plastic bins down quickly, backing away as Mamá began unpacking spray bottles and brushes. Mamá was about to wage a war of vinegar and Pine-Sol, and she did not want to get caught up in it. There were three whole bedrooms upstairs, and one of them was waiting for her.

The first bedroom definitely had something living in the closet. *Seventy-three percent chance it's mice*, she thought, retreating from the scurrying noises. The second bedroom had a sagging piece of tile rimmed with brown stains smack in the middle of the ceiling. Having a contractor dad had taught Wendy enough to know what *that* meant. A leaky roof. *Which they just fixed*, she reminded herself.

A grimy tarp dangled in the doorway to the third bedroom. Wendy pushed it aside gingerly, took one step inside, and froze. An inch in front of her blue Converse shoes, the floor ended. She could actually see the downstairs between the beams and unidentifiable house guts. One more step and her leg would have gone straight through the ceiling into the dining room. "Okaaay, I guess that's not my room," she whispered, backing slowly away.

"Wait, the room without a floor is *my* room? Why can't that be Tom's?"

Papá's hand reached out from under the kitchen sink. "Pass me something to catch this water! ¡Apúrate! Hurry!"

Wendy grabbed one of the disposable food containers Mamá reused until the lettering on the side was impossible to make out anymore. Maybe yogurt. Or sour cream. Papá slid it under the water spraying from the sink trap. It smelled like something dead. Wendy's eyes watered and her throat hurt. *Don't cry*, she told herself. *It's pointless, illogical.* But she couldn't ignore the sinking feeling inside. With everything else this house needed and Papá's contracting work already booked up for months, there was no chance she'd have a room by the end of the year.

Wendy whirled toward the door that led from the kitchen to the backyard. The rusty hinges screeched horribly as she pushed outside. Through blurry eyes, she saw a large stump near the back fence and shoved through the weeds toward it, her breath short and labored. Alicia was gone and their old street was empty anyway and she couldn't even unpack her stuff. Her books and binoculars, her lamp that projected stars on to the ceiling—all in boxes for who knew how long. She collapsed onto the stump's flat surface, trying to breathe in between the sobs that now shook her body. Her throat was too tight. Wendy coughed, rubbing her hands on her shorts, and reached for her inhaler, just in case. Her pocket was empty. A sudden jolt of panic hit her in the stomach. The air felt heavy now and she gripped the stump with her fingernails, gulping oxygen. She should stand up, go inside, and find the inhaler. But her body was betraying her, still heaving with sobs, and she had to focus all her energy on breathing.

"Hey, are you okay?"

Wendy jumped. She'd felt completely alone out here, with the high wooden fence surrounding this abandoned jungle of a yard. Her crying shuddered to a stop as she looked around.

"Sorry, didn't mean to scare you."

The voice came from the other side of the fence. Wendy couldn't see anything over the top except the back walls of the church across the alley. She leaned closer and squinted at a gap in the wooden boards. A wide grass-green eye looked back at her.

"I've cried like that before. Where you, like, cry so hard you can feel your throat almost touching your tongue in the back? Like your tonsils are turning inside out, you know?"

Wendy took a breath, letting oxygen fill her throat. She wasn't ready to say anything.

The girl—she thought it was a girl—didn't give her much time to answer anyway.

"Do you live here now? Is it scary inside? Is that why you're crying? I've never seen anyone go in there."

Wendy leaned closer to the crack in the fence. The eye leaned closer, too, the face around it pressing against the wood so closely that the tip of an upturned, freckled nose poked through.

"Do you speak English? Or . . . habla español?" the fence asked. "I'm learning. Un poquito."

This time Wendy had to answer. Quickly. "Of course I speak English!" She tried to sound clear, and very, very American. "I'm American," she added. Just to be sure.

"Oh, okay. Me too. But it'd be cool if you're not. I wish you spoke Spanish. My mom and I are learning so we can talk to Luz. What's your name?"

"Wendy!" called a voice loudly from the back door behind her.

Wendy jumped again. She had to stop doing that. Mamá was peeking out of the house toward the weedy corner where she sat. "Wendy, carry your things to the upstairs, please," Mamá called in her not-clear, not-American voice. "I have to clean the downstairs, and your things are under the foot."

Oh, no.

"Just a second!" she called, willing Mamá to go quickly back to the safe cocoon of walls and grime-covered, impenetrable windows. *Please*, she thought, *don't say anything else.* She wasn't sure if she meant Mamá or the fence. She felt her chest relax a little as Mamá disappeared into the house.

"I have to go," she whispered to the fence.

"Was that your mom?" the fence whispered back. "Does *she* speak Spanish? Is your name Wendy? Like in *Peter Pan*?"

The question immediately made Wendy more irritated than nervous. "No! Wendy like Wendy Freedman, the astronomer."

That wasn't true even a little bit. Her mother had no idea who Wendy Freedman was and would never have named her after someone who spent their time "looking up to the heavens and not to where you put your feet," as she was constantly scolding Wendy. But Wendy had gotten so sick of kids asking her about Neverland that one day she googled "Wendy" and "astrophysics" and found Wendy Freedman's name. Astronomy was way better than some fairy tale.

"Why are we whispering?" whispered the fence. "Hey, you should come over to church later. I have to be there all day."

"You have to be at church all day?" Wendy asked, glancing at the church steeple. They were more of a special events churchgoing family, but even on holidays they never stayed all day.

"Well, my mom's the pastor. So sometimes it's really boring. But today is actually not bad. We're getting the room ready for Luz. Do you know about Luz? From the news? I made a sign for her with glitter, but I don't know if I wrote the Spanish words right. Hey, maybe your mom could help me with it?"

"Um," Wendy said, glancing back toward the house. She was pretty sure asking Mamá to help Fence Girl with Spanish was not the kind of blending in Papá had in mind. "I don't think so. We're moving in today, so, you know. Kind of a lot to do." Wendy slid off the stump.

"Really? Luz is moving in today too!"

Wendy frowned back at the fence. "Moving in? To the

church?" Just then she heard Mamá call her again and she hurried away with a quick "Goodbye!" to the fence.

A whisper of "Bye, Wendy!" followed her but she didn't turn around. Fence Girl seemed nice, but Wendy definitely hadn't wanted the first person she met in their new place to find her sobbing in the backyard. Or to ask for help with Spanish. And what had the girl meant about someone moving into the church? She sighed and rubbed her neck. Her lungs ached.

Her inhaler was nowhere to be found. After looking in three different boxes, Papá gave up and called the closest pharmacy. Mamá made her a cup of tea on their little camp stove while they waited. Wendy closed her eyes, breathing in the warm scent of chamomile as she listened.

"Yes, sir," Papá said, sounding as white as a Southern gentleman. Papá's voice always changed a bit on the phone, like he was sitting up straighter and answering a question from a teacher.

Unlike Mamá, Papá was born and raised in the US, and he could flavor his voice with a bit of his South Carolina twang whenever he wanted. Usually it would switch on around the older white ladies, the ones that shot quick, nervous glances at his black hair and dark eyes, scanning his clothes as they edged away. That voice would sweep in, and the fingers clutching at purses would relax under the comfortable warmth of a "Pardon me" or "You have a fine day now." On the phone his voice was especially different, like there was nothing keeping him from creating a whole invisible identity. Wendy was pretty sure he didn't even notice he did it.

"Wendy *Toe-lee-doe*. T-o-l-e-d-o. Yes, just like the city."

Tom had figured out that their Spanish last name was actually the same as a city in Ohio. He'd quickly learned that pronouncing it the American way made school roll calls easier, and by the time Wendy started school, all the teachers knew them as the *Toe-lee-doe* family.

After a hearty "Well, that's real kind of you," Papá hung up. Mamá took off her apron and reached for her purse, but Papá shook his head no. He called Tom over instead, directing him to the pharmacy and handing him some cash.

"You go too, Wendy," Papá said, beckoning her to the door. "The fresh air will help."

"Espera." Mamá reached for the door before he could close it.

"Dulce, no," Papá said, too quickly. It seemed he'd been waiting for her, expecting Mamá to follow them. "You stay inside. Tom will watch her."

Wendy tried not to notice the look on Mamá's face. This neighborhood wouldn't have immigration agents watching everyone like back in Melborn. And even if there were, Mamá had her papers. There was nothing to worry about. Papá was just being cautious.

"Yes, okay." Mamá's voice was stiff. "But they need to take this."

She handed them Wendy's health insurance card.

As they walked down their new street, Wendy pictured Mamá turning back to the kitchen and tying her apron on again, hidden inside behind the dirty windows.

THREE

TOM PUT ON his friendliest smile as they walked through the door of the pharmacy, and Wendy automatically looked for the security guard. The stores in their old neighborhood all had them, but there was only a bored teen who droned "Hellohowareyou" from behind the register.

If the pharmacist had expected them to look different after hearing Papá on the phone, he didn't show it. Wendy was grateful for that, but then he asked warmly how they liked it here and if it was very different from where they were from. Wendy tensed but Tom worked his usual magic. Soon he and the pharmacist were sharing opinions about college basketball while Wendy poked around racks of magazines and school supplies. She glared at a purple notebook with a fluffy cat wearing glasses on the cover. Cats wearing glasses made no sense. Alicia would love it, though. Alicia loved everything ridiculous—unicorn kitties and rainbow pandas and roller-skating llamas. Wendy looked away. She couldn't think about Alicia.

A white kid on a bike pulled up outside the front window and stopped to look at his phone. He was about her age, with honey-colored hair that fell in waves over his eyes. She wondered if it was hard for him to see. Suddenly he looked straight at her and smiled. Wendy gulped and glanced around. She was the only one anywhere on this side of the store. With a deep breath, she turned slowly back toward the boy. He was holding his phone in one hand and combing his hair with the fingers of his other hand. She smiled hesitantly back at him. What now? Wendy wanted very much to walk away. But wasn't that exactly why she could never make friends? This boy was giving her a chance. Should she wave? It looked like he was raising his hand. Feeling self-conscious but a bit brave, Wendy waved through the glass just as the boy on the bike lifted his phone and gave a strange, cool look somewhere above her head. He held the expression for a second, then glanced down at the screen. Wendy's brain flashed a warning as she mentally connected the dots. The sun was behind him, but his face was lit up. Which meant the light must be bouncing off the glass window, making it pretty hard to see inside. So he hadn't been looking at her . . . Wendy sucked in her breath and froze as the realization hit. He'd been looking at himself in the window. And he had just taken a picture of his reflection with his phone.

Please don't look up, Wendy thought frantically, her hand frozen midwave. Of course she was doing the only thing that might attract his attention. And of course he did look up. His blue eyes came into focus, locking onto her horrified face with a flash of surprise. Wendy dropped her hand and whirled away from the window. Her ears burned as she rushed around a shelf of batteries and straight into Tom. The paper bag in his hand crinkled as she pushed past him.

"Whoa, Chiquitín," he said, reaching out to stop her. "Where're you going?" He held up the bag. "I got your magic potion."

Then he noticed her bright red face and followed her darting eyes to the window.

"No, Tom! Get down!"

She pulled him around the corner, clipping a display and sending a couple bottles of suntan lotion rolling into the aisle.

"What?" His voice was suddenly tense, and he peered past her warily. "You see something?"

"Oh, no, it's—it's nothing," Wendy said, scrambling for the bottles and feeling a stab of guilt. It wasn't anything, not really. It was just—

"A boy?" Tom was leaning around the corner, looking at the street. "Who is he?" He sounded more curious now than worried. Wendy sank back, mortified.

"Hey, he's cute." His voice was definitely lighter now. Wendy could hear the teasing tone taking over.

18

"Was he checking you out?" Tom asked. Wendy glared. "Want to meet him?" Her brother continued. "Let's go say hi!" Tom barreled out of the aisle and toward the door and Wendy felt her stomach plummet.

"No way!" She shot after him, grabbing the back of his T-shirt. "Don't you dare!"

Tom was laughing. "Okay, okay. Look, he's gone anyway."

Wendy risked a glance at the empty window. The golden-haired boy was nowhere in sight.

It wasn't until they passed the library that Wendy finally forgot about the boy. Books about outer space lined the long row of library windows. Rocket-shaped posters proclaimed, "Blast Off with a Book!" Foil stars dangled from the ceiling and in the center of it all hung a giant, glittering sun with "READ TO WIN" emblazoned across it. Wendy stepped closer, her breath catching as she read the list of raffle prizes. There were passes to visit the Slettebak Planetarium at The Ohio State University. A year's subscription to *Sky & Telescope* magazine. A star map and a calendar of astronomical events for the next year. And the grand prize "Star Pack," which included all of the above plus a ticket to this year's Astronomy Convention at the planetarium in November. One entry with each completed Fall Reading Challenge.

"Tom," Wendy murmured. No answer. She turned to look at him. Her brother was absorbed in his phone, his face serious as he scrolled. Wendy looked away, her chest tight.

Alicia didn't have email or a phone, so Wendy had no way to contact her friend after she disappeared. But Tom had called Gina constantly after she left, leaving hushed, pleading messages, until that day Wendy found him staring straight ahead, his face drained and thin. She asked him what was wrong, her stomach knotting, and he held out the phone so she could hear *"This number has been disconnected"* looping in an efficient female voice. After that, Tom just waited. He wouldn't put his phone down, even during meals, his hand jerking for it every time a text came in, his eyes hopeful, then disappointed. The messages were never from Gina. Papá had finally snapped, threatening to cut off Tom's service if he couldn't look away from the screen, so he stopped checking it in front of their parents. Wendy wasn't sure which was worse—Tom never getting an answer or Wendy not being able to send any to begin with.

"Anything?" she asked quietly.

He blinked, as if coming up from an underwater dive. "Nah." He shrugged, pocketing his phone, then nodded over her shoulder. "Looks like this is your kind of place, nerd."

She looked back at the library display and grinned.

"Tom, I *need* to sign up for this!"

"Not now, Einstein." He grabbed her shoulder and there was something tense in his voice. Wendy looked at him, confused, just in time to see his face switch into the friendly and respectful expression he used with adults he didn't know.

Wendy turned to see who had prompted "the look" and a cool, strong voice said, "You kids heading down to the church?"

A black SUV had pulled up next to them, two white men in the front. They both wore plain T-shirts and baseball caps. The man on the passenger side had measuring, hard blue marbles for eyes, and they were locked on Tom's face. He draped one arm casually out the window, a smartwatch glinting on his wrist. His smile didn't show teeth, but he seemed like the kind of guy whose teeth would be white and straight.

Tom's hand was still on her shoulder and Wendy felt his fingers tighten.

But he responded easily, "No, sir, just heading to the library." Tom started to turn, gently nudging Wendy away from the strange car.

"Hang on." There was no hurry to the voice. The man expected to be obeyed. "You must be friends with Luz, right?"

Wendy swallowed, remembering the chattering girl behind the fence and the woman she'd made a sign for in Spanish. The woman who was moving into the church. The woman named Luz. Tom shook his head no, and Wendy gave hers a shake, too, hoping they looked convincing. Of course they did, she told herself. They *were* telling the truth. Still, she could feel her eyes aching to dart suspiciously away from that blue marble gaze and she forced herself to meet it head-on.

"Your parents must know her, then? Luz Ramos?"

Wendy could feel her heart pounding and she took a deep, slow breath. She thought of the inhaler in the paper bag.

The man glanced toward the end of the street.

"You kids live near here?" he asked. He was looking almost directly at the crooked house.

She heard Tom inhale a fraction, about to speak. Then his phone buzzed loudly. As he glanced at the screen, Wendy blurted out, "We can't talk to strangers!" She grabbed Tom's hand. "Come on. We need to go."

She pulled him swiftly toward the library entrance. Inside she let go of Tom's hand, wiping the sweat on her shorts and sucking in the cool AC. Tom looked back out to the street, biting his lip.

"Hey." She tried a little laugh. "That was weird, huh?"

He frowned down at his phone, not answering.

"Maybe they thought we were someone else," Wendy babbled on. "We don't know any Luz."

Nothing. A big black hole of nothing.

"Also, what kind of creeps are driving around asking kids questions anyway? We should report them." It sounded right. Like the kind of thing a teacher would say in one of those safety talks. Not safe. Uncalled for. Report them.

"You know exactly why they asked us questions, Wendy," Tom snapped. "Because we're brown. We're brown and they think we don't belong. Like Luz. So yeah, we're not reporting anyone! Got it?" He whirled away and punched numbers into his phone. "Go get yourself signed up to read," he told her over his shoulder.

Wendy stared in disbelief, her jaw hanging open. She was the one who had gotten them away, after all. And she hadn't actually meant they should report them. Not with ICE picking up people off the street just for looking like immigrants. *ICE*. Immigration and Customs Enforcement. La migra. Of course she knew all that. She felt a prickle of tears, but gave herself a mental shake and stomped away, determined to distract herself.

Wendy got a library card, found three astronomy books, and signed up for the Reading Challenge. To enter for the raffle prizes she needed a parent's name. Wendy had to spell *Dulce Ortiz Toledo* for the librarian twice. By the time she was done, Tom was waiting, looking distracted.

"Papá," he said, holding up his phone. "He said something's going on at the church across the alley. He wants us to get home and go straight inside."

"Because of a church thing?" Wendy asked, following him outside. A church gathering wouldn't have anything to do with them. Unless it was some super-white church that didn't want them moving in next door. She shivered at the thought. In their old neighborhood, lots of kids had the same dark hair and brown skin as her. But outside Melborn, like in the big country houses Mamá used to clean, plenty of people had thought they didn't belong.

A blue van drove past them and Tom nudged her, pointing

to the *NEWS at 4* logo on its side. It turned onto their street. And then she noticed the noise. It rumbled like thunder—a distant drumming rhythm. As they drew closer Wendy could make out music coming from the church around the corner. Some of the crowd spilled into view and stood on the sidewalk, holding signs and singing half a block from their front door.

Wendy sped up, ready to get inside and away from it all, when Tom pulled at her arm.

"Here." He thrust the pharmacy bag into Wendy's hands. "Tell Papá I'll be home soon."

"What? Tom, no!" She felt a sudden panic twist in her chest. "Papá said to go home now!" They were supposed to go home, each of them following along the same, safe path, no matter what was pulling at them from outside.

But he was already hurrying past the chipped cement steps of the crooked house, toward the voices on the corner. He did not look back.

FOUR

PAPÁ'S MOUTH DREW in hard and tight when Wendy told him where Tom had gone. When Tom didn't respond to his texts, Papá set to unpacking boxes in distracted silence. Wendy shot him sidelong glances as she unwrapped the dishes from the crumpled newspaper. She wasn't even sure why he seemed so worried, but she wished she could reassure him. Tom was the one who always knew the right thing to say, not her. She tried desperately to think of something.

"I signed up for the library reading thing," she blurted.

Papá made a *hmmm* sound.

"I might even win a ticket to the Astronomy Convention," Wendy continued. "It's at the planetarium and they said astronomers come from all over. Only, I had to put an adult's name down, so I gave them Mamá's. . . ." She trailed off because Papá was obviously far, far away.

Mamá walked to the table and shifted boxes and tools

aside to make space for plates of steaming beans and rice. "Óscar?" she said softly.

Papá made a grunting sound and shook his head. "We wait," he said stubbornly, carrying a lamp into the other room.

Wendy's stomach growled and she looked pleadingly at Mamá, but she only sighed. "It is important to him, mija. The family eating together. You know this."

Just then the door opened and they all looked up.

"That was amazing!" Tom swept into the room, his energy so different from Papá's that Wendy felt the air shift. Tom's cheeks were flushed and his copper eyes sparkled with excitement. "I know who Luz is now, Chiquitín," he said to Wendy. "And we were right about ICE. They are looking for her. But she's safe because the church is letting her—"

"Tom, stop," Papá said firmly. "We do not need to hear—"

"Papá," Tom said. "This is a big deal! Luz might actually win this, according to this one lawyer—"

"I don't want to talk about it, mijo." Papá hadn't raised his voice, but Wendy saw something in his face that made her want to step back.

"But listen," Tom insisted, "she's fighting back! She has a deportation notice—"

"Enough!" Papá slammed his hand on the table, and Wendy jumped as a crate of dishes clinked. "This has nothing to do with us! We came to this country the right way."

Tom flinched, and Wendy couldn't tell if it was from the sharp sound or Papá's sharp words. Papá kept talking, not seeming to notice. "We paid our dues and put in our time and we are American! What that woman is doing back there"—he pointed a trembling finger out the back window to where the church steeple stood against the darkening sky—"has *nothing* to do with *us*!"

Tom frowned. "You already knew about Luz?" he asked.

Papá sighed. "I saw a bit," he said. "On the news today. If I had known before . . ." He rubbed his face with his rough hands, his shoulders drooping.

"It will only bring attention." Now he sounded almost pleading. "It will bring people, people looking for illegals."

Wendy looked at Tom. Her brother's expression had darkened at the word "illegals." They knew people who'd been deported. The immigration police came for them and sent them back to whatever country they had been born in. That's what had happened to Alicia's dad. Their family had tried to do things the right way, too, but it hadn't helped. It wasn't Alicia's fault her dad's green card expired and his renewal was denied. Or that her whole family had to run away in the middle of the night. But here, in this neighborhood, Wendy's family was supposed to be safe. They were supposed to be far away from people with deportation notices—far away from ICE.

"We keep away from all of it. Do you understand?" Papá said.

Wendy looked at Mamá, whose hands were bunching the bright fabric of her apron into knots at her side, and thought of Papá telling her to stay inside. Mamá had stayed inside more and more the past year. She'd stopped cleaning houses and instead took on sewing jobs she could do from home. Wendy had noticed. She had wondered if maybe Mamá's green card had expired too. And if what happened to Alicia's family would happen to them. So one day, she'd finally asked. Mamá had frowned and said her documents were fine and that all Wendy should worry about was doing her chores. But then why was Papá so concerned about this woman next door? Why did he think Mamá should stay indoors? Wendy's throat tightened. She wanted nothing more than to dive into her new library books and ignore all of this.

"Do you understand?" Papá asked again.

Wendy met Papá's eyes and nodded. Tom looked grim, and he worked his jaw back and forth as if tasting a retort. But then he gave a quick nod, too, and Papá's face brightened.

"Now," Papá said, clapping his hands, "let's see what magic your mamá has made without even a real stove!"

But as they sat down at the table, Mamá looked out the window toward the church and Wendy heard her voice, barely above a whisper. And this time, she understood her.

"¿Porqué aquí? ¿Porqué tenia qué ser aquí?"

"Why here?" she had said. "Why did it have to be here?"

FIVE

IT TOOK WENDY a long time to fall asleep that night. The whirring fan only pointed her way every eleven seconds and her sleeping bag was hot and slippery. Tom's bed with his cool cotton sheets sat against the wall. Papá had offered to set up her bed, but Wendy had refused. That felt way too permanent and this was *not* her room. This room was a stranger. She knew every shadow in their old room, the feeling of the furniture in the dark and the way the sound bounced off the walls. Here, sounds seemed to come *from* the walls. Creaks and squeaks and rustles. This whole house felt unpredictable.

Unpredictable like Tom. He wasn't himself. He hadn't been for a while, really, but today felt different. The way he had jumped down her throat at the library—that wasn't like him at all. Wendy looked at her brother, the glow of his phone making his face the only bright spot in the dark.

"Hey, Torpedo?" she whispered.

She used to make fun of that nickname. Back when he

was in middle school, some of the other kids had laughed at him for pronouncing his last name the English way. *Se cree gringo*, they said. *He thinks he's white.* Then they started repeating his name with bizarre American accents whenever they heard it. "Toe-leeee-do Tom." But Tom had a way of taking whatever anyone dished out and flipping it. No one ever figured out where it started, but "Toledo Tom" soon turned into "Torpedo Tom" as he raced through his track meets. By the time he left for high school, Tom held the all-time track record at Melborn Heights Middle School: the entire auditorium had chanted *"Tor-pe-doooo, WHOOSH!"* when they called his name at eighth-grade graduation.

He looked up, blinking at Wendy in the darkness.

"Hey, Chiquitín."

"I'm not little," she answered automatically.

Tom half laughed, then sighed. "I was kinda a jerk earlier, wasn't I?"

Wendy snorted. "Ya think?"

"Yeah. Sorry."

Wendy shrugged even though he couldn't see her.

"It's okay."

The fan whirred and she heard the house creak.

"Do you think those men *were* ICE?" she whispered.

She probably shouldn't ask. But she couldn't get those hard eyes out of her mind.

She wasn't sure Tom had heard her at first, then he answered, "I think they might have been."

Wendy tensed.

"But they were there for Luz, not us." He kept his voice low. "She's undocumented and ICE wants to send her back to Mexico. But instead of going to her check-in and probably getting deported, she went into sanctuary. She's staying in the church."

Wendy propped herself up on one elbow, staring at his dark shape.

"So she's hiding out from ICE *here*?"

"Well, not exactly hiding. ICE knows she's here. That's the whole idea." Now he sounded excited. "See, they won't go into churches, right? So instead of Luz just running away and always being scared they'll catch her, she's got this whole crowd of people that are standing around taking pictures, telling her story and stuff. And as long as she's inside the church, she's safe. That's what sanctuary means. A safe place."

"Why?" Wendy didn't get it. ICE had raided the factory in Melborn; they had raided that farm up north; they had been at her school one morning stopping parents when they dropped off kids. She had even heard about them going into a hospital in another state and picking up someone from their sick kid's room. "They know she's here. Why wouldn't they just go in and get her?"

"Because it looks bad! There's like this whole army of people ready to flip if their church gets invaded. These are religious people. Probably mostly white people. You know what it's like. People listen to them." She saw his shadow shrug in the glow of his cell phone.

"I mean, it's not for *sure* she's safe. It might not stop them. But at least people are paying attention." He held up his phone. "There's articles and interviews on the news. It's kind of a big deal."

"But she's illegal?" Wendy asked.

Tom's eyes flashed in the dim light. "Don't use that word," he said.

"Papa does," Wendy muttered, frowning. Why didn't Tom understand? Papá didn't want this Luz woman here, not next door to them. He didn't want an army of white people ready to fight for some illegal. He didn't want ICE agents. He just wanted a new neighborhood where they could live in peace.

"Well, she's been trying to get papers," Tom said. "She came here, like, twenty-five years ago, Wendy. She has a whole family here, kids and everything. She just wants to live a normal life."

"So do we!" Wendy said. She wasn't sure why she said it like that, like they were arguing or something. But their family had papers. Papá was American and Mamá had a green card. So they should be allowed to just live in peace, away from stuff like this, right? Maybe she was still thinking of Mamá whispering, *"Why did it have to be here?"*

Tom didn't say anything for a moment. Then he shrugged.

"Yeah, you're right again, genius."

His bed creaked as he switched off his phone and shifted under his sheet.

"We're gonna be super normal here," he said. "It's a normal kind of place."

She couldn't tell if he was being sarcastic. That was usually her thing. She settled back onto her pillow, feeling the warm air buzz in her direction.

"I was hoping normal life would mean my own room, though," he added sleepily.

Wendy stuck her tongue out in his general direction.

"Don't think I didn't see that," she heard him whisper, even though there was no way he had. She smiled. At least she was still predictable.

SIX

WENDY'S INSIDES CHURNED as she walked toward Leopold Preparatory Academy with Papá. Every time she almost met the eyes of a kid about her age, Wendy dropped her gaze to her brand-new galaxy shoes. When Papá had given her the deep-blue high-tops with their swirling starbursts, Wendy had immediately fallen in love with them. But now she wished she had opted for the plain black flats. She'd kept everything else so basic—black shirt, jeans, a simple braid. Just the right amount of unremarkable to blend into the crowd. Weren't these shoes a little . . . extra?

"This is quite a school, mi bella estrella," Papá said. *My beautiful star.* He always called her that when he was feeling sentimental. She looked up at the school and felt a little thrill.

The one big plus to moving over an hour away was how close they were to Leopold Preparatory Academy. When the guidance counselor at her old school first told her about it, Wendy's excitement had been tinged with guilt at the thought of leaving Alicia. Still, it had been impossible to not feel goose bumps when she read about the school. LPA was the only public school in Ohio specifically for seventh and eighth graders identified as gifted and talented. According to the counselor, LPA had recently partnered with surrounding school districts to "broaden their admissions base." And Wendy had been offered a spot. Her parents hadn't been too sure about the hour-and-a-half bus ride, but when Papá found a house in the exact same neighborhood as LPA, it only made sense for her to enroll. And she hadn't had to leave Alicia behind. Because Alicia was gone anyway.

Wendy shook that thought away and focused on the dignified stone-and-brick building ahead of them. A stone crest hung over the door and Wendy craned her neck to read the words. Non ducor, duco. *That must be Latin*, she realized. This school had an actual Latin motto. And, according to the shiny brochure, it had a state-of-the-art science lab. But what she was most excited for didn't happen until next year. Eighth graders at LPA spent part of their class time each week learning from different community partners, like the art museum and the history center. And the Slettebak Planetarium. Wendy could just see herself learning from real astronomers. *First, let's get through seventh grade*, she thought, tugging on her backpack straps. She had double-checked her supplies. Binder, folders, unicorn-kitty tape dispenser—everything was there. She had triple-checked the new inhaler.

"I'm sure it'll be great, Papá." Wendy turned and gave him a bright smile. "Thanks for walking me here. Bye."

She turned away before he could respond and hurried toward the entrance. It was like ripping off a Band-Aid. She just had to jump right in.

Whoever had designed the old building had not made it easy for kids to find their way around, especially in three minutes before the bell rang. Wendy was searching for the third-period art room when she turned through a doorway and nearly walked out onto a stage. Two other girls were running off the stage toward her, gasping with nervous laughter.

"Oh my god, how did we even get here?" one of them squealed. "I didn't even know there *was* a stage!"

"The staircases move!" The second girl wore a *Doctor Who* shirt and her shaggy black ponytail swung in panicked excitement as she talked. "I *swear* the staircases move!"

Wendy saw the sketchbooks and packs of colored pencils in their arms and followed them down the stairs. But at the bottom they all just stood looking down the hall, first one way, then the other, like they were kindergartners learning to cross a street.

"This place is haunted," the ponytailed girl moaned. "For real. The stairs used to be, like, right there."

"Mal, what do we do?" the other girl said, tugging nervously on a strand of wavy blonde hair. "We are totally late!"

"So what if we're late?" someone said from behind them.

A girl about their age, her short black hair pulled into two high knots, walked up, shifting her art notebook in her arms. "It's day one. What are they gonna do?"

She looked down the hall, then turned to the other girls. Her light brown eyes were small, but her dark eyebrows curved elegantly over them, and it made them look bigger. Wendy suddenly thought of her own bushy eyebrows and considered whether she should start plucking. But the thought of intentionally causing herself pain made her shudder. The girl looked at Wendy.

"What do *you* think?" she asked. "Art room. Which way?"

Wendy hated being wrong about anything. But she was 85 percent sure which way to go.

"Art's this way," Wendy said, pointing to the left.

For a second she was sure the girls were going to laugh again and go the other way, but then the girl named Mal shrugged and hurried down the hall, the others tagging along behind.

The art room was at the top of the next staircase, and they all heaved a sigh of relief when they saw it.

"Oh, thank you, LPA spirits!" Mal declared dramatically to the ceiling, and they all burst out laughing.

"Are you guys in art?" said a voice behind them. They all spun around. The golden-haired boy from the Walgreens window was walking straight toward them. Wendy gulped. It was as if Earth had suddenly developed the gravity of Jupiter and her insides were plummeting to the center of the planet.

"Hey, Fiona." He grinned at the blonde girl, who had grabbed onto Mal's arm when he startled them.

"Hi, Brett." The girl named Fiona giggled again. "We thought you were a ghost."

Mal gasped, "Well, he might be!" She leaned toward him and whispered eerily, "Maybe he's a former student haunting the halls!"

"Huh?" Brett leaned away from her, his eyes looking worried under his sun-streaked hair.

Fiona elbowed Mal. "Cut it out, Mallory. This isn't one of your weird fandoms."

"Excuuuse me?" Mallory's eyes widened behind her glasses. "Which fandom is weird? And you better not say *Supernatural*," she added emphatically.

"Oh my god, Mal." Fiona rolled her eyes. "I promise you, Brett Cobb is not a ghost. We go to the same summer camp." She stepped up to Brett and put her hand on his arm. "See? Totally real flesh and blood." She giggled again, looking at Brett.

"Yep, I'm for real." He shrugged. "Sorry, who are you guys?"

Fiona waved her hand to introduce them. "This is Mallory. We were in the same group at orientation. And . . ." She trailed off, looking at the Black girl. "I met you earlier, right? Kalifa? Kajima? Something like that." She shrugged and smiled at Brett again.

The girl arched one perfect eyebrow. "Kha," she said, forming her lips precisely around each syllable, "di"—she took a small step forward, her eyes locked on Fiona's—"jah." She lifted her chin a tiny bit and added, "I go by K.K."

"Why do you go by K.K.?" Mal asked curiously. "I like Khadijah."

"Hey, it's cool," Brett said. "I'd shorten it, too, if I had a weird name. K.K. is way easier."

K.K. narrowed her eyes. She walked past him, keeping her laser gaze on Brett for a second more until she turned her head and entered the classroom. Fiona giggled, letting go of his arm to cover her mouth, like she was embarrassed to be laughing. Mal looked at her, her eyebrows scrunching together under her shaggy fringe. Fiona shrugged. Wendy just wanted to slip into class before Brett recognized her. No such luck. Mal noticed her hovering behind and waved a box of colored pencils.

"Hey, you with the cool shoes." Mal smiled at her brightly. "You saved us. What's your name anyway?"

Brett was now definitely staring directly at her. She swallowed.

"Wendy," she said, ducking into the classroom just as the bell rang. She slid into the seat next to K.K. and glanced at her face. K.K. was staring, thin-lipped, at Brett as he walked in, her manicured nails tap-tapping on the table. Wendy tried to think of something to say.

"Hey," Mal whispered from the seat behind them. "First of all, Khadijah is *not* weird. I mean, if people can figure out Pokémon names, they can handle it."

K.K. turned toward her and smiled. "Right?" she agreed.

"Second," Mal continued, "it's your own business what you want to be called. I have a Korean middle name but only my grandma calls me that. I like it too much to let anyone around here butcher it. But if you want me to call you Khadijah, I will."

"Thanks," K.K. said. She sounded surprised but pleased.

Their art teacher called the class to order, and K.K. turned back around. She wasn't frowning or tapping her fingernails anymore, Wendy noticed. Mal had known exactly the right thing to say.

SEVEN

ART SEEMED LIKE it would be a fun class. The teacher, Miss Hill, was a Black woman with a wide smile, braids that swung almost to her knees, and a patchwork skirt printed with superhero comics that Mal couldn't stop talking about. But the class Wendy was looking forward to most was science. She was desperate to latch on to something solid in the middle of all this newness. Science was predictable and comforting. Like the law of gravity. The earth kept spinning around the sun, tethered to it by that invisible force whether Wendy made friends at school or not.

Brett and Fiona were both in her science class. She watched them snag a table near the back and wave over a friend. Wendy assumed it was someone else they knew from camp, and she tried not to think of Alicia.

"They're so lucky they know each other," a soft voice murmured.

A girl in a pink headscarf was setting her bag on the table next to her.

"I'm Yasmin," she said with a smile that dimpled both her cheeks. It was such a sweet expression that Wendy automatically smiled back at her.

"Wendy," she said.

Bursts of laughter came from Brett and Fiona's table. Wendy and Yasmin both glanced over.

"I don't know anyone here," Yasmin sighed.

Just then, Brett looked up at Wendy and one side of his mouth slid up in a crooked smile. He raised his fingers off the desk. She gulped and lifted her own fingers to wave back, dropping her pencil. Wendy ducked her head, turning her back on Brett's table. She felt the heat rush to the tips of her ears. It was always her ears that turned red. Why couldn't she just blush like a normal person? She slid her seat back so she could pick up her pencil and the foot of her chair landed right on it, snapping it with a soft crunch. She snatched up the broken pieces, groaning quietly. It was the first day and she'd already broken a pencil.

"Need a new one?" said a voice behind her, and Brett Cobb reached over and set a perfectly sharpened pencil in front of her. "I have extra," he said.

"Thanks," Wendy said in a voice that she hoped sounded normal.

He smiled and walked back to his seat. Wendy resisted the urge to plant her face on the table.

"You know him?" Yasmin whispered loudly.

"No!" Wendy said, hunching over. She was sure her ears were like red beacons on either side of her head. She'd bet anything Yasmin blushed like a cartoon princess. Roses on her cheeks, for sure.

Yasmin looked delighted. "You do! And he's cute!"

"I just moved here," Wendy hissed, trying to motion for Yasmin to stop staring at him. "I don't know anyone, I swear!"

"Wendy, right?" chirruped a voice near her elbow.

Wendy and Yasmin whirled around. A wisp of a girl had materialized at their table. She seemed to float there for a moment, staring at them with huge eyes. Wendy blinked.

"You *are* Wendy! I knew it!" The girl took Wendy's hand in a surprisingly strong grip. A collection of woven fabric and leather bracelets jiggled on her skinny arm as she shook hands. Wendy stared at her, sure she would have remembered if they had already met. Her chunky pixie haircut was topped with bright turquoise streaks that might have looked edgy on another kid. But this girl looked more like a wood sprite than a rock star.

"So, that house swallowed you up before I could introduce myself," the pixie continued. "I'm Coretta Carpenter. We are basically neighbors. Because of the church."

She beamed at Wendy, who squinted back at her. Yep, there were the high, pale eyebrows and the slightly freckled little nose. And that voice . . . it was Fence Girl.

"Most people call me Etta," she said matter-of-factly, pumping Yasmin's hand.

Yasmin gaped at her, just as surprised as Wendy at the formal introduction. But she dimpled into a smile again and said, "Most people call me Yasmin."

The fairy girl nodded and took a deep breath, as if preparing to blow up a balloon. "It's science time, friends!" she declared.

Right on cue, the bell rang. Wendy wasn't sure if Etta was trying to be funny or if she was just a bit odd. But their teacher didn't give her time to wonder. Ms. Park was a short woman in a stiff white lab coat and she got straight to business. The handout she gave them was dense and full of detailed class goals. Wendy flipped to the calendar and saw the words "Science Fair." She sat up as straight as she could in her seat.

"Some of you may incorrectly assume one month is plenty of time to prepare." Ms. Park's lips squeezed together in disapproval. "Do not squander your time," she warned. "The LPA Science Fair has sent scholars on to win top place in the district competition every year since we began. Some other schools would love a chance to push us down a notch or two." She raised her eyebrows at them. "I would prefer that did not happen on my watch."

Wendy nodded seriously, her brain already charging ahead. Some kind of water-powered device might be fun. Or maybe something that mixed chemicals to get a cool reaction.

"Additionally," Ms. Park said, raising her voice over students who were now murmuring about project ideas, "the Astronomy Department at OSU has agreed to participate in judging this year."

Wendy grinned. That settled it. If someone who did actual astronomy research would be evaluating her project, it definitely had to be about the stars.

"And I have it on good authority," Ms. Park said, sounding pleased, "that their representative is interested in scouting out candidates for a junior internship program at the Slettebak Planetarium for upcoming eighth graders."

Wendy sighed happily. Science class was 100 percent going to be excellent.

She could still feel the smile on her face as they filed out of the room after class. Ahead of her, Yasmin and Etta had fallen into easy conversation. Suddenly a stocky white boy pushed past Wendy, slamming into Yasmin as he passed them. She stumbled, and Etta's arms flew up to steady her.

The boy didn't slow down. He just said, "Oops, sorry," in a mocking voice that made a girl next to them giggle nervously.

Wendy pulled back from him as he jogged away. Yasmin's knuckles tightened as she clutched her books to her chest. She bent her head down, the pink fabric smooth across her forehead.

"Watch where you're going, P.J., you ignoramus!" Etta shouted after him.

He looked back, surprised, then his grin widened.

"Oooooo, is wittle Etta mad?" P.J. said in a whiny baby voice.

He caught up to a group of boys who were all snorting with laughter. They jostled each other and one of them said loudly, "Yeah, P.J., you *ignoramus*!" P.J. pretended to punch at the boy's stomach. Wendy pressed against the wall, wishing she were invisible. And then, from the middle of the crowd of boys, Brett's steely blue eyes met hers. He gave her a quick wink and followed his friends around the corner.

Wendy let her lungs fill up like a balloon before blowing air out slowly. Yasmin looked shaken and Etta looked furious. But nothing had actually happened. Just an accidental bump in a crowded hall and some guys laughing. And Brett. Winking. At her. Wendy gave herself a little shake. She just had to stay out of trouble and blend in. She edged slowly past Yasmin and Etta, muttering a quick bye as she hurried to her next class.

After a full week of smiling at strangers, floods of names and room numbers, assignments and procedures to remember, all Wendy wanted to do was curl up in her own room and digest it all.

But of course her room had no floor. And of course Mamá had chores for her to do.

She was putting away the mop in the bathroom closet when she saw it—a latch halfway up the closet wall. Wendy reached for it and pulled. And a door in the wall swung open to reveal a creaky staircase. She only hesitated for a second before climbing cautiously up, step by step, into a musty attic streaked with sun. She hadn't even realized the crooked house had an attic. Thin glints of silver cobweb caught the light all around her, sparkling in corners and hanging from the rough ceiling beams. Something about it made Wendy think of a barn. It felt like it didn't quite belong to the rest of the house, like the outside was leaking in. But it had a floor.

Papá wasn't thrilled about the idea. He said it wasn't up to code. Wendy calmly pointed out that this entire house wasn't up to code and maybe they shouldn't have moved in if it wasn't livable. She had to do penance for that comment by helping Mamá clean the secondhand stove. She bit her tongue, put on rubber gloves, and climbed halfway into the bottom of the oven, scrubbing and thinking dark thoughts about Hansel and Gretel.

The next morning Wendy woke up to muffled noises coming from somewhere above. She rushed up the hidden stairs to find Mamá, her hair tied back in one of her colorful fabric bandannas, mopping the attic furiously. The windows glittered with clean morning light and there was not a single cobweb in sight.

"You know the door is in the bathroom? You are okay with this?" Mamá asked, pausing for a moment and gesturing with the dripping mop.

Wendy threw herself at her, wrapping her arms around the mop, too, for good measure.

47

"Gracias," she whispered.

By Sunday it almost looked like a bedroom. There was a little nook in the corner with a round window set so low in the wall that Wendy could sit on the floor and look out. She decided to leave her sleeping bag there for stargazing, even though her bed would fit better across the room. The window had a clear view of the church, too, she couldn't help noticing. Her eyes ran over the full parking lot, and she wondered if Etta was inside. Then she spotted a black SUV and pulled away. It probably wasn't the same car as the one the man with the hard eyes drove. But she still wondered if ICE was out there, watching the people going into the church. She needed to remember to stay out of sight on Sundays.

EIGHT

THERE WAS A static electricity experiment Wendy had seen once where little balls of tin foil danced around on a pane of glass, bouncing off and away from each other in constant motion. Even when they weren't skipping along the surface they quivered in place, waiting for something to come close and set them off again. She thought of that experiment more than once those first days of school, skittering through the halls and classrooms with the other students, each of them drawing close to each other and then jumping away, trying to find their place.

By the middle of their second week the electricity in the air had settled a bit. Until Principal Whitman announced during assembly that today was the start of clubs. Clubs were held during the final class period each Wednesday and all students were required to sign up.

"Fun! I didn't know about this," Yasmin whispered. Etta had waved her and Wendy over to sit with her, K.K., and

Mal in the auditorium. They all watched eagerly as the principal projected a list of all the options on to the Smart board, then introduced the student body president to talk about student council.

"We have to decide today?" Mal said, her eyes wide behind her glasses.

"I can't wait!" Etta said, bouncing up and down in her seat.

"Shhh!" K.K. hissed. She was leaning forward, her back straight and her eyes bright. As the eighth grader explained how elections for student council would work, K.K. pulled a spiral notebook from her backpack and started jotting down notes.

"Are you running for student council?" Mal asked.

K.K. gave a determined nod, her focus still on the speaker. He was holding up a banner with the school crest on it and talking about leadership and purpose. Apparently the Latin motto *Non ducor, duco* meant "I am not led, I lead."

"K.K. was student body president last year at our elementary school," Etta said in a stage whisper. "She's gonna run this world pretty soon."

K.K. shushed her again, even though she looked pleased. "I can't be president this year," she said. "It's always an eighth grader. And he was already elected last spring."

"But vice president is always a seventh grader," Etta responded, her eyes sparkling. "And you would be an epic VP!"

Mal leaned forward, looking down the row toward Yasmin and Wendy. "What are you guys doing?" she asked.

Wendy looked at the list on the Smart board, considering. Definitely not student council. She was not the leader type. Maybe Math Club? Or yearbook. That sounded logical and focused. She wished there were an astronomy club.

Another kid was talking now, telling everyone about the Gay-Straight Alliance. As he finished speaking, he lifted his arms with a flourish and spun around to show off his rainbow cape. Etta nearly popped out of her seat she was cheering so hard.

"I might join the Green Team," Yasmin said quietly.

Mal looked relieved. "Oh, yeah! Me too. That's super important."

Etta stopped midcheer and whirled toward them. "Yes! It is SO important! Educating people about our environment and global warming? I mean, our world is *burning*—"

Someone shushed them loudly and she stopped, turning toward the front. A girl was holding up a cardboard cutout of a chess piece, but she was so quiet it was hard for Wendy to hear what she was saying about Chess Club. Besides, Etta's jittery excitement was distracting.

"They need a social justice club," Etta said. "To organize protests and to make sure the school is being inclusive and stuff."

Wendy felt herself shrinking in her seat. Etta's voice was

too loud and Miss Hill was looking their way. K.K. nudged Etta and nodded toward the teacher. Etta lowered her voice a notch but kept talking.

"Seriously, K.K., why isn't there one? I'm going to talk to Ms. Whitman. We can start one ourselves!"

"Etta, girl, look." K.K. pointed her pencil at the board and read, "Unity Club—developing a diverse, equitable, and inclusive student body."

"Oh," Etta said, deflating.

"You're actually disappointed, aren't you?" Yasmin asked, her face dimpling in a smile.

K.K. grinned. "She is! Etta's mad she couldn't start it herself."

Etta shrugged good-naturedly. "I do like to start things. Hey, how many clubs can we sign up for?"

Mal shook her head in exasperation. "One! You are only one person, Etta!"

"Miss Hill," a voice called from the row behind them. "Some people are being very noisy and I can't hear the speakers."

Wendy looked at the girl who had spoken. She was pretty, her hair falling in glossy brown waves over her shoulders, and she had a self-satisfied smile that made Wendy instantly dislike her. Then she felt bad. After all, she'd been wishing Etta would be quiet too. Fiona was sitting next to the girl, giggling with one hand over her mouth.

Miss Hill leaned forward. "I do need everyone to hold

their talking until after the presentation, please," she said, mostly to Etta. Then her gaze shifted to the girls behind them and she added, "That goes for you as well, Avery."

Avery's smile turned to a full pout. Before Wendy could turn back around, Avery narrowed her eyes at her and glared. Wendy shrank down more in her seat and stared straight ahead. She didn't want any run-ins with Avery. And, she thought, glancing down the row to where Etta was still radiating energy, maybe she should steer clear of Etta too. She didn't need friends who liked to "start things," not when she was trying to keep her head down.

The hall outside the art room buzzed with activity all day as kids chose their clubs and wrote their names on the sign-up sheets posted on the wall. Wendy was trying to decide between Math Club and Robotics when K.K. stopped next to her and sucked in her breath. Wendy looked over in surprise, following K.K.'s gaze to a blank spot on the wall.

"What?" Wendy asked. K.K. hadn't signed up for a club since she was running for student council. But now she was staring at the wall, her eyebrows drawn together.

"It's gone," K.K. muttered. "Unity Club."

Wendy ran her eyes over the sheets of paper lining the walls, reading the titles: Choir, Green Team, Chess Club. No Unity Club. "Maybe it's full already?" she asked.

K.K. shook her head. "There were only, like, five names on there last period." She reached up and pulled off a corner of torn paper that was still taped to the wall. She held it up between her coral fingernails and frowned. "Do you think someone tore it down on purpose?"

"*Excuse* us."

Wendy felt a nervous twist in her stomach. She recognized that voice already. Avery was standing behind them, arms crossed and tapping her foot. Fiona and another girl were with her.

"Some of us are trying to choose our clubs, you know," Avery said pointedly.

"Really, Captain Obvious?" K.K. said. "Why do you think everyone is here?" She waved her arm at the students in front of the wall of sign-up sheets.

"So, sign up already and let us through," Avery said.

Wendy made a quick decision. She leaned forward and wrote her name on the Robotics Team sign-up sheet, then stepped away.

"There you go," K.K. snapped. "All yours." She moved away from the wall and crossed her arms over her notebook, leveling her gaze at Avery.

"You're not signing up?" Fiona asked K.K. as Avery moved forward.

"I'm running for student council," K.K. told her, ignoring Avery's look of surprise. "I was going to sign up for Unity Club just in case. But someone tore it down."

"Oh please," Avery said, rolling her eyes. "You really think anyone is that worried about your stupid club? *We* are signing up for Choir." She wrote her name with a flourish and passed the pen to Fiona. "And you should definitely sign up for another 'just in case.' Because you"—she gave K.K. a pitying smile—"are not going to make student council."

Avery and her friends sauntered off. Wendy stared at K.K., the tension in her stomach knotting. But K.K.'s light brown eyes shone, and she tapped her fingernails against her notebook. "I am, though," she said quietly, lifting her chin. "I am going to make student council."

Wendy stared at K.K. She would make a great seventh-grade rep. But how could anyone be so certain of something that was impossible to predict? Wendy would never be so bold as to set her heart on improbabilities. She just hoped K.K. was right.

NINE

MISS HILL HAD images of collage art on the projector. She was explaining how the class would be illustrating scenes from history for their next project, but Wendy was having a hard time paying attention. Her thoughts kept getting pulled toward science project ideas.

"Wendy?"

Her brain clicked back into focus. Miss Hill was looking at her curiously.

"Um, what?"

Miss Hill smiled. "I asked if you could please give Etta a hand."

Wendy nodded quickly and jumped up. Etta was already passing out papers with "Setting the Scene with Mixed Media" printed across the top. Wendy grabbed a stack and snaked her way down the other side of the room. As she handed Brett's to him, he smiled at her and slipped a folded paper into her hand. Wendy glanced down, her heart thumping. It was folded over several times, and the name Yasmin was written neatly across the top.

Wendy slid the note into her sleeve. She held it in place awkwardly, handing out the last papers with her thumb and forefinger. As she neared the end, she looked over at Brett. He jerked his golden head slightly toward Yasmin's table. Did he like Yasmin? Wendy hated that she felt a twinge of jealousy at the thought. She'd never seen him talk to Yasmin. But P.J. was sitting next to him, tearing strips of paper off the bottom of his packet and scrunching them into spitballs. Her brain flashed back to P.J. slamming into Yasmin in the hallway that first day and how he mocked Etta for defending her. What if this was a different kind of note?

But Brett wasn't P.J. She took a step toward her seat, feeling like she was dragging her Converse shoes out of a mud pit. The note burned hotter in her sleeve with each step. She could look at it first, then she'd know if it was something mean. But the thought of Brett seeing her look at it made her ears burn worse. It wasn't right to look at someone else's note. *Neither is passing notes at all*, she reminded herself. Yasmin was sitting two steps away, her covered head bent over the handout. There was a vomit-colored plastic trash can just under the end of the table. It would be easy to throw the note away and pretend it never happened. But then what? She imagined Brett coming up to her later, asking her why she'd done it.

Wendy's chest tightened as she walked forward, working

the note out of her sleeve and cupping it in her palm. One more step to the trash can. She reached out her hand, shooting a glance at Miss Hill. But instead of her teacher, she locked eyes with Brett again, one arm slung over the back of his chair, confident and relaxed. He leveled his gaze on her, his chin slightly lifted. There was so much sureness in that look. He already knew what she was going to do, and Wendy felt herself responding instinctively to the pull of his will. There was a whisper of sound as the note landed on Yasmin's paper. Wendy hurried to her seat, her head lowered. *On my safe orbit*, she thought dimly.

When a muffled gasp came from behind her, Wendy didn't look up. Maybe it was Yasmin. Maybe not. She kept her eyes glued to the handout. After a moment she heard a small sniff and her heart sank. But she couldn't be 100 percent sure that Yasmin was crying. Not even 70 percent. Then Yasmin stood and hurried out of the classroom. Okay, that was definitely not good. What had Wendy done? And what should she do now?

Before Wendy could decide, Etta rushed up front to whisper in Miss Hill's ear. Their teacher had been facing the projector and hadn't noticed when Yasmin left. But now she looked toward the door, her face concerned, and nodded to Etta. Immediately Etta collected her things and Yasmin's and was gone. Just like that. She didn't hesitate; she didn't stall. She just went after her friend. Wendy slid lower in her chair, trying to ignore the tightness in her chest.

Wendy saw Etta's brilliant turquoise hair at the end of the hall and dipped her head into her locker, hurrying to grab what she needed before—

"Wendy."

She jumped. How had Etta made it through that crowd so fast? She was like a fairy ninja.

"Hi." Wendy barely glanced at Etta.

"Wendy. What's going on? Did you see what happened? Do you know why Yasmin left?"

Wendy pulled her notebook out with a jerk that sent several things clattering to the floor.

"Ugh," she muttered, bending down.

"Wendy! Stop ignoring me!" Etta crouched next to her. She picked up Wendy's unicorn-kitty tape dispenser and leaned forward, her green eyes huge. "You were right in front of her. I saw her face when she left. She was crying and I'm pretty sure someone said something awful to her. What was it?"

Wendy could feel her throat constricting. Not too much, but enough that she could imagine it closing. She sucked air into her lungs slowly.

"Etta, I don't know what it said. Give me my tape dispenser."

"What *it said*?" Etta gasped. "It was a note, wasn't it?"

"Just leave it alone, Etta! It has nothing to do with us!"

Wendy stood and shoved her things into the locker. She was supposed to keep her head down. For her family. And

Coretta Carpenter was making it way too hard not to get involved.

Etta stared at her for a moment, then looked down at the tape dispenser. It had a rainbow tail on one end and a unicorn horn poking out from between pink kitten ears on the other.

"I didn't know you liked unicorn kitties. It's cute." Etta handed it to her with a sad smile and walked away.

Etta's disappointment in Wendy was so real she could almost taste it. Wendy stared down at the dispenser, wondering what Alicia would have done with the note. She pushed the tape dispenser roughly into her locker and looked into the ridiculous, oversized kitty eyes, blinking back tears.

The next day the school sent home a letter to all the school families about bullying and acceptance. Wendy couldn't help but wonder if it had something to do with that note. The note that she had passed to Yasmin. She bit her lip and tried not to think about it. She hadn't written the note, after all. It didn't really have anything to do with her. Besides, Yasmin was fine. Wendy, her stomach twisted up like a guilty pretzel, had tried to apologize the next morning, stammering that she didn't know what the note said. But Yasmin just gave her that sweet, dimpled smile and waved it off. And Yasmin insisted she was fine every time Etta asked what had happened.

Thankfully Etta had plenty of other things to keep her attention. Even though their sign-up sheet had gone missing, Etta managed to track down the kids who had signed up for the Unity Club. She'd gotten them to join forces with the Gay-Straight Alliance to launch an inclusivity campaign, so, in a way, she had joined two clubs after all. They called themselves "GSA United" and they spent lunch periods in a whirlwind of glitter and oil pastels, decorating posters and notes of empowerment to distribute in the halls.

Meanwhile, K.K. was in full campaign mode. The vote for vice president was next Wednesday. It didn't give her much time, but K.K. had set a goal of meeting every seventh grader in person before the election and had started switching lunch tables every day.

Their lunch table was quieter without Etta and K.K., but Wendy felt a tiny, guilty flicker of relief that Etta was so busy. Wendy spent all her time trying to not attract any trouble and Etta seemed like a lightning rod for it.

The weekend was a relief, especially with her own space waiting for her. The attic felt cozier every day. Papá had put together her actual bed, and falling asleep was getting easier, even if the strange room did creak at night.

Tom didn't seem to care all that much that he had his own room. He was hardly ever there. Cross-country and track were a big deal this year, with Nationals looming. Papá had always been ridiculous about mealtimes, insisting that families should sit down and eat together at the same table every day. As Tom's practices took up more and more time, Papá's forehead would crease in deep lines at the missed family meals. Then his eyes would dart to the stacks of college flyers that had begun arriving in the mail and the furrows would soften. If Torpedo Tom placed well at Nationals, his college chances would skyrocket.

That Saturday Tom slept until noon. Papá, his work pants speckled with bits of insulation, had come home for lunch in between work site inspections. They had just sat down to eat when Tom, rubbing his face with the palms of his hands, stepped into the room. He grabbed an empanada from the table, mumbled something about training, and headed for the door.

"Mijo, don't move," Papá said calmly.

Tom stopped.

"Is this a drive-through window?" Papá's finger, grimy from work, pointed menacingly at the table in front of his plate.

"No, sir," Tom said, looking at the floor.

"You are correct. It is a table," Papá said slowly. "Where we sit to eat our lunch. Together."

Papá let that hang in the air for a beat. Then he reached for the plate of empanadas. "These are riquísimas Dulce." He smiled at Mamá and helped himself to another.

There was a tense moment where the only sound was the clinking of the spoon as Papá poured crema over the empanada and Wendy felt a desperate urge to laugh.

Then Tom grinned and slid into his chair. He plopped the empanada from his hand onto his plate. "Looks good, Mamá," he said lightly.

Wendy breathed and smiled. Okay. Yes, this is how things should be. Tom smiling and Mamá cooking good things and Papá home.

"The family that eats together," Papá began, and Wendy mouthed the rest of the familiar refrain as he continued, "sticks together." She smiled at Tom to see if he'd mouthed it, too, as they usually did every time Papá repeated his favorite phrase. But Tom didn't look up, and her smile faded. So much for together.

Papá looked pleased, though, and he smiled at Mamá. "I will fix the hot water tonight, Dulce. This will soon be the most magnificent house you've ever lived in! Our own castle."

Mamá let the corners of her lips slide into a skeptical smile. Wendy loved that smile. She was 85 percent sure she had no chance of ever replicating Mamá's gentle beauty. Her own face was too plain and too critical. Tom said Wendy looked like she was judging everyone all the time. But every now and then, Mamá would give this smile that had a smirk hidden inside it and Wendy would see a little flash of herself.

"Maybe a castle of spiderwebs," Mamá answered drily. A flicker of disappointment crossed Papá's face and Mamá winced. "Ay, sorry, Óscar. I did not mean it."

Wendy glanced at Tom. He was looking out the back window, his mind far away. Was he wondering about his old girlfriend? Or thinking about the woman at the church? Or something else?

"Spiderwebs don't stand a chance around Mamá," Wendy offered, her voice a little too cheery. "So it's not a spiderweb castle. Just a kind of . . . crooked castle." Her voice dropped at the end as she realized this might not be the most helpful thing to say.

But Papá let out a muffled laugh around his mouthful of food. Then he swallowed and looked at Mamá. "You know, mi Dulce, you make any place into a castle. That is what queens do."

Mamá blinked and reached across the table to lay her soft hand on Papá's square, hard one. Something passed between them that felt as foreign and unknown to Wendy as the words they whispered in Spanish when she was not meant to hear. It made her wish for her science books with solid answers and explanations.

Then Tom stood up and the spell was broken.

"Thanks for lunch. I'll be out late."

His bag was still slung over his shoulder and he stood and left the house, the door banging shut unceremoniously behind him.

Papá's fist clenched under Mamá's small hand. Her thumb rubbed a gentle circle on his calloused skin.

"He is hurting, Óscar," she said quietly. "He needs to look for his way."

"He had better remember how we raised him," Papá said gruffly. "There's hurt in life. But we still need to walk the right way."

Mamá said, so quietly Wendy wasn't sure she heard correctly, "The right way or the safe way?"

That night, Wendy woke up to a muffled shouting making its way from the bottom floor all the way up through floorboards and insulation to her attic. Papá's voice. And Tom's.

She flipped open her phone. The glowing numbers said two a.m. She rubbed at her crusty eyes and tried to listen. Tom had stayed out late when they lived in Melborn, but only until midnight, and their parents always knew where he was. He had probably just been playing Xbox at some friend's house and lost track of time. But still. This wasn't like Tom.

There was another burst of Papá's angry voice, then she heard stomping on the squeaky stairs and a door slamming. Wendy pulled her knees up to her chin and strained her ears. Tom's room was dead silent. He must have fallen straight into bed, even with Papá still stomping around downstairs. That wasn't like him either. Tom was usually the one who soothed ruffled feelings in their house. At least, he used to be. Before Gina disappeared. And before Tom started talking about people fighting deportation orders. Now he was the one stirring things up. Every few minutes she could hear Papá's voice again from the first floor as Mamá calmed him down.

Still clutching her pillow, Wendy slipped her bare feet onto the rough floorboards and tiptoed to her round window. She peered out the murky glass. The moon was waxing. It looked like a deflated soccer ball on its side, the church steeple jutting up into the night sky next to it. Wendy sank onto her sleeping bag. Even though it wasn't full, the moon was bright—so bright that the stars were hard to see at first. Wendy waited, her eyes still grimy and tired, blinking at the window, trying not to think of Tom's empty chair at the dinner table every night. Or Papá's angry voice. Then she saw the zigzag of Cassiopeia's friendly stars winking back at her and a warm, soothing feeling filled her chest. She imagined the starlight racing thousands of light-years, passing nebulae and meteors and whole galaxies just to dance through the little window to reach her. The worry creaking around her felt a bit farther away. Her eyes darted to other familiar shapes in the velvety sky—Orion, Canis Major, Cepheus—each one making her world feel a little more solid and friendly.

Her parents' footsteps finally squeaked up the stairs to their room and the stillness of a sleeping house filled the angled space around her. Wendy's body felt soft and heavy against the old chest behind her back. Just as she started to drift asleep, she saw a figure standing in the dark emptiness of the church parking lot. The shape was blurry to her sleepy eyes, but it looked like someone tilting their head up toward the sky, hands stretched out, cupped open as if to catch the starlight.

TEN

ETTA SURPRISED WENDY by dropping by the crooked house on Sunday afternoon. Papá was at a job site and Tom had gone to some kind of cross-country team meeting, so Wendy had talked Mamá into making her favorite lunch—baleadas. Mamá took one look at Etta's fairy face and the thin legs sticking out of her rainbow shorts and sat her down in front of a plate of refried beans and scrambled eggs. Wendy had already wrapped hers in a warm tortilla and was halfway through the baleada.

"Gracias, Señora Toledo," Etta said seriously. Wendy's eyebrows shot up. Etta's Spanish was careful and slower than her usual chatter. It was actually pretty good.

Mamá beamed at Etta, patting her shoulder. She was obviously thrilled that Wendy had a friend over, especially one she could feed. Wendy, on the other hand, wasn't sure she wanted Etta visiting her house. It still smelled slightly of mold.

"My mom is at a team meeting with Luz," Etta explained

brightly, looking at Wendy's baleada and filling her own tortilla the same way. "There's a TV reporter coming to interview Luz tomorrow so they have to get ready. But when they're done I thought you could come with me to meet her." She took a giant bite.

Wendy stared at her. She wondered what Papá would make of this pixie girl who seemed to think giving TV interviews about defying the immigration police was totally fine. And she wanted Wendy to meet the woman with a deportation order.

Before she could answer, Mamá bustled out with fried plantains and Etta started talking about the food. In Spanish. Wendy shook her head and sighed.

Mamá had spoken Spanish to Wendy when she was little, enough to leave her with a wistful memory of lullabies and disjointed words. But as she got older, her parents became more and more strict about their "English only" rule. In the last couple of years Papá had started getting angry whenever Wendy would slip up and use a remembered Spanish word. Of course, Wendy couldn't blame him. Not when people looked at them the way they did.

She remembered the first time she'd felt ashamed of speaking Spanish. They had been driving to Tom's championship track meet when they stopped for gas. Mamá took them inside for snacks, and while they waited in line she had said something to Tom in Spanish. A woman behind them remarked to the white kid at the cash register that people should learn English if they are going to come to this country. Wendy had been eight or nine. She'd clutched at Mamá's skirt and stared. The woman's mouth was pink and there was a little fleck of spit on her bottom lip. At first Wendy just felt confused. The woman wasn't talking to them, but she spoke loudly, like her words were meant for them to hear. If she thought they didn't speak English, why did she want them to hear? Mamá's face went pale and tense, and she kept her eyes facing forward, as if she hadn't heard. Maybe that's why the woman kept talking. Mamá's hands trembled as she placed their things on the counter. It made Wendy want to run out the door and away from the words that made Mamá shrink. From behind them, the woman complained to the cashier about people who got food stamps while poor Americans like her were out there struggling. Wendy wanted to tell her that they *were* American and they had never used food stamps but she was having trouble breathing. Then Tom turned around. He looked right at the woman and actually smiled. Like he thought he could charm her. It didn't exactly work. But she did stop talking. The little fleck of spit stayed on her lip, though, while Mamá paid and the cashier bagged up their things. Mamá took the bag and hurried away, tugging Wendy along. But Tom turned back and in his perfect, All-American English wished the shocked woman a wonderful day. The whole time the little fleck of spit trembled on her lip. Wendy had not been able to eat her snack in the car. She wasn't hungry after that.

Wendy blinked away the memory and looked at Etta, who seemed completely comfortable sitting in the crooked house, eating Guatemalan food and talking in Spanish with her mother. Wendy scrunched up her face at Mamá, wishing she'd tell Etta about their "English only" rule, but Mamá just said, "Your friend is so nice! I will make tea." And she scurried to heat up some water.

Wendy bit her lip. Etta *was* nice. She was also . . . kind of a lot. But for some reason Etta didn't seem like too much here, the way she sometimes did at school. She seemed relaxed and not at all weirded out by Wendy's home. Wendy had almost forgotten what it was like to have a friend over, sharing your space like this. She hesitated, then asked, "Want to come up to my room?"

Everything about the unfinished attic seemed to enchant Etta. She poked into each little corner, plopped herself onto the bed, then jumped back up. Wendy couldn't help grinning at her excitement.

"Is this a star lamp?" Etta asked, holding up a geometric cardboard dome.

"Yeah, astronomy is kind of my thing," Wendy admitted.

"Luz likes the stars too," Etta said, peering at the lamp. "She said she loves looking at them at night. You should talk to her about it sometime."

Wendy immediately felt a squirmy feeling in her stomach. Etta kept talking about Luz like she was just a friend to hang out with after school—but she was basically a criminal.

"Did you make this?" Etta asked. "The holes are different sizes. Wait, did you make them all different to match the real sizes of the stars and stuff?"

Wendy stood up a little straighter. "Yeah, I did," she said shyly. "I mean, not technically the real sizes. Just how they look from earth."

Etta tilted her head to one side and stared at Wendy like a puzzled bird. "Not their real sizes? What do you mean?"

"Well, it's just how they look. From different places," Wendy tried to explain. "It's perspective. Or parallax actually."

Etta's eyes lit up.

"Ooohhh!" She skipped onto the bed again and crossed her legs, her eyes looming up at Wendy. "I love new words. What does *par-a-lex* mean?"

Wendy looked at her skeptically, but Etta's huge, expectant eyes were completely serious.

"It's *parallax*," Wendy corrected. "It means that things look different depending on where you are when you look at them."

Etta scrunched her eyebrows together and pointed at Wendy. "Explain further, oh great astronomer."

Wendy sat on the bed next to Etta, holding the star lamp carefully in her lap. She thought about the giant expanse of the universe where she loved to escape in her mind.

"You know how if you were drawing the stars, you'd just put yellow dots on a black paper or something?" Wendy asked. Etta's eyes were scrunched shut, but she nodded.

"Well," Wendy continued, "the sky isn't flat like that. It's more like . . . like a swimming pool full of . . . I don't know. Glowing sea creatures? Or something?"

"Oh! Or glitter!" Etta squealed, her eyes still shut. "I love glitter."

"It has to glow, though," Wendy said. "And it has to be heavy enough to sink a bit."

"Okay, so big, chunky, glowing glitter!" Etta nodded her head up and down. "That is totally genius, and I would definitely buy it."

Wendy laughed. "Fine. So, you throw these chunks of glowing glitter in the pool, and it floats around and maybe sinks a bit. And if you look down into the water, the glitter closest to you might seem brighter than the rest. But if you dive in and swim past the closest spots of light, you'd see them from totally different directions. So, the faraway ones look brighter when you swim up to them. *That's* how the sky is. The whole universe is 3D; we're just floating in one particular spot." Wendy ran her fingers lightly over the holes on her cardboard lamp. "So, if we looked at a star from two different places in the universe, or even two different places on Earth, it would look different. Because of the angle. That's parallax. Things look different depending on where you're floating."

Etta's eyes popped open. "You are astronomically smart."

Wendy looked down and shrugged, feeling a smile spread over her face. Talking about the things she cared about with a friend felt really good. *Maybe that's how Etta feels when she talks about the woman in sanctuary*, whispered a guilty voice in her head.

Before she could follow that thought, Etta hopped up from the bed. "Let's decorate your room!" She gave Wendy a sly grin. "Do you have any glitter?"

"Absolutely no glitter," Wendy said, setting down the star lamp. "But I still need to hang my science posters. Want to help?"

Moments later, Etta had clambered onto a heavy trunk and was smoothing a poster with pictures of famous scientists against the angled ceiling. Wendy pulled off pieces of masking tape, rolling them into sticky-side-out loops and passing them up.

"It's too bad these are pretty much all men," Etta said, trying to get the corners to stick. "I mean, we totally know that lots of women never got the credit for their work." She glared at a man with wavy white hair and said accusingly, "Who'd you steal ideas from, mister?"

Wendy laughed. "That's Isaac Newton. He discovered lots about how the universe works." She passed Etta more tape. "They named tons of stuff after him. The force of gravity is measured in newtons. And there are Newton's laws of motion. Those are super important. They explain all about what keeps our solar system together."

Etta harrumphed and gave the poster one last smack before plopping down on the old wooden trunk. "Well, I think *you* should have a science law named after you," she said defiantly. Her heels kicked against the side of the trunk, making a soft thudding sound.

"What's in here?" Etta asked, running her hands along the top. "It looks like it's from an old movie set."

"I don't know," Wendy said, stepping closer. She couldn't remember seeing the trunk before. It must have been stored away in her parents' room at their old apartment.

"Can we peek in?" Etta asked, jumping up and down. "Maybe there's treasure!"

Wendy laughed but helped Etta pry at the lid until it finally gave way. The smell that drifted out made her think of old dresses and sawdust. A shallow tray in the top of the trunk was divided into compartments for small items— yellowed papers, folded cloth, a set of old keys, unfamiliar jewelry. Aside from a rosary with a tiny crucifix that might have been real gold, nothing looked that expensive.

Wendy had a nagging feeling that they shouldn't touch anything, but Etta lifted out the tray and set it on the floor to reveal stacks of boxes underneath.

"This *is* like a treasure chest!" she squealed.

"Just try to keep everything exactly as we found it," Wendy said. She couldn't shake the thought that they were uncovering some kind of secret. The chest hadn't been hidden. And no one had said she couldn't look in it. But neither of her parents talked much about their past. And this chest was full to the brim of the past.

Most of the boxes held yellowed papers, mostly in Spanish. In one box they found tins of shoe polish, a stiff brush, and a neat stack of stained polishing rags. Another was full of worn-out books, the edges bit into with age. Some of them were in English—*Pippi Longstocking, Charlotte's Web,* and of course, *Tom Sawyer,* the American name that Mamá had given her son so he could blend in. Wendy peeked in the front cover and saw "Dulce" written in faded ink. This was her mom's book. Underneath, she spotted *Peter Pan.* Wendy tried to picture Mamá as a schoolgirl, following the English words haltingly with her small finger as she struggled to learn the strange language. It was hard to imagine. From the way Mamá closed up whenever Wendy asked questions, it seemed like her childhood was mostly colored by loss and pain, not learning. Or maybe she'd gotten these books later, after crossing the border and getting her green card. Either way, she must have loved the idea of Wendy Darling's world where little girls could go off on fantastical adventures yet still grow up happy and secure. Wendy looked guiltily at Etta to see if she'd noticed the book. Did Etta remember her story about being named after an astrophysicist?

But Etta had moved on to the last box, a rectangular leather case with a metal clasp that gave a satisfying click as it flipped open. Inside they found a manila envelope full of printed pamphlets and posters in Spanish. Wendy held up one that said *"El Salvador Unido"* with a cartoonish drawing of fists in the air. The pamphlets were full of words like "Resistencia" and "Justicia."

"Hey, look at this," Etta said excitedly, holding out a yellowed newspaper clipping. It was a picture of a priest in a long robe with a gentle, scholarly face. He was smiling down at a chubby baby in a white bonnet, one hand raised to bless him and the other tickling his chin. The baby was laughing and reaching for the priest's glasses.

"I've heard of this guy," Etta said, pointing to the caption. "Óscar Romero. From El Salvador. We have a quote from him hanging on our wall at my house."

Wendy leaned closer and read haltingly, *"Monseñor Óscar Romero bendice el hijo de periodista Jesús Herrera y Celestina Toledo de Herrera."*

The names *Jesús* and *Celestina* were underlined in faded blue ink, and underneath was written, "Óscar Jesús Herrera Toledo" with a thin arrow pointing to the baby.

She stared at the words, reading them again and again, her brain racing. Her eyes jumped back and forth from the round-cheeked baby profile with the little fingers lifting toward the priest to the name written in blue.

"Wendy?" Etta put a hand on her shoulder. "Are you okay? You're all . . . frozen up."

Without realizing it, Wendy had begun to do her calm breathing technique that was supposed to steady her when her brain fired too fast.

"This . . . this is my dad's name," Wendy whispered. "Óscar Jesús Toledo. But my dad was born in South Carolina. It can't be him."

She looked from Etta's wide eyes back to the faded newspaper clipping in her fingers and bit her lip.

"Right?" she whispered.

ELEVEN

"HOW OLD IS your dad?" Etta asked.

Wendy had to think about it. "Thirty-eight? Or thirty-nine. I think."

Etta's eyes loomed wide in her thin face. "Wendy, this article is from 1980. That's thirty-eight years ago. That baby could definitely be your dad."

Wendy looked at the name again. *Óscar Jesús Herrera Toledo*. She shook her head disbelievingly. "No, it couldn't. His parents left El Salvador before that. My dad was born in South Carolina. And his last name is just Toledo, not Herrera. And those aren't my grandparents' names."

She looked at the names again. *Jesús. Celestina*. These people couldn't be her grandparents. Papá's father had died before she was born, but she remembered his mother, her abuela. And Abuela's name wasn't Celestina. But Wendy's was. Her pulse raced and she could feel her throat getting tight. She couldn't bring herself to tell Etta that Celestina was her own middle name.

Wendy tried to sound casual. "Maybe—maybe it's a relative?"

"Maybe." Etta did not sound convinced.

Etta tipped the rest of the contents of the manila envelope onto the attic floor. Wendy picked up a small stack of papers and photos tied together with a fraying ribbon. She untied it carefully and unfolded the first paper. It was another newspaper clipping with a picture of people crowding around something on the floor. The headline read, *ROMERO ASESINADO*.

"*Asesinado?*" Wendy whispered. "What does that mean?"

Etta shrugged, squinting at the article. "Romero. That's that priest guy, right? And look. Jesús Herrera's name is on here. He wrote this article."

Wendy scanned the picture of white-robed nuns bending low, their arms reaching out to something on the floor—or someone.

"Oh, no!" Etta gasped softly. "*Asesinado*. That kind of sounds like *assassin*. You think it means . . ."

"Assassinated?" Wendy finished, eyeing the shape on the floor at the nuns' feet. She shivered and moved the clipping to the back of the stack. "Oh," she said quietly, holding up a small card with an ornate border around a picture of the priest. "Yeah, I think it does mean that."

She showed the card to Etta. The Spanish text said "En memoria" and underneath was the name *Óscar Romero, 1917–1980*. On the back was a time and date for a funeral at the cathedral in San Salvador.

"They look so sad," Etta murmured, looking at the next clipping in the packet. Faces streaked with tears marched behind a banner with Romero's name on it. Wendy picked it up and concentrated on the words, trying to understand the headline.

"Etta, do you know what *muertos* means?" she asked hesitantly.

Etta shook her head. She looked over Wendy's shoulder and read slowly, translating what she could. "Forty muertos . . . Romero's funeral service . . . explosiones . . . víctimas . . . I mean, those have to be explosions and victims, right? That doesn't sound good."

The last paper was another "In Memory" card, like the one of Óscar Romero. But this one had a picture of a young woman on it with a border of pink roses. She had a playful, alert smile and short, tightly curled hair. The name across the top read "Celestina Toledo de Herrera" and below her picture was printed "1961–1980." Wendy flipped it over and compared it to the other funeral announcement.

"Look," she said to Etta. "The date for Celestina's funeral was a few days after Romero's."

Etta knelt next to her, holding the newspaper clipping with the names of the baby's parents printed under the photo.

Celestina y Jesús. Wendy took the clipping and held it next to the picture of the pretty woman framed by roses.

The air in the attic room wavered. Wendy felt like she was holding pieces of a puzzle, trying to understand how they fit together. So, Celestina had died around the same time as Romero's funeral. There were explosions and victims at the cathedral. Had she died *at* Romero's funeral? She looked down at the picture of the priest and the laughing baby. Celestina and Jesús's baby. Jesús who wrote newspaper articles.

Who were Celestina and Jesús? Why did her dad have the same name as their baby? *And* the same first name as the dead priest? If that baby *was* her dad, then who was the woman she remembered as her abuela?

"Etta," she said quietly. "I . . . I don't think we should have opened this trunk."

She stacked the papers, tapping them on the floor to straighten the edges, and began tying them together again. "Let's put it all back."

Etta was watching her curiously. *Please don't go all Nancy Drew on me*, Wendy thought, sliding the packet into the manila envelope.

"Okay," Etta said, repacking the boxes into the trunk. "If it weirds you out, I get it." She lowered the lid of the trunk and gave Wendy an impish look. "But *I'm* going to find out more about Óscar Romero."

TWELVE

ON MONDAY MORNING the wall outside the art room boasted a handful of campaign posters. This election was only for vice president, so there were only five kids running. K.K.'s poster read "Make Way for K.K." across the top in green block letters. Her picture smiled out from the center with a speech bubble that said, "I'll be your voice" and a black-and-green border. The K.K. in the picture looked confident and put-together in a black outfit with earrings shaped like tiny green turtles.

"Nice color coordination," Wendy told her.

"You think?" The real-life K.K. was wearing the same outfit, but her smile looked a little less sure.

"It looks amazing," Mal said firmly. "Especially next to P.J.'s."

She nodded her head toward a piece of lined notebook paper with a stick figure in the middle. "Vote P.J. bc u know i'm the best!" was scrawled on the bottom in pen.

"That's just a joke, right?" Yasmin asked, raising her eyebrows.

"It must be," K.K. said. "He wasn't at our candidate meeting. Besides"—she pointed at a professionally printed red, white, and blue poster with Brett Cobb's name emblazoned across the top—"he wouldn't run against Brett."

"*No one* in their right mind would run against Brett," said a voice from behind them. Avery was walking past, her arms linked with two of her friends.

K.K. started to say something, but Mal pulled her away, muttering, "Come on, just ignore her."

Avery smirked at their backs, then saw Wendy staring at her and wrinkled her nose. She pulled her friends down the hall, whispering something that made them lean their heads close to her. They all giggled, looking back over their shoulders. Wendy felt her ears burn.

"You shouldn't worry," Yasmin said softly. Wendy looked up, embarrassed, but Yasmin was talking to K.K. "Everyone is new here, so no one has any advantage. Besides, you're the one who's put in the most work."

Wendy wasn't sure that was true. K.K. did seem to have put in more work, but there were quite a few kids who had gone to school with Brett last year. Avery obviously knew him already. And she was clearly on his side. Wendy looked up at his poster. Somehow, even printed on that sleek paper, Brett's smile had that same magnetic pull that she'd felt when he gave her the note for Yasmin. That note that made Yasmin cry. Wendy shivered and pulled her gaze to K.K.'s bright smile instead. She knew who had her vote.

After math class, yellow half sheets of paper were sticking out of all the lockers. Wendy pulled hers out and looked it over. It was about the school skate party next Thursday. She read the date and realized with a start that next Thursday was her birthday.

Usually, a birthday meant tostones and tres leches cake and an apartment full of neighbors. Even last year, when they had just heard about the raid at the factory up north and the grown-ups' voices had been getting more and more tense every day, they'd still had fun. Everyone sang "Feliz Cumpleaños" while Tom strummed along on his guitar.

She tried to imagine the scene this year, music ricocheting off the warped floorboards in a mostly empty house. The smells of baking and pork mingling with the paint thinner and musty air. A birthday in the crooked house would be miserable. She would have to convince Mamá to just let her celebrate with her new friends at Skate Zone 71 instead. It shouldn't be too hard. She wasn't even sure anyone at home had remembered her birthday. With Papá so busy at work and everything that still had to be done at the house and Tom going to practice every day, no one had mentioned it. She had almost forgotten about it herself.

Wendy walked toward her next class, her mind full of birthday smells and sounds. Then something caught her attention. A few kids were gathered around the campaign posters, whispering and pointing. Wendy looked up and froze, staring at K.K.'s poster. Someone had drawn a turtle with black Sharpie—right over the top of K.K.'s smiling face.

"Oh, come on," Yasmin muttered next to her. "Why are people like that?"

More kids stopped next to them, nudging each other and looking at the drawing. It was a simple cartoon turtle and the round hump of its shell had been filled in with scribbles that completely covered K.K.'s eyes. A few people giggled, but Wendy saw Fiona purse her lips in disapproval and shake her head. Wendy's eyes flicked over the faces crowding the hall. Had K.K. seen it yet?

"Scholars!" A commanding voice reached down the hall, the *clip, clip, clip* of Principal Whitman's heels echoing toward them. "Where should you be right now?"

For a second everyone froze, suspended between the ruined poster and the swiftly approaching principal.

"Miss Adams," Principal Whitman called as she drew closer, her pale face stern.

Avery squealed and slipped her phone guiltily into her pocket. *Did she just take a picture of it?* Wendy thought. *That seems messed up.*

"The next time I see your cell phone out in the hall—"

Principal Whitman's voice cut off as her gaze landed on the poster. Her steps slowed and the throng of kids shuffled aside until the principal stood staring up at the wall, her blue eyes wide under her round, gold-rimmed glasses.

"Well," she said briskly, "let's take care of that." She reached up and pulled K.K.'s poster down in one quick motion. "And unless one of you," she added, peering at the kids in the hall, "knows anything about this, then you had better get on to class." There was a half second of silence, then rustling and scurrying as everyone did as she suggested.

"I'm going to find K.K.," Yasmin said. "She should know about this."

Wendy looked back at the wall as Yasmin headed away. The principal was folding the poster carefully, over and over, until the scribbled photo was hidden under several layers. Wendy thought about K.K.'s little green turtle earrings and how meticulously she had matched the colors on the ruined poster to her photo. She had a sudden urge to cry. *Ridiculous*, she thought, turning away. Crying wouldn't do any good. Not that she could do anything about this anyway.

Suddenly an Etta-shaped blur sped past her.

"Ms. Whitman," Etta said, skidding to a stop in front of the principal. "You can't just take down K.K.'s poster. It's an unfair advan—"

"Miss Carpenter," Ms. Whitman interrupted, in a voice that made Wendy think this was not the first time she'd had to say this to Etta, "what have we said about using our walking feet in the halls?"

"That we . . . should use them?" Etta asked. Then she added earnestly, "But my feet were powered by righteous indignation." Ms. Whitman blinked at her. Etta plowed ahead. "It is completely unfair for K.K.'s poster to come down just because some racist, bigoted—"

"Now, now," Ms. Whitman said firmly. "There is no need for name-calling. It's just a drawing of a turtle. We have no idea who defaced the poster or why." She looked at the clock in the hall. "You had better get to class and let me handle this, Miss Carpenter."

"But you could at least take down the rest of the posters so that everyone's campaign has the same visibility," Etta insisted. "That would make it fair, right?"

Ms. Whitman took a breath and held it for a moment before letting it out, slowly. She seemed to be considering Etta's suggestion. Or maybe she was just doing some deep breathing. Wendy could understand the need for mindfulness exercises with Etta around. "Thank you for your recommendation, Miss Carpenter," Ms. Whitman said. "I know that all the candidates worked hard on their posters, and I would hate to take this away from them because of the irresponsible actions of one person."

Etta opened her mouth to protest but Ms. Whitman held up a hand to stop her. "I will make sure Miss Braun knows that she is welcome to put up another campaign poster. And I'll see that she is given some time today to work on it. Right now I need you to run to class. I will not ask you again." As

Etta turned away, Ms. Whitman corrected herself. "I mean, *walk* to class, please! Just . . . walk quickly."

K.K. brought in a new poster the next day. It was almost the same as the last one except for a row of adorable little cartoon turtles along the bottom.

"Those turtles are so cute!" Yasmin said.

"Mal drew them," K.K. explained. "I was ranting to her about the way that jerk messed up my picture." She stuck putty on the corners of the poster. "It was, like, weirdly aggressive."

"Your exact words were 'Who weaponizes a turtle?'" Mal said with a giggle.

"Yeah," K.K. said, lining the poster up with the others on the wall. "So I decided to lean into the whole turtle thing instead. Mal's into drawing cartoons like that so she offered to help."

"They're kawaii style," Mal said, helping K.K. press down on the corners. "It's Japanese for cute. The whole kawaii aesthetic is pretty much just extreme adorableness."

"I love it," Yasmin said. "They look so much cuter than that scribbled turtle."

Wendy nodded. That was a clever way to flip things on whoever had ruined K.K.'s poster. It showed that she wasn't going to let them push her around.

"Slay the Sharpie vandal with cuteness!" Etta cried, raising a fist in the air. She lowered her arm and added conspiratorially, "Want me to set up a stakeout to catch them?"

K.K. snorted. "I can't let myself worry about that. I have a speech to write. But you do you, Etta."

Even though Etta insisted on popping by the wall in between every class the rest of the day, there was no sign of further sabotage. On Wednesday morning all the seventh graders filed straight into the auditorium after homeroom for the VP candidate speeches.

"She looks amazing!" Yasmin whispered to Wendy, pointing to the row of chairs where K.K. sat on the stage. Her hair was pulled back in a sleek low puff and she had redone her nails in mint green to match her shirt. She tapped them against her notecards, mouthing the words to her speech with her eyes closed.

Wendy had listened to her practice. It was pretty good for a one-minute speech, especially since she'd lost some prep time making that new poster. The candidates had been warned that the mic would cut off after exactly sixty seconds, so K.K. had stressed a lot over her timing.

The student council adviser, Miss Carol, welcomed everyone, reminded them that voting would open after the assembly, and went over the rules about being a respectful audience. Then she motioned to the row of candidates and took her seat. Brett was first. He hadn't worn a suit like the only other boy running, but his shirt was the same light blue as his eyes. As he walked across the stage, Wendy couldn't help but notice how good that color looked on him.

Brett placed both his hands on the podium and paused for a

moment. He leaned forward and said into the mic, "I'm Brett Cobb. Vote for me." Then he walked calmly back to his seat.

There was some feeble clapping. Someone hooted and a couple guys cheered Brett's name. Wendy looked at her friends, but they all seemed just as puzzled as she was.

The next candidate walked up. They looked back at Brett, then out at the audience and shrugged. Everyone laughed and the kid launched into their speech. It was mostly about their plan for stocking the cafeteria with toasters and Pop-Tarts, but the mic cut out before they could finish their last sentence. Still, everyone clapped and cheered as the kid walked back to their seat.

But before the next girl could stand up, Brett got up again. He walked back to the podium, casually, just like last time, looking out at the audience with a smile on his face. Nervous laughter rang out and a handful of people started to clap, but Miss Carol stood up.

"Brett, you had your turn," she said, motioning for him to sit down.

"I have sixty seconds," he said. "I've only used five." She opened her mouth to say more, but he cut her off. "The rules say I get sixty seconds, not when I have to take them." He spread his hands out palms up, as if he were helpless in the face of the rules. He turned to the podium, leaned forward, and said, "I'm Brett Cobb. Vote for me." He lifted one hand in a wave and walked away.

This time the response was quicker. Kids were laughing

and clapping all at once. There were more cheers now, too, and Wendy heard P.J.'s voice call out, "Brett Cobb!"

The other kids onstage appeared confused. She saw them look at Miss Carol, but the adviser seemed just as unsure as they were. Ms. Whitman hurried over and they spoke together quietly for a moment. Wendy was sure they would call Brett off the stage, maybe even ask him to leave. Then Miss Carol motioned toward the podium, and the next girl got up uncertainly. She was shaking as she gave her speech and she spoke so fast that she finished a bit early. They all clapped politely as she hurried back to her seat, but when Brett stood up again, the applause grew much louder. He walked to the podium for a third time, leaned forward, and said, "I'm Brett Cobb. Vote for me." Then he walked back as the room exploded in cheers.

Ms. Whitman motioned Brett over to the edge of the stage. He leaned down to speak to her, but they were too far away for Wendy to hear. Besides, there was still too much clapping and laughing. The kids loved Brett's move, but Wendy was sure Ms. Whitman wouldn't allow it. But when Ms. Whitman turned away from the stage she was smiling and shaking her head in admiration. Brett straightened, walked to his seat, and sat back down. He looked out at the room and gave a cocky little wave.

"Wait, they're just letting him do this?" Etta said. "That is so not fair."

K.K. was next in line, but she hesitated, looking toward

the adviser. The noise finally died down, and Miss Carol, looking a bit frazzled, waved for K.K. to take the podium.

"But he's just going to get up again," Etta hissed. "He's going to get more turns than anyone else!"

"It isn't more *time* than anyone else, though," Wendy whispered. "Not technically." Etta glared at her and she slid down in her seat. "But yeah, it really does seem unfair," Wendy agreed.

"I can't believe this," Etta muttered.

"Shh," Mal said. "It's K.K.'s turn."

K.K. smiled out at the room, her head held high. Wendy had no idea how she could look so relaxed and confident with the excitement of Brett's stunt rippling through the room. But K.K. spoke clearly about fair representation and better lunches and school dances that gave back as fundraisers. Her speech was perfect and she timed it to the exact second. Wendy's whole row whooped and cheered as loudly as they could when she finished. But it didn't matter. Because when K.K. sat down and Brett stood up again, the volume of the cheers drowned all of them out. This time the cheering hardly even stopped when he leaned into the mic and said, "I'm Brett Cobb. Vote for me." It just kept on going until he was in his seat.

Even wearing a suit, the last kid never stood a chance. As soon as he left the podium, Brett was standing up, waving to the rows of kids applauding him. As he leaned into the mic to use his last seconds of speech time, a crowd of voices chanted along with him as he said, "I'm Brett Cobb. Vote for me."

He won the election by a landslide.

THIRTEEN

THURSDAY MORNING WAS rainy, naturally. Wendy's expectations for her birthday were so low it didn't surprise her to wake up to the sound of a steady drizzle. When she came down for breakfast Mamá waved her into the living room. A sparkling blue ten-speed bicycle leaned on its kickstand by the window. Hanging from the handlebars was a white helmet with retro stripes and a heavy-duty bike lock. Wendy ran a hand over the sleek frame of the bike.

"It's perfect, Mamá!" she said, smiling.

"Only, maybe not today," Mamá said apologetically, looking at the drizzling sky. Her shoulders slumped a bit, and Wendy gave her a quick hug and a thank-you kiss.

Even as she walked to school under her umbrella Wendy felt her spirits lift. The rain would clear up soon and she couldn't wait to ride her new bike. It was the one slightly athletic thing that she was good at, and just thinking about the wind blowing against her skin as she rode made her smile.

When she opened her locker twelve mini balloons fell out and floated to the floor while Etta led her friends in an energetic rendition of "Happy Birthday!"

"This is from me and K.K.," Mal said, handing her a gift bag. "She's at her student council meeting, but she said I could give it to you."

K.K. had gotten the most votes after Brett, so she was now the seventh-grade representative on the student council. It wasn't quite VP, but K.K. would make a great class rep.

Wendy peered inside. *We are all made of stars.* The words glittered up at her from a pale lavender T-shirt nestled in fluffs of tissue paper. Tom had shown her this quote once on a poster. She'd told him, "It just means we're the leftovers some old ball of gas vomited out during its death throes billions of years ago." He'd told her it was supposed to be cute and magical. She'd punched his arm.

"Thanks," she said. "It's so . . . cute and magical." And she was surprised to realize she didn't mind it. Yasmin gave her a set of gel pens and a bag of Wendy's favorite sour gummies.

"And this is from me," Etta said, handing her another gift bag. "Well, this and the balloons."

It was a set of artistically designed posters, one for each of Newton's laws of motion. And one blank poster, which Wendy held up questioningly. "And that," Etta said, "is for Wendy's Law!" She beamed at Wendy. "If that old guy gets science laws named after him, then so do you. We just need to figure out what it is, and I'll design your poster."

Wendy laughed and stashed her gifts before hurrying after her friends.

In science class Ms. Park held up a list and announced she had their team pairs for the Science Fair. An excited buzz filled the room. Wendy had decided to build her own telescope and she had already started researching it. But she'd spent so much thought on what her project would be that she hadn't really considered who she'd have to work with. What if it was someone who didn't like her ideas? Or someone who insisted on making something boring, like a baking soda volcano? She sat up straighter, her shoulders tight.

Ms. Park read the first team. "Avery Adams and . . . José Rodriguez."

Avery tucked a glossy strand of chestnut hair behind her ear and wrinkled her nose. "Josie," a voice called from the back. Someone laughed. Ms. Park's beady eyes glared in the direction of the laughter until it choked to a stop. Wendy didn't need to turn around to know where it had come from. P.J. had been making fun of José's name since the first day, pronouncing it with an English "j" instead of the soft "h" sound it made in Spanish. And so had Avery, she realized with a sinking feeling. The thought entered her mind that maybe she should offer to switch partners, but then she glanced at the other kids in the room. Even though there were a decent number of Latinx kids at LPA, she and José were the only two in this class. Wendy imagined what

Avery and P.J. would say about the "Mexican Team" and she sank down into her chair.

"Brett Cobb and Wendy Toledo."

Wendy looked at Brett. She gave a weak smile, and he lifted his chin in a half nod, then turned back around. *At least it's not P.J.*, Wendy thought. Brett seemed pretty smart. And ambitious. He'd want to do well. She just had to convince him about the telescope.

It turned out to be easier than she had expected. During their first planning session Brett seemed distracted, looking around the room as if hoping for inspiration from everyone else.

Wendy cleared her throat.

"I think a telescope would be good." She raised her voice a little to be heard over the other groups. "We could make a Galilean telescope and then measure the positions of the stars or maybe compare two different stars."

Brett looked at her skeptically. "What's that?" he asked, pointing at the notes she had scribbled in the margin of her Science Fair packet.

"Oh, um"—Wendy slid it toward him—"I was just brainstorming."

Brett examined her notes, his eyebrows scrunched together as he scanned her ideas about tubing and her diagrams of lenses.

"You really think you can make a telescope? Like, a legit one? That works?"

Wendy hesitated. She had been reading about telescopes for a while. She'd seen plans online and looked at materials before.

"I'm ninety-four percent positive?" she said.

"Okay." Brett nodded. "Cool." He pulled out his phone and took a picture of her notes. "Let's keep pictures of the process. For the report."

Wendy nodded, impressed. That was a good idea. He was really behind this.

He grinned at her. "You going to the skate party?"

Wendy hadn't expected that. "Oh, yeah. Yeah, it's my birthday." *Oh, shoot*, she thought. *Why did I say that?*

"Nice. Guess I need to find you a gift." The bell rang and Brett grabbed his things. "See you, Wendy." He gave her a crooked smile and left.

Wendy blinked, then let out her breath in a relieved huff. That hadn't been too bad, actually. Brett seemed to believe she could build a telescope. And . . . had he meant it when he said he would get her a birthday gift? The idea warmed her inside and Wendy felt a twinge of guilt. It was so hard to know what to think about Brett. *Why can't feelings just make sense, like Newton's laws of motion?* Wendy thought with a sigh as she packed up her things. Sometimes it seemed like her emotions were operating on a completely illogical orbit.

Tom was in a good mood that afternoon. Maybe he was just happy to be borrowing Papá's truck. Tom and Wendy sang loudly the whole way to the roller rink, and it reminded her of how they used to sing together in their tiny Melborn apartment. Lately whenever Wendy caught a bit of what Tom was listening to with his headphones it was all news or politics. Things that made Papá narrow his eyes and frown. Definitely not music. But now, with the world whipping past them outside, they belted out lyrics together and she couldn't stop smiling. When they pulled into the parking lot, Tom rolled down the windows and sang along to "Here With Me" in a remarkably good falsetto. Wendy slid down in her seat, giggling and trying to stay out of sight of anyone from school.

Inside, kids were already orbiting the rink, disco lights and music cascading over everything. Tom settled into a seat in the corner with his phone, and Wendy scanned the room until she saw Etta and Mal. Then K.K. arrived and soon they were all clinging to each other, laughing and wobbling on their roller skates. None of them was very good, but it didn't matter. They all leaned together, their own little constellation in the moving swarm of kids.

Brett glided by with Fiona, both of them skating in rhythm. They looked good together. Wendy found herself wondering how it would feel to skate in unison with Brett, with his crooked smile and those blue eyes flashing her way under the lights. *Stop it. You don't really even know him*, she told herself. *And there's a good chance he wrote something awful to Yasmin, even if he is cute. Be logical.*

She turned her focus to her feet and the feel of her friends steadying each other as they skated under the dizzying colors. Etta's grip was strong and Mal's hand in hers was warm and safe.

Suddenly Yasmin skated by backward, her feet weaving in an easy motion. She smiled at them shyly and spun around again, graceful and fluid. Her head covering matched her bright pink roller blades that flashed under the lights as she wove effortlessly around the rink.

"Whoa, Yasmin, you're amazing!" Mal gasped.

When the girls were too out of breath to skate anymore, they collapsed in a booth, panting dramatically. Wendy offered to buy them drinks with her birthday cash and headed to the line.

"Hey, Chiquitín." Tom's hand landed on her shoulder. "You having fun?"

But before she could answer he said, "I'm going to hang with my friends out back. I'll check in later." He gave her shoulder a pat and was gone.

Wendy stared as Tom walked away, wondering which friends he was talking about. She was sure Papá didn't know he was meeting anyone here. She thought about all the times Tom had come home too late or hurried out of the house with a vague comment about "training." Sometimes it felt like he had a whole other secret life. A sour feeling knotted in her stomach.

"What did he call you?"

She turned to see Brett carrying slushies away from the

counter. Avery, Fiona, P.J., and a few other kids were with him. Brett's steely blue eyes followed Tom and he asked, "Was that your Mexican name?"

The knot in her stomach tightened.

"I'm not Mexican," Wendy said. She was going to clarify that her parents were from El Salvador and Guatemala, but that felt too complicated. And then Brett might have more questions. Questions that she didn't want to answer. Instead she said, "I'm American," and felt a pang of guilt.

"Wait, really?" said a curly-haired girl. Avery laughed.

"Be nice, Morgan," Brett chided.

"What?" Morgan asked, her eyes wide. "How was I supposed to know?"

"Morgan," Avery said, in the tone of a teacher explaining a new concept, "our wonderful country is a very diverse place." She waved her hand toward the booth where Wendy's friends were sitting. "May I direct your attention to Exhibit A."

"Oh my god, Avery," Morgan said, slapping her arm playfully. She blushed and looked at Wendy. "I just meant, like, you all look . . . you know." She tilted her head toward the booth.

Wendy glanced at her friends. K.K.'s short afro was pulled up in a high puff today and her head was bent next to Etta's turquoise-streaked pixie cut. Mal's shaggy black hair and Yasmin's hijab bent next to them, all of them looking at something on Mal's phone and giggling.

"Kind of like a diversity ad?" Avery asked helpfully.

Morgan giggled. "I guess? I mean, is that okay to say? Cuz you are, like, super diverse."

Wendy didn't know what to say, so she turned toward the counter and ordered. They hadn't really said anything bad. Not exactly. She didn't want to make a big deal out of nothing.

"For real," Avery said. "Remember what your dad said, Brett? How the school has to prove we're diverse enough or something because the district doesn't like us taking all the gifted kids?"

"Something like that," Brett said, slurping his blue raspberry slushie. "He talks a lot."

The person at the counter handed Wendy a pitcher of Coke and a stack of plastic cups. She took them and stepped carefully away from the counter on her skates, focusing on her balance. Out of the corner of her eye, she could see Avery watching her.

"They should totally put a picture of you all on the LPA website." Avery swirled her straw in her cherry slushie. "It would make us look super exotic."

Wendy felt her ears turning red as she tried to maneuver past the group of kids.

"Yes! You guys are so photogenic," Morgan gushed, looking at Wendy and then back to the booth. "There's the pretty Arab girl and Etta, who is so . . . colorful."

"You're allowed to call her gay, you know," Avery said in a fake whisper. "She's proud of it so it's okay."

Morgan giggled and kept talking. It was like she was going down a checklist. "And there's the Black girl."

Wendy tried to ease her way past them, and Fiona stepped back with an embarrassed smile. "Oh, sorry, go ahead," she said, not quite meeting Wendy's eyes.

"And you're Latina," Avery added, pointing her straw at Wendy as she passed by. "And isn't that one girl Chinese?"

"Mal's part Korean," Wendy snapped. "She's Korean American. We have names. And we are *all* American, by the way. We aren't *exotic*."

Avery frowned in annoyance. "You don't have to say it like that. I just meant you all look interesting. It's a compliment. Geez."

Wendy teetered away from them, her throat tight.

Behind her she heard Morgan's voice. "I said photogenic! You guys heard me say photogenic, right?" She sounded hurt.

Sure. Photogenic and exotic. Like imported animals or some kind of food. She wished they had just ignored her. *I also wish I weren't wearing skates*, Wendy thought, stumbling and slopping some Coke over the edge of the pitcher.

"Here, let me get this." Fiona appeared next to her and took the pitcher from her hands.

Wendy looked at her in surprise. Fiona's eyes flicked back to Avery and Morgan. She didn't say anything, but she turned and walked over to the table with the pitcher.

"Oh, hi, Fiona," Mal said, giving her a friendly smile.

"Hi." Fiona stood there for a moment, looking around the table.

Wendy looked at her curiously, wondering what was going through her head. There was an awkward silence, then Fiona set down the pitcher and said quickly, "Okay, bye!" She hurried away.

"What's up with her?" K.K. said.

Wendy shrugged it off. It didn't seem like it would help anything to repeat what she'd heard. Besides, she'd much rather just drink carbonated sugar while laughing at cute animal videos. Mal shared a stash of jelly beans and Pixy Stix and pretty soon they were all hopped up on sugar and giggling at everything. They skated some more, and Wendy let her friends' energy and the lights and music of the skate rink drive out the tight feelings in her chest.

A staff member wheeled out the cart full of light-up souvenirs, and they started trying on different accessories and laughing at each other. K.K. bought a glow necklace and Mal and Etta bought cat ears. They tried to force glowing cat ears onto Wendy's head and she skated away, giggling. Mal and Etta chased her around the skate floor and Yasmin skated after them like a figure skater, a plastic crown flashing red, white, and blue lights over her pink hijab.

Suddenly there was a rattle of wheels from behind. A bunch of boys skated straight into their group, bodies weaving around them and jostling against each other. One of the boys stumbled against her and Wendy felt her skates roll backward as she lost her balance. She threw out her hands as she hit the floor.

"Whoops. Sorry!" The boy who had bumped into her was on the floor, too, but he climbed back up quickly and left with an awkward laugh.

Wendy looked at her friends. It was like a meteor shower of bodies had swept through their group. K.K. clung desperately to the short wall that circled the rink. Etta and Mal had their arms around each other for support, giggling. Yasmin was standing alone, looking a little dazed and adjusting her head covering. Wendy got to her feet, skated over to the wall, and grabbed on next to K.K.

"Good call," K.K. told her, still clutching the top of the wall. "It's wild out here. I'm about done with this skating business."

"Those boys are a menace to society," Etta said as she and Mal joined them.

"I feel like we survived a tornado," Mal said, laughing.

"Yasmin, what's wrong?" Etta asked.

Yasmin was running her fingers along her forehead and fiddling with the fabric. "Oh, just . . . fixing this. It kind of slipped a bit."

"Did those boys pull your hijab?" Etta asked, her voice rising with each word.

"No!" Yasmin said quickly. "I mean, I think one of them

slipped and his hand just grabbed at the air and kind of got a corner . . . but, no. It wasn't like that."

"Are you sure? Because that is a huge deal, Yasmin! If someone tries to pull off your hijab? That's religious bullying!"

"I know, Etta!" Yasmin's eyes flashed. "I'm the hijabi. I don't need you to tell me about bullying."

Etta, who had already opened her mouth to say more, snapped it shut. She gave Yasmin an apologetic look and blew out a puff of air like a balloon deflating. "Right," Etta said. "Okay, just . . . just know I've got your back."

Yasmin gave her a little nod of thanks, but she still looked slightly annoyed.

"Hijabi?" Mal asked.

"Someone who wears hijab," Yasmin explained. "And, yeah, there may be bullies, but I knew that before I decided to wear this." She tucked the ends of the pink scarf over her shoulders and looked across the rink toward the rowdy boys. "Can we sit back down for a minute?"

"Have you ever had anyone mess with your hijab?" K.K. asked as they skated back to their booth.

"No. I've heard about that happening before, though." Yasmin slid into a seat, biting her lip. "I guess that's why it kind of shook me when I felt someone grab at me."

"That would scare me too," Mal said.

Wendy hesitated, imagining what that must be like. She always tried so hard to dress so she wouldn't be noticed.

"Do you ever think about . . . not wearing it?" Wendy asked. "I mean, if it doesn't feel safe?"

"Wearing hijab isn't what makes me feel unsafe," Yasmin said firmly. "Bullies make me feel unsafe."

Wendy hadn't thought of it like that. It wasn't Yasmin's fault if someone else was mean about her hijab. It was on them, not her. "That makes sense," Wendy said, even though she couldn't imagine being as confident about it as Yasmin.

"Yeah, what you wear isn't the problem," Etta said, nodding vigorously. "They are." She glared at the boys.

"They didn't actually do anything, Etta," Yasmin told her. Even as she said it, though, Yasmin didn't sound 100 percent certain.

Etta sighed and raised her hands in surrender. Wendy thought about the way Brett had called her Mexican and Avery had said exotic was a compliment. They hadn't actually done anything either. So why did those things make her throat feel tight? And make Yasmin want to be done skating? Suddenly Wendy didn't want to be here anymore, with all the people and all the lights and all the feelings. She wished, for probably the hundredth time that week, that she could drift off into outer space.

"Hey, let's go to the arcade," Mal said eagerly. "There aren't many people over there and I brought coins."

The mood shifted and everyone started piling out of the booth. Wendy glanced at the arcade games in the corner and saw Morgan and Avery at the claw machine.

"Actually, I need to get going," she said. "My brother is supposed to drive me home now."

It sounded like a pathetic excuse to her, but her friends just waved, and Etta gave her "one last birthday hug." She was on her way to return the Rollerblades when someone skated up fast, swinging around to slow to a stop in front of her.

"I got you something," Brett said. Wendy stared at him, startled, as he smiled his adorable, crooked smile and pushed something into her hair. She lifted her hand and felt the spiky shape of a plastic headband.

"See, Birthday Girl? Red, white, and blue. It's an American crown." Brett leaned in. "Just like you. Consider it an apology for calling you Mexican."

Wendy's stomach twisted and each breath squeezed out of her chest too fast. He was giving her a gift. So why was her body acting like it was a threat?

"Well? You like it?" Brett asked.

She licked her lips. "Thank you," she whispered. The words tasted wrong in her mouth, and she kept her eyes on his chin.

Brett laughed and said softly, "Happy birthday, Lady Liberty."

Wendy practically fell onto the bench as he skated away. She scrabbled to untie her skates and return them to the counter. He had apologized. Well, he'd apologized for calling her Mexican. *Like it was an insult*, she thought with disgust. But it *had* bothered her, the way he talked as if all of

Latin America was just one country. And then he had come to apologize and give her a gift. Wendy groaned. Her emotions were a tangle. She didn't know what to think, but she knew she wanted to go home.

She was jamming her feet back into her galaxy shoes when she heard Etta's curious voice. "Oh, you found Yasmin's crown?"

Wendy's hand flew up to her head and she pulled the headband off, staring down at it. It was Yasmin's. She pictured Yasmin, insisting that the boys hadn't really done anything, but looking uncertain as she patted her head. Wendy hadn't realized her crown was gone. Her stomach sank.

"Yeah, um . . . here." She shoved it at Etta. "I have to go. My brother's waiting. Bye."

She didn't wait to hear a response. As soon as the door swung shut behind her, muffling the music, Wendy pulled out her inhaler and took a deep breath from it, blinking rapidly. She stood for a moment, letting the outdoor air fill her lungs again and again while she stared into space. The dull gray sky looked empty and sad.

FOURTEEN

SHE HAD JUST thanked Brett Cobb for giving her a stolen headband—one he had ripped from her friend's head. It had all happened so fast. She hadn't even seen him with the boys who crashed into them. But that crown looked just like Yasmin's. And Wendy had *thanked* him. Actually thanked him! Tears burned her eyes. What choice did she have? Yasmin spoke perfect English. Wendy was pretty sure her entire family was born in the United States. That was supposed to protect them. Wasn't it? Suddenly she was furious at her brother for calling her Chiquitín in public. And then abandoning her.

She let out an angry huff of air and started toward the pickup, scanning the lot for Tom. A car drove up and in the sweep of headlights Wendy saw Tom leaning against Papá's truck, deep in conversation with a few older teens she didn't recognize. She knew most of the kids from his track team and his friends from school. But these teens were unfamiliar and again she had the strange sense that Tom had another world out there that the rest of the family knew nothing about. The car backed into a space across from them and she saw Tom squint in the sudden brightness. Just as she opened her mouth to call out to him, the slam of a car door sounded out like a shot. The car that had just pulled in still had its headlights on, and a broad-shouldered man stood behind the beams of light.

"You kids here to skate?" he asked, and something about his voice made Wendy freeze.

"We look like we're skating?" one of them retorted.

Someone else barked out a laugh, but a young woman said something sharp under her breath and he quieted. She stepped slightly forward, and in the lights Wendy saw a pretty Latina with half her head shaved. Despite the tension in the air, she looked completely relaxed, her hands in her pockets.

"May I help you?" she asked the man in a voice that somehow sounded both authoritative and mildly amused.

In the dimness Wendy saw him rest his hands on his hips. A walkie-talkie on his belt crackled with static and a garbled transmission flicked on and off.

"Dude, he's a cop," someone whispered. Wendy looked at Tom uneasily. What was he doing out here? Who were these people and why were they worried about the cops?

"It's all good, man," someone else called out. "We're just here chillin'."

"See, this isn't really a chillin' spot," the man said coldly. "This is where folks park so their kids can have a nice, safe time skating. So maybe you should find somewhere else to . . . chill." He stared at them, and even cloaked in shadow his eyes were like a freeze ray.

The woman with the shaved head smiled and looked back at her friends. She gave her head a nod. As if it were a signal, they all began to move, murmuring goodbyes and shooting looks at the man.

Tom turned away, too, but his eyes met Wendy's and he stopped. Guilt flickered over his face for a brief second, just a twinkle in the dark. She stepped forward quickly, longing to climb in the truck and drive away and forget this miserable night. Too late, she realized the man was still watching them.

"This your truck, son?" he asked. Wendy couldn't shake the fear that trickled down her back when she heard that voice, but she wasn't sure why.

"My dad's," Tom answered, smiling pleasantly. Turning to her he said, "Let's get going, kid."

"Hold up." The man reached out a hand, his white palm facing toward them like a stop sign. "You have a license, son?"

Tom didn't move for what felt like an eternity. She stepped closer to him and said quietly, "Come on, Tom, show it to him."

The man stepped closer and suddenly Wendy knew that she *had* seen him before. He was the man from the black car by the library, with his steely jaw and hard eyes like blue marbles. Her fingers closed around her inhaler in her pocket, and she reminded herself to breathe slowly.

"Where are you from, *Tom*?" His voice leaned heavily on

111

the name. Then he repeated himself, in Spanish. "¿De dónde eres?" His accent was careful like Etta's but with none of the warmth. Unbidden, stories of American citizens being arrested by the immigration police for speaking Spanish came to her mind. Her legs locked into place as she waited for Tom to explain his way out of this.

"Um . . . sorry?" Tom asked with an awkward laugh.

"I believe I asked you where you're from, son," the man drawled, his hands on his hips. "Which didn't you understand? The English or the Spanish?"

Tom swallowed and said, "I was born in South Carolina. Been here in Ohio for a while, though."

"Ahhh," the man said. Then he stepped forward. He was within arm's reach of Tom now. Even under her fear, Wendy was fiercely proud of her brother for not backing away.

"The thing is, Tom—" This time he said it as if they were old friends on a first-name basis. He was proving something by using his name, and Wendy bit her lip. She shouldn't have said his name. *But it doesn't matter*, she told herself desperately. *He didn't do anything!*

"I'm off-duty at the moment," the man continued. "So maybe it's your lucky day. Maybe you and your sister here can just drive away and never see me again." His walkie-talkie crackled again, and he leaned toward them, talking over the static. "But I've got a kid inside and I don't like to see thugs like you clogging up our safe spaces. My memory's real good, Tom. And the next time I see you, I'm gonna be asking for more than a license." He straightened and took a lazy step back, but he didn't turn around. "Váyanse a casa," he said. *Go home.*

"Get in," Tom told her, his voice low and tense. Wendy had to try the handle three times before her shaking hands pulled open the door to the truck. She kept her eyes glued to the side mirror as they pulled away, watching the man's shadow. As they reached the corner, he turned, and his back faced their way in the headlights. Three white block letters were clearly visible on his dark jacket. *ICE.* He wasn't a cop after all. He was something much worse.

"Why didn't you show him your license?"

Tom didn't answer. The streetlights swept over his profile, all angles and tension.

"You're American, Tom! Why not just show him?"

"Don't you get it?" Tom said roughly. "I'm not the one with the problem. ICE doesn't just look at your name, then forget about you if you're clear. They look up everyone you live with too."

Wendy stared at him, her brain racing. The photos from the trunk in the attic expanded in her mind, crowding out everything else.

"But . . ." She searched for words. "Papá is American. He was born here." She stubbornly ignored the Salvadoran baby who had her father's name. "And Mamá has resident papers. She has a green card."

Tom glanced at her quickly. "Have you seen her papers?"

Wendy opened her mouth to answer, then stopped. She'd never asked to see their papers. Her parents had told her they had them, and she'd wanted so much for that to be enough. A sick feeling rose in her chest. She'd been telling herself that Mamá was just scared because people were mean about her English not being great. But was that really enough of a reason to move? Or was there more to it? If ICE looked up her parents, what would they find?

Wendy took deep breaths and made herself think logically. Nothing had happened. Everything was fine. She repeated the words over and over in her head the whole drive home.

Wendy stepped through the front door, wondering what to say to her parents. But immediately the sounds of "Happy Birthday" rang out through the darkness, Papá's deep voice and Mamá's clear one rising in unison. She saw Mamá's face floating into the room in a halo of birthday-candle glow over a cake that was way too big for just their family. Tom joined in the singing and Wendy wrapped her arms around herself as her family's voices washed over her. She felt like she was watching everything through a telescope, the candlelight flickering like far-off stars in the darkness.

The song ended, but Wendy knew it wasn't over yet. Papá insisted on singing at least four different variations of birthday songs every year, until the candles were little stubs surrounded by a melted pool of colored wax mixed with frosting. He launched into "Feliz Cumpleaños" and Wendy groaned loudly, as usual, trying to pretend she was anxious to blow out her candles. But her heart wasn't in it. She didn't even have a wish. What was the point? There was too much, and it was too impossible. Should she wish for Brett and his friends to be nicer? For their project to win the Science Fair? For Mamá to be more American? She felt a stab of guilty pain at the thought. In the dim light, she could see Mamá's face smiling gently and singing along with Papá, who was now clapping boisterously to a different birthday song in Spanish. Why should Mamá have to change who she was? And who even decided that American looked or sounded a certain way anyway? None of it was fair.

Wendy blinked, her eyes dangerously close to leaking, and suddenly realized that everyone was waiting for her.

"Wish, mi estrella!" Papá bellowed, his party voice echoing off the walls. Wendy swallowed, her wishes all a muddle in her head, and took a breath. Which of them would have the best chance of actually coming true?

"Come on, Chiquitín." Tom smiled faintly at her.

Even though Wendy had been thinking about the Science Fair, the thing that jumped into her mind as she blew and the last star flickered out was a wish that ICE would just disappear.

FIFTEEN

"HEY, WANT TO come with me to visit Luz this weekend?" Etta leaned over her lunch tray, dipping her veggies into Wendy's hummus.

Wendy gulped, then pushed the hummus across the table. "Here, I don't like this anyway."

"I know you don't. You never eat it." Etta picked up her clementine and set it on Wendy's tray. Wendy looked at it, surprised. She'd never told Etta clementines were her favorite. This girl saw everything.

"So, want to?" Etta continued. "Luz gets lonely. Because, you know, she can't leave or anything and it's just a church. I mean, it's fine. But I wouldn't want to live there. Especially when it's empty and all . . . tomblike. Not that I've ever been in a tomb. Anyway, I want to go and see if she can teach me more Spanish."

Wendy took a huge bite of her cheese sandwich as Etta talked. Even though her parents had stopped speaking

Spanish around her, she'd learned some from Alicia. Maybe she could learn more from Luz. *No*, she told herself. *I'm supposed to stay away from her.* Papá's words echoed in her head. *"That woman has nothing to do with us."*

"Etta, you're doing it again," Mal said, sipping her orange juice.

"What? Talking too much?" Etta asked.

Mal peered at Etta over her juice and nodded.

Etta grimaced. "Yeah, I know. But the words—they just keep coming! Oh, hey!" She leaned forward. "Have either of you seen Yasmin?"

Mal and Wendy both shrugged.

"I think she's eating in the library. Again. And I *know* why." Etta's eyebrows dove downward into an angry V and she shot a glance toward Brett and his friends. "P.J. had better quit messing with her or I'm going to *end* him."

Wendy snorted through her mouthful of food. Tiny, pixie-like Etta *ending* anyone was ridiculous. Especially P.J., who was almost as tall as Tom with arms like tree trunks.

Etta squinted at Wendy over a celery stick.

"Don't underestimate me, kid," she said. Then she fell eerily silent, munching her veggies with quiet menace.

Mal caught Wendy's eye and gave her a worried look. Wendy shrugged. She 100 percent didn't want to think about P.J. or about Brett. She could picture his smile and hear him calling her "Mexican." But he'd apologized. The familiar tight feeling hovered in her chest, threatening to creep through her lungs and wrap around her throat. She blinked the thought away and forced herself to finish her lunch.

But putting off Etta was not easy. She cornered Wendy on their way to free period, dragging her into an empty classroom.

"So here's the deal," Etta told her, eyes blazing. "I know Yasmin said nothing happened. But she doesn't *ever* come to lunch anymore. And I know those boys pulled her crown off at the skating rink." She leaned closer and said intently, "I think they were *trying* to pull her hijab. So I went to Principal Whitman because this is racial and religious bullying. But then she asked me who exactly pulled off her crown. And I didn't actually see anything happen and Yasmin won't say." She huffed in annoyance. "So did *you*?" Etta snapped her mouth shut and waited, fixing her fiery gaze on Wendy. The sudden silence caught her off guard.

"What?" she asked weakly.

"Did you," Etta said with excruciating patience, slowing down each word for emphasis, "see who pulled off her crown?"

Wendy gulped, discomfort crawling in her belly. She pictured Brett, pushing the flashing crown onto her head, with his crooked smile.

"I . . ." Wendy felt her mind racing. Maybe he found it on the floor. Or maybe it wasn't Yasmin's. There had been a pile of headband crowns in that cart. But a sinking feeling deep inside told her it had been Yasmin's. And if it wasn't Brett who pulled it off it was probably one of his friends. But what would Brett do if she told? She was supposed to blend in, for her family. For Mamá. And who would believe her over Brett, student council vice president and golden boy? Her windpipe was freezing up. She could feel the tension clamping around her neck.

"Wendy!" Etta's voice was not patient anymore, and she grabbed Wendy's arms, giving her a shake. "Snap out of it! You had the crown. You know who took it! Was it P.J.?"

"Etta." Wendy said her name around gritted teeth, trying to force her throat to relax. She could feel the tension all over her body, spreading like a fog threatening to fill her lungs. "Etta, just drop it."

Etta let go of her arms and stepped away, her sharp eyes boring into Wendy's.

"I don't get it," Etta said. "Brett and P.J. and them aren't just randomly mean, Wendy. They are mean to people like *you*!" Etta's voice rose and Wendy could feel her own tension rising with it. "Why would you let them do it?" Etta continued, high and loud and accusatory. "Why, Wendy? You have to stick up for your people, you know!"

Wendy's dark brown eyes snapped back to Etta's bright green ones, the rumbling inside her now a roar in her head. She was breathing too fast, not slow and steady, but she couldn't help it.

"*My* people?" she asked quietly.

Etta blinked, registering what she had just said. "I . . . I just meant you need to do what's right," she clarified.

Wendy took a step forward. "It must be nice to always know what's right," she hissed, surprising herself with the venom in her voice.

Etta stared back. "But . . . I mean, it's obvious what's right. You know what's right too! You're just scared."

The accusation stung, and Wendy felt something crack inside her. "Of course I'm scared!" she exploded, her hands clenching into fists at her sides. "I'm scared because one day, ICE raided a factory and Alicia's dad never came home. I'm scared because I watched my best friend cry her eyes out for weeks and stop eating." She gulped down a sob. "Because she knows that if they send him back to El Salvador the gangs are waiting for him. I'm scared because one morning Alicia's sister told me she was too sick to come to school, but when I got home her house was totally empty." Etta was staring at her, and Wendy registered her shocked face but couldn't stop. The words poured out as quickly as the tears streaming down her cheeks. "They had all just *left*, and she didn't say goodbye. She didn't even take her unicorn-kitty tape dispenser. She just left it in her locker with all her stuff and Mr. C was just throwing it all out, but I made him give it to me because it was her favorite and it's all I have left of my best friend, and I don't even know where she is or if she's okay. *That's* why I'm scared!"

Wendy stopped, trying to steady her breath, but the sobs kept wrenching out of her.

"I—I didn't know all that," Etta said. "But . . ." She swallowed, her pixie face thoughtful and a touch defensive. "Well, isn't that just as much reason for you to help Yasmin? And, I mean, Luz is trying to stop that exact same thing from happening to her, and she's fighting—"

"NO! Etta, you don't get it at all!" Wendy could feel her throat clenching. "You want to know why else I'm scared? I'm scared because *your friend Luz* is hiding practically IN MY BACKYARD and my mom might be next! It doesn't matter that Luz is nice or that she likes the stars. It's not that simple. It's my MOM, Etta! Isn't protecting my family more important? Can't that be what's right?"

Wendy knew her voice was too loud in the empty classroom. She was practically screaming at Etta. But Etta and her self-righteousness were too much. Etta and her inclusivity posters. Etta and her meetings with Principal Whitman. Etta constantly pulling Wendy out of her safe zone and into some intense crusade.

"Maybe there's a reason I don't want to go around drawing all this attention to myself, Etta. And maybe Yasmin doesn't want more attention either. Did you ever think of that?" Wendy felt like her anger was pushing the words out of her.

"You—you never told me any of that," Etta said, sounding hurt. "About your mom."

Of course she hadn't. Wendy had never meant to tell

anyone. She didn't even like to admit her doubts about Mamá's papers to herself. She'd just been so mad and mixed up inside, and Etta had kept pushing at her and now . . . She squeezed her eyes shut.

"Why can't you just leave me alone?" Wendy choked out.

Etta's mouth fell open.

"I'm trying to be your *friend*!" she snapped.

A voice cut into the charged atmosphere. "Um, ladies?" K.K. was leaning through the doorway, watching them under arched eyebrows. "You sure you want to broadcast this all down the halls?" Then K.K. looked closer at Wendy's tear-streaked face and her heaving shoulders. "Are you okay?" she asked.

Wendy started to nod, but fumbled for her inhaler, sobbing and dropping it to the floor with a clatter. Etta looked at it, startled, then scooped it up and stepped toward Wendy. Without thinking, Wendy pulled away from her. Etta froze, hurt filling her face. Then she shoved the inhaler at K.K., spun on her heels, and ran out the door.

Silently K.K. handed Wendy the inhaler and led her to a chair. Wendy counted steady beats as she breathed in the medicine, grateful for K.K.'s hand on her back. When her breath had evened out, she opened her eyes to see K.K. watching her cautiously.

"So," K.K. asked, "what did Etta do?"

Wendy licked her lips, ashamed of her outburst.

"Nothing really. Just . . . she just wants to be a good friend."

She didn't know what else to say, but K.K. nodded as if she had given an explanation.

"Coretta Carpenter can be a bit extra." K.K. grinned. "You know, last year she started a Black Lives Matter club at our elementary school. Pretty sure she thought it was gonna fix racism." She shook her head affectionately. "I love the girl, but sometimes she makes zero sense."

"What happened?"

"Not a whole lot." K.K. shrugged. "We handed out BLM buttons to everyone and set up a 'safe space' in the library to talk after lunch every day. Only, like, four kids ever came. Etta had other ideas, but we all mostly just wanted a place to talk. She just . . . doesn't always get it. Don't get me wrong, though; she's nothing like Avery and her squad."

K.K.'s face clouded, and Wendy thought about the girls who usually orbited Avery Adams. Girls like Morgan, who had told Miss Hill yesterday that she couldn't participate in the racial equity art project because she "didn't see race." Or Fiona, who looked embarrassed but still giggled whenever P.J. said something horrible.

"I mean, Etta's great. And she will definitely stick up for you no matter what," K.K. continued. "But she's got her own black-and-white world she lives in. She can't know your life."

Wendy took a shaky breath, the guilt in her heart easing up a smidge.

"A bit extra" was an understatement. Etta was all or nothing—usually all. It was part of what Wendy liked about her. Etta could make you feel safe and warm and fill your locker with balloons for your birthday. But around Etta you never knew when she'd see some wrong that needed righting and go into battle formation, regardless of what might get trampled along the way. Regardless of how the people she was fighting for might feel.

It was better that Wendy had been honest with her. Now she could just lay low and let Etta do her own thing.

"What crusade is she on about now anyway?" K.K. asked.

Wendy wiped at her eyes. "About Yasmin getting bullied."

K.K. furrowed her brow. "Yasmin's getting bullied?"

"I guess that's why she's been eating lunch in the library," Wendy explained. "Etta thinks it's P.J."

K.K. let out a laugh. "Oh, that's perfect!"

Wendy looked at her, startled. But K.K. just shook her head and said, "That's so Etta. Full speed ahead without all the facts. Wait until Yasmin hears about this."

"So, she's not being bullied?" Wendy asked slowly.

K.K. grinned. "Don't worry. Yasmin is fine. If anyone was actually messing with her, I don't think she'd just hide. Yasmin may look real sweet with her dimples and all, but she's no pushover. And Etta is dead wrong about what's going on at lunch. I'll let Yasmin tell her that, though. In fact, Yasmin might enjoy setting her straight."

Wendy could not imagine confronting Etta on purpose. Etta was terrifying even when she was on your side.

K.K. saw her skeptical look. "No, really. She might be

quick to lose it, but Etta's also pretty good about admitting when she's wrong. And that girl *needs* people to tell her when she's wrong. She'd walk straight off a cliff if she got it in her head there was a good reason to and no one stopped her."

"She is . . . a lot," Wendy agreed.

"You gotta admit, though," K.K. said, "life's a lot more interesting with Etta around."

Wendy nodded slowly. Interesting, maybe. But was it safe?

SIXTEEN

BRETT HAD SAVED her a seat in science, which was just as well since Wendy was trying desperately not to look in Etta's direction. She slid into the seat next to Brett, her insides churning. All she could see when she looked at him was Yasmin's crown flashing at the skating rink. But K.K. had insisted Yasmin wasn't being bullied. Maybe that whole thing had been an accident? Brett gave her his signature crooked smile, brushing his hair out of his eyes as he leaned forward.

"Ready for a killer project?" he asked, sliding a book toward her. It was a library book about telescopes. Wendy reached out a finger and flipped through the pages. She stopped on a diagram of a Kepler telescope and examined the images.

"This is a lot like what I was thinking, actually," she murmured.

"Do you mean you understand it?" Brett asked eagerly. "I stared at that page for, like, ten minutes and couldn't figure out how it would work."

"Um, yeah, I do," she said, with a glimmer of pride. "I think the Kepler telescope would be better than the Galilean for actual experimenting. It'll give a wider field of vision. Here's what I was thinking."

She opened her folder and took out the stack of papers she had covered with notes and sketches. A prickle of discomfort crept up the back of her neck as Brett thumbed through the pages, but she shoved it aside. It wasn't like it was a private journal or something. And he was looking over the papers with undisguised admiration even though they were pretty messy.

"I'm really bad at drawing," she admitted as he examined her drawing of the lenses.

"I'm decent," he said. "I can take a shot at them." He took out his phone and snapped pictures of her diagrams. "I'll look over these and draw up something."

Wendy found herself relaxing a bit, and when Brett offered to buy what they needed she was happy to hand over the list of supplies. By the time the bell rang, Wendy was feeling better about her project and even about Brett. He had been so nice today. Sure, that note to Yasmin hadn't been good. But she hadn't even seen what it said. Maybe he'd meant it as a joke. Or maybe it was a misunderstanding. Maybe he really was just a cute guy who thought she was smart enough to build a telescope. She slung her bag over her shoulder and headed to her next class.

The wall across from the art room had turned into a

notice board of sorts. It was covered with posters of upcoming events, and Wendy stopped to look at the Science Fair notice. She let herself imagine winning for a moment, her beautifully designed telescope and Brett's drawings impressing even the rep from the planetarium.

"Are they serious with this?" said an angry voice behind her. Wendy turned, startled, to see K.K. glaring at the wall. "Look at what the PTO is up to," K.K. said, pointing to a flyer from the Parent Teacher Organization. "*'Race-based or merit-based? Parent discussion of admission policy.'* They're really trying to say kids are either getting in *because* of their race *or* on merit?" K.K.'s face flushed in anger. "Like it can't be both!" For a moment she reminded Wendy of Etta.

"Oh yeah," Mal said, walking up and peering at the paper. "My mom got an email about that this morning, and she went into a full-on rant about the wording. I'm guessing she'll be at that meeting for sure." Mal grimaced. "And probably in lawyer mode."

Wendy looked closer at the notice, forgetting about the Science Fair for a moment. "'Race-based or merit-based?'" she read aloud. "What does that mean?"

"It's about how they admit kids to the school," Mal said. "Merit-based means you get in on test scores only."

"I thought that *was* how they admitted kids to LPA," Wendy said.

"Well, it used to be," Mal explained. "But it was pretty unfair to some kids. Parents with money would get tutors for their kids and send them to all these extra camps and stuff. So kids from poorer families who were just as smart didn't usually test as high because they didn't have the same experiences and opportunities."

K.K. looked at Mal, impressed. "Good explanation. You should join the debate team."

Mal shook her head no, so vigorously that her glasses slid down her nose. "No way. My mom's the lawyer, not me. I'm just repeating what I've heard her say a million times," she said, pushing them back into place. "Anyway, I guess some people don't like that it's changed. Now LPA has spots just for kids from low-income families who score high on tests. Or for kids who aren't native English speakers."

Wendy had grown up speaking English, but she thought about José and some of the other kids who hadn't. "And people are complaining about that?" she asked.

"Well, for a school like this one that has been around a long time, it means that it looks . . ." Mal hesitated. "Different than it used to."

"You mean there are more Black and brown kids going here now," K.K. clarified, her lips tightening.

Mal shifted uncomfortably. "Well, no one actually says that. But yeah. My mom was practically the only Asian kid when she went here. It's obviously way less white now. One of the moms at the last meeting was trying to say LPA lowered their standards just to look more diverse."

K.K. made a disgusted sound and Wendy swallowed. If

parents didn't like how the students looked, then it didn't matter if she spoke English. She was still brown.

"Well, whichever parent made this flyer already knows what they think," K.K. said. "They're implying that kids are getting in just because of their race." She raised an eyebrow. "Wanna take bets on whose parents are on that side?"

"No bets!" Mal said. "All I have is candy and I'm not gambling away my sugar. Besides, my mom can take them all on. She lives for a good argument." Mal sighed dramatically. "How I am even her child is a mystery. Do you think Etta and I were switched at birth?"

Wendy giggled, and Mal grabbed K.K.'s arm and led her away. "Not to totally change the subject or anything," Mal said brightly, "but what season of *Supernatural* are you on? Because I NEED you to get caught up!"

"You can't just bring up *Supernatural* whenever you're trying to avoid conflict, Mallory," K.K. said, laughing. But she answered her question anyway as they walked.

Wendy tuned out their talk about demons and complicated family relationships. She had enough of that in real life. Well, the complicated family relationships part anyway. She hoped her parents weren't planning on coming to this PTO meeting. If it was going to be as messy as her friends seemed to think, her complicated family should probably stay away.

Between spoonfuls of lentils and pork that night Wendy stared vaguely at the wall, wondering how much magnification they would need to really do a proper study of the stars. Her bowl was nearly empty when the tension in her parents' lowered voices finally cut through her thoughts. Papá's lips were tight, and his breath huffed in between bites in irritated grunts. Wendy's attention suddenly came into focus, shifting from her telescope plans to the charged air around them. Her eyes flew to the paper in front of Papá. His rough fingers pinned it to the table, and Mamá kept glancing between the paper and the door. Wendy craned her neck to read it. It was Tom's cross-country practice schedule. *They must have been talking about Tom*, she realized with a sinking feeling. That schedule was the reason he'd been out late almost every night. Wasn't it?

Just then the door banged open and Tom's clear voice singing along to Beyoncé drifted into the room. He dropped his bag by the stairs and pulled his headphones down until they hung around his neck. The last few notes died out as he saw Papá's glare.

"How was practice?" Papá asked, too casually.

Tom's face turned wary. He looked from Papá to Mamá.

"Ummm, okay." He shrugged and stepped into the room, eyeing his bowl of stew, the chunks of pork floating in broth long since gone cold.

"¡Qué rico, Mami! I'm starved."

Before he could sit, Papá's hand stretched across the table, slapping the paper next to his bowl.

"And this, Tomás? Monday, Wednesday, Thursday. Today is Friday. There's no practice on Fridays, Tomás!"

Wendy sank down in her seat. Papá almost never called him Tomás. It wasn't even his name, actually. He was officially just Tom, like in the dusty *Tom Sawyer* book from the attic, a name brimming with quaint American boyhood.

Tom had looked almost happy when he came in, but his face was changing now. The line of his mouth stretched thin and tight, mirroring Papá's.

"I had other stuff to do."

"Other . . . stuff?" Papá stood, glaring up at Tom. When had Tom gotten taller than him? Wendy wondered. "You told your mother you had practice because you had *stuff*? You had *stuff* on Tuesday too? And last weekend? You do a lot of this *stuff*?"

Tom's defiant chin tilted upward. "Yeah, I do. And it's more important than running in circles around some field."

Mamá sucked in her breath and made her disapproving *aaiii, aaiii* sound.

"Running is important, mijo!" she said. "You love to run. This year you go to the Nacional."

Tom's eyes softened slightly, but he shook his head. "There's things that actually matter out there, Mamá."

"What are you saying?" Papá's anger had worry in it now. "You have been running, haven't you? You've been training?"

Tom looked down and shrugged. "Yeah, mostly." Then his shoulders straightened and he looked up again. "But I'm gonna quit."

A stunned silence enveloped the room. Wendy's mind

wandered to the vacuum of space and imagined how quiet it would be there. She waited for an explosion from Papá to jolt her back.

Instead Mamá's soft voice insisted, "Pero, mijo, you cannot mean that! You have the beca, the scholarships to get. And— and your team needs you."

Tom's eyes flashed. "How am I supposed to care about sports when there's families like ours being ripped apart?"

"No, stop—" Papá started, but Tom cut him off, his voice growing stronger.

"*You* need to stop! You need to stop pretending! There are toddlers in prison at the border and kids coming home to find their parents deported! There are people who have never committed any crime getting arrested illegally and they're never heard from again!"

Tom's voice was clear and solid. Wendy had never seen him like this, so sure of something. Her brother was easy-going and quick to please, never saying anything that anyone would disagree with or question. Tom was the one who could slip into any situation and be whatever he was supposed to be, right there and then. Not this angry teenager staring down Papá.

"That has nothing to do with us!" Papá insisted.

But Tom was done listening to Papá tell them to stay out of everything. Wendy could see it in his face. This time he wasn't going to back down.

"Oh, sure, nothing at all," Tom said sarcastically. "Don't

think we haven't noticed how scared you are. How you ran away from Melborn when the raids got bad. How you found a nice white neighborhood where no one knows us and a junky old house to hide us away in!"

"Enough!" Papá roared, louder than Wendy had ever heard him before, but Tom barely flinched.

"No! It's not enough! Why don't you DO something? How can you just watch this all happen? It's not going to stop! Hiding and pretending is not enough!"

"And what are you going to do then?" Papá yelled at him, his finger now pointing at Tom's chest. "You are somehow going to stop it?"

Surprisingly, Tom's face cleared. He almost smiled. Then he said quietly, almost to himself, "I'm sure going to try."

And with that he left the room, taking the stairs two at a time and leaving only the sound of his bedroom door closing firmly upstairs. Wendy, slouched so low in her chair that her eyes were nearly level with Tom's abandoned bowl of stew, watched her parents. Papá's shoulders slowly fell into a soft, round shape. Mamá slipped quietly around the table and rested a hand on Papá's back.

"He just . . . he can't." Papá still spoke in English even though Wendy was sure he'd forgotten she was there. "He doesn't understand."

"He has the fuego inside him." Mamá's voice was strangely proud, and Papá turned to her with a harsh laugh.

"Fire? Is that what it is?"

Mamá lifted her head to face him, smiling sadly. "Yes, it is the same fire you had. I remember."

Papá snorted and began pacing, hands on his hips. "I know that fire." Bitterness laced his words. "I know what that fire asks of you." He stopped, looking at Mamá desperately. "I won't let it burn up this family too." He reached for her and pulled her into a rough hug. "We must keep him safe. We must all be safe."

After a moment, Mamá's arms circled around him, and her cheek pressed against his work-stained shirt. But Wendy saw a disapproving frown tugging at her mouth.

Why can't life on Earth be more like the stars? Wendy wondered later that night as she gazed out her attic window. *Easy to predict. Dependable. Important.*

She wrapped her fingers around her binoculars, focusing on the familiar weight of them in her hands. Something settled deep inside her when she looked out into the universe. It was so incredibly huge, so impossibly beyond anything on Earth. Yet somehow, those giants of gas and dust were also familiar. Just like this one . . . "There you are," she whispered, feeling a smile stretch across her face. "Hello, Polaris."

Wendy loved the North Star. No matter how the earth spun, the North Star stayed suspended in place, a safe and solid anchor. Of course it wasn't an anchor, she corrected herself. It was moving through space just like everything else. But because it was lined up with the earth's axis, the human eye saw that star as always pointing toward the North Pole. That's why it was called Polaris. She stared at it for a moment, wondering if somewhere out there other eyes might be gazing at Polaris from a totally different planet, watching it dance through the sky just like all the other stars. How different things looked, depending on where you were standing. *Parallax*, she thought with a smile.

A sudden movement pulled her eyes downward. The backyard gate leading into the alley swung open and Mamá stepped through, closing and locking it behind her. *It's kind of late to be taking out the trash*, Wendy thought, leaning forward. There was something in Mamá's hands. An empty Tupperware—no, *two* empty Tupperwares. And not the dinky little yogurt containers she insisted on reusing a million times. These were the good ones that she used when she made extra food and shared it with their neighbors back in Melborn. Mamá walked into the house and out of view. Wendy's mind raced. She thought of the figure she had seen, standing in the parking lot, staring up. She remembered Etta talking about how much Luz liked looking at the stars. Suddenly she was pretty sure she knew who Mamá had been carrying food to so late at night. Wendy climbed back into bed with the uneasy feeling that somewhere deep in her world an anchor had shifted.

SEVENTEEN

WENDY RODE HER new bike to the library Saturday afternoon and found Brett already waiting.

"Here's the stuff," Brett said, pushing the cardboard tubes and a box across the table.

Wendy felt a thrill as she opened the box of lenses and examined the two glass discs nestled in their padding. She lifted the larger one gingerly, careful not to touch the surface with her fingers, and held it up. The table with its jumble of papers and materials warped in a wavy image on the other side of the smooth glass.

"What are you doing?" Brett asked.

"It's just so cool!" Wendy said, grinning. "See, this big lens just gathers the light. So it won't magnify by itself. But when we put the two together . . ." She lifted the smaller lens, looking through it to the larger one. Wendy laughed delightedly and leaned over so he could look through them too. "See how it bends the light?"

"Just tell me what we need to do," Brett said, not even glancing at the lenses. "I don't really need to understand how it works."

Wendy felt her ears burn.

"Okay, let's fit the lenses in," she said hastily.

"Hang on." Brett pulled his phone out of his pocket and handed it to her. "Get my picture with the lens."

After some trial and error, Wendy found the perfect distance between the lenses. She had to trim away the cardboard with an X-Acto knife to make the pieces slide together, then fit the lenses into their proper place. While they waited for the glue to dry, Brett pulled out his drawing pad.

"Tell me if I got this right," he said, flipping it open.

Wendy gasped. He had redrawn all of the scribbled notes and messy diagrams she had shown him the day before. They had been completely transformed, carefully inked on thick, satisfying drawing paper. He'd even shaded the telescope with inked lines that made it pop off the page. If Wendy hadn't spent the time designing them herself, she probably wouldn't even have recognized them as hers.

"That's great!" Wendy said truthfully. "It's way better than mine." Brett smiled his crooked smile at her and Wendy's stomach quivered. "Um, maybe we should add labels?" she asked. So with Wendy pointing out the different parts to him, Brett labeled the sketches with his India ink pen, his letters neat and narrow. *It looks like it belongs in a science book*, Wendy thought proudly. They had soon finished all they could do for the day. The rest would require tools. Wendy wanted to take it home so Papá could help her finish it. He had already promised to make the base she had designed. This way she could put the telescope and base together and bring it on Monday. But Brett looked at her bike helmet and frowned.

"You can't bike home with all this stuff." He pointed at the stacks of papers and books and the heavy cardboard tubing longer than a yardstick. "No, my dad'll help me finish it. Just tell me exactly what we need."

Wendy swallowed and explained carefully, using a pencil to make exact marks on the tubing for the drill. "And if you get it to me on Monday," Wendy told him as he gathered up the supplies, "I can attach the base. And I can chart the stars for the next two weeks and put it in our report—"

"As long as we have a telescope that works," Brett interrupted, "we'll nail this thing. Don't worry, Wendy. You did great today." He flashed her a smile and headed for the door.

Wendy tried not to feel uneasy on her bike ride home. It seemed like Brett had paid close attention, even taking notes. *He'll do fine*, she told herself. Her job now was to focus on actually using the telescope. Which would be tough in the city. Nowhere around here was really dark enough, but if she could find an open space close by, she might be able to see something on a clear night.

As she came to the corner, a poster in the window of a cafe caught her eye and she braked to a stop. "Let Luz Stay" stretched in block letters across the top of the poster. In the center, a woman sat in front of a stained-glass window, staring at the camera with a directness so intense it was hard to look away. Wendy had imagined Luz as someone sad and scared, but her dark eyes had something defiant about them. Wendy examined her face, thinking about the figure she had seen from her window, standing in the dark parking lot and gazing at the sky. She grinned. She knew the perfect place to try out the telescope.

A knock on the cafe window made her jump. Etta's upturned nose was pressed to the glass inside, and she gestured frantically for Wendy to wait, then rushed for the door. Wendy gripped the handlebars, biting her lip and thinking about the words she had screamed at Etta the last time they'd talked. When Etta barreled outside and stopped in front of her, fists on her hips, Wendy was certain she must still be furious with her.

"So listen," Etta said briskly. "You were totally right. I don't know what it's like to be scared like that." Her pointed chin jutted out as she spoke, her eyes darkening. "It's not fair to you and I need to stop expecting everyone to do things just like me. I should have been a better friend."

Wendy opened her mouth to protest, but Etta raised a hand and continued. "I didn't know you had asthma. *And* I didn't know about your friend's dad. And I *really* didn't know you were worried about your mom. I . . . I can't even imagine that." Etta took a deep breath, closing her eyes for a moment.

"Anyway, I'm sorry." She straightened up, standing as tall as her tiny frame allowed. "You need to do what's right for you, and I need to support that."

Wendy looked down at Etta, who somehow managed to look imposing. Relief filled Wendy's chest. "Thanks," she said. She started to say, "I'm sorry too," but Etta threw her arms around her, cutting her off and nearly knocking her off balance. Wendy planted her feet on either side of her bike and hugged her back.

Etta, her face pressed against Wendy's helmet, said, "I just get so stuck in my own head sometimes."

Wendy let out a small laugh and pulled back to look at her friend. "We all do now and then," she said.

Etta ran her fingers through her hair until it stood up even more than before. "Um, yeah, but especially me. It's just that . . . things are so *unfair* sometimes! And I hate it and I get so mad that I sometimes get it wrong." Etta stuck her hands in her pockets and kicked at the ground. "Did you hear about Yasmin?"

"No. Did something happen?" Wendy asked.

"Well, you know how I thought she was hiding from bullies at lunch? That wasn't it. She was just eating in the library because the librarian lets her pray in there." Etta gave Wendy a sheepish grin. "She prays every day at noon. That's all."

"Oh." Wendy felt a sudden urge to laugh out loud and she bit her lip to stop herself. Classic Etta.

"I did tell her that I'll stand guard so she doesn't get

interrupted, though," Etta said, grinning. This time Wendy let herself laugh and Etta joined in.

"You would make a great personal bodyguard," Wendy admitted, and Etta snapped to attention and gave her a salute.

"I gotta get home," Wendy told her, smiling. "See you, Etta."

"Hey, Wendy?" Etta said before she could ride away. "I'll always fight just as hard for you as I do for Luz. No matter what."

EIGHTEEN

SUNDAY AFTERNOON, AS Wendy leaned against the old trunk and tried to do her assigned reading, she found her mind wandering to her telescope instead. *I should name it something,* Wendy thought suddenly. *What's a good telescope name? Maybe some astronomy term? Or a constellation?* Wendy set down her book and turned, hoping a look at the outdoor sky would inspire her. But instead she found herself looking down at the trunk sitting quietly in a streak of sunlight. Without overthinking it, Wendy creaked the lid open.

Everything inside was just as she and Etta had left it—the rosary, the old keys, the cloth. She hadn't really looked at the folded cloth last time, and now she picked it up, wondering if it was something Mamá had sewn. A faded photograph slipped out of the fabric and landed facedown on the floor. It was torn slightly in one corner and creased through the middle as if it had been folded and tucked into a pocket for a long time. It looked fragile and precious in the dusty beams of attic light.

Wendy picked up the worn photograph and turned it over. A family stood in front of a thatched-roof hut. The man had some kind of tool over his shoulder and the woman wore a long skirt with a wide fabric belt. Her face was serious and the baby in her arms looked at something in the sky over the photographer, the tiny pink mouth frozen in a cry. But Wendy's eyes were drawn to the two children. A boy and girl, exactly the same size, stood in front of the woman. The boy grinned at the camera, his hands shoved into the pockets of his blue shorts, the elastic waistband pulled up high over a button-up shirt. Even though the picture was a little fuzzy, his smile gave the impression he was about to pull a prank on someone. The little girl smiled at him adoringly.

Wendy turned the picture over again. Tight cursive writing scrawled across one corner. In slightly smeared ink it read, "*familia Ortiz Najarro, 1987*." Her fingertip touched the name *Ortiz*. Mamá's family name. She turned it back over, examining the parents' faces. Was she looking at her maternal grandparents' faces for the first time in her life? Her eyes went again to the little girl, and then to the baby. Was one of them Mamá? Wendy held the photo for another moment, then carefully folded it back in the fabric, feeling a twinge of guilt.

Her abuelo, Papá's father, had passed away when Wendy was a baby, and her only memories of Abuela were of a distant woman, polite but disapproving of Wendy whenever she spoke too loudly or ran in the house. She'd been sad when Abuela died, but mostly because Papá had been quiet for days. Part of her always wondered if Mamá's parents would have been a little more like the grandparents in books and movies. Grandparents who asked about her day, offering her cookies and hugs and stories. But Mamá's past was one of those dark things they didn't talk about.

Wendy shivered, feeling a deep, tugging urge to close the chest and leave all its mysteries alone. But it was too late to pretend that she hadn't seen what was in it. Besides, there was one more thing inside that had her in its gravitational pull. She riffled through the chest until she found the small card lined with roses. The woman's eyes glittered up at her, framed by two dark eyebrows. Wendy read her name out loud.

"Celestina."

It had been eerie enough to see Papá's name written next to that baby in the newspaper clipping. Maybe that's why she hadn't told Etta about this name. Wendy swallowed hard, staring down at the card. Celestina—her own middle name. She'd always loved that it meant heavenly. Now she wondered if this woman, whoever she was, had looked at the heavens the same way she did.

Mamá was sewing at the kitchen table when Wendy came downstairs. "Ah, Wendy," she said, glancing over her shoulder. "Pass me the scissors, please? They fell on the floor."

A long, bulky piece of fabric hung over the edge of the table. Wendy retrieved the wayward scissors and sat down, watching as Mamá fed the fabric through the machine. The precision of the sewing machine and the neat, sharp edges when Mamá ironed the seams into their straight lines was always satisfying to her. The cloth Mamá was working on now looked difficult, much bigger and thicker than the soft, colorful fabric she had used to make their curtains. The machine hummed as her mother's quick fingers pushed the rough cloth under the needle.

"Mamá," she said tentatively, "did your mom teach you to sew?"

Mamá's hand jerked, and the hum stopped abruptly. "*Ay*, it has broken," Mamá muttered to herself, carefully picking the needle tip out of the fabric. Wendy bit her lip, waiting. Mamá replaced the needle and threaded it in silence. Wendy had given up on getting an answer, when Mamá finally said, "No. At the factory they taught me." She pressed the foot pedal and the machine buzzed to work again, drawing a dotted line of tan thread all the way to the end of the canvas-like cloth. Then, to Wendy's surprise, Mamá added, "My mother did not have a machine. She sewed by hand, but . . ." She trailed off, her hands pulling the fabric from the machine and laying it across the table. "She did not have time to teach me."

Wendy's whole body tilted toward Mamá, trying to catch everything she could. "Because she worked a lot?" Wendy asked, her voice hushed.

Mamá's fingers, running along the seam, froze. "Because she was killed," she whispered. Wendy swallowed, watching Mamá's eyes cloud over. "She did not have time," Mamá repeated, and this time Wendy understood. The heavy fabric began to slide toward the edge and Mamá caught it. She blinked down at it and Wendy saw something close shut in her mother's face. "You have homework, mija?" Mamá said briskly, her hands moving quickly again over the cloth. "Please finish it now."

And Wendy knew that was all she would get. For now.

NINETEEN

ALL WEEK, WENDY waited anxiously for Brett to bring in the telescope. The Science Fair was next weekend and they still had to run the experiments. There wasn't time to mess this up. Papá had agreed to build a base for it, but for that she had to bring him the actual telescope. She contented herself with double-checking her sketches and adding a few details to the notes. After the third day of Brett saying he would bring it in tomorrow, Wendy frowned at him.

"Okay, well," she said, tearing a page from her notebook and handing it to him. "Can you just make sure this part is right?"

He took it without comment and looked away again.

"You—you *are* working on it, right?" Wendy asked. Her heart thumped as he turned his bright blue eyes on her, an injured look in them.

"Why are you acting like this?" he asked her. "Do you

think I'm not good enough to do this? Or do you just not trust me?"

"No!" Wendy gasped, her fingers tightening around her pencil. "No, that's not what I meant!"

"Well, that's what it sounded like." He shook his head. "I told you I'd finish it, so stop being judgy." He turned in his seat to watch P.J., who kept sticking his hands in the bowl of slime Fiona was mixing and yelling, "It's alllliiiiivveee!"

Wendy fixed her eyes on the star chart she was trying to plot. He was right, of course. She shouldn't have said that. She took a deep breath. He was working on it, and she just had to wait.

Brett left with P.J. and Fiona before Wendy even had her stuff packed up. *I should apologize*, she thought, hurrying after them. *I wasn't being fair to him*. But as she came up behind them, she heard her name and her mouth snapped shut.

"Yeah, I know," Brett was saying. "She just keeps trying to check up on my work."

"Well, it's a joint project—" Fiona started, but P.J. interrupted.

"Bet she smells like tacos!" He snorted and Brett laughed.

Wendy's throat clenched.

"I mean, whatever," Brett said. "I'll just be glad when it's over and I can focus on student council. If I get a bad score on this project, my dad will be pissed."

"Just tell him it's her fault," P.J. said.

"Oh, he'd believe that," Brett said. "He'd say she only got in because of 'diversity,' you know." Brett put air quotes around the word. "He'd be all like, 'If you're smart enough to come here, fine. But don't take spots away from people just because they're white.' He kept going on about it after that PTO meeting."

Wendy remembered the PTO meeting flyer on the wall outside the art room. The flyer that made it sound like kids were getting admitted because of their race. She felt herself shrinking inside.

"Yeah, like, remember Jeremy?" P.J. said. "Dude totally should be here!"

"Right." Brett nodded, brushing his hair out of his eyes. "Bet you anything one of those kids took his spot. My dad says they just check some ethnicity box and boom—here they are."

The sick feeling spread up to her throat and Wendy swallowed hard, trying not to cry. Brett's dad thought she didn't belong here. Did Brett think that, too?

"Wendy is smart, though," Fiona said.

"Yeah," Brett said. "Avery is stuck with Josie and she said he barely even talks. She has to do all the work."

"It's José," Fiona corrected him. She sounded annoyed, and Wendy felt a miserable flicker of gratitude for Fiona.

"Josie," P.J. called out. "Hey, Josie!" Wendy saw José in the hallway ahead of them speed up at the sound. P.J.

cupped his hands around his mouth and shouted, "Yeah, run, Josie!"

José started to jog, his backpack bumping against his back as he hurried away. He threw a panicked look over his shoulder just as the band teacher turned the corner in front of him and they collided in a flurry of papers.

P.J. swore and ducked into a classroom, but Brett cracked up, leaning against the wall like his laughter might knock him over otherwise. Fiona turned away, her hand over her mouth to hide a giggle, and her eyes locked on Wendy's. Her smile faltered. For a second, Wendy thought Fiona was going to say something to her. Instead she looked down at her binder, letting her blond hair fall over her face. Wendy put her head down and rushed past them. She hated herself for pretending she hadn't heard them and for walking past José as he struggled to collect the sheet music. Her chest was tight and her eyes were stinging, and more than anything she hated not knowing what to do about any of it.

In art class, they were discussing the completed historical scene collages. Miss Hill put K.K.'s scene up on the Smart board so the whole class could get a good look at the details. It showed a group of people moving together against a background made from a map. Real bits of cloth formed bundles that hung from real sticks over their shoulders. They all walked forward, gazing at a bright star made of foil and paper strips.

"This old map truly gives the whole piece the feeling of a journey," Miss Hill said, zooming closer. "And what are these lines on the map you highlighted?"

"Those are the routes of the Underground Railroad," K.K. said. "They are real routes that went through this part of Ohio."

"The Underground Railroad went through here?" Mal asked.

"Yup," K.K. said, pointing at the lines on the map.

Miss Hill beamed. "What wonderful attention to detail, K.K. And it brings it so close to home." She looked at the class. "Just imagine for a moment that you lived a hundred and fifty years ago, right here, and this group showed up at your house," she said, waving at the image on the screen. "What would you do?"

K.K. said, "You're asking the white people, right?"

Harry, another one of the Black kids, spoke up. "Yeah, cuz we all know which side *we'd* have been on."

Miss Hill looked thoughtful. "Oh, I don't know. This was a free state. That means free folk of all colors lived here. If you were free, white *or* Black, and Harriet Tubman knocked on your door one night, what would you do?"

Hands shot up around the classroom, Etta's among them. But Miss Hill shook her head, her long braids swinging. "Hang on. *Really* think about it. Let's say you're a poor farmer, your crop went bad this year, and you have five children to feed. Would you risk a hundred-dollar fine, which was a whole lot of money for someone back then? Or a flogging? Or an arrest, which could be even worse for your family?" The room was silent as she looked at each of them.

"Would you risk it? If it endangered the people you cared about most?"

A boy said hesitantly, "But it's the right thing to do."

Miss Hill lifted up one finger in the air and repeated excitedly, "The *right* thing to do!" She turned to the Smart board, switching off the projection. "Tell me about that. What makes something right?"

Someone murmured, "Helping people." The teacher wrote the answer on the board, waving encouragingly toward the room to keep them coming. Kids warmed up and ideas came faster. Saving lives. Protecting the weak. Respecting others. Listening to your parents. Obeying the law. Miss Hill pounced on this one.

"Yes, Fiona, what do you mean by that?"

"Oh, you know," Fiona said. "Like, we don't steal or break the law. That's doing what's right."

"So, it would follow that breaking the law would be wrong?"

Fiona nodded, twirling the end of her blond hair around her finger. "Obviously."

"And if you knew of someone who had broken the law, would helping them be considered right or wrong then?"

"Um . . ." Fiona fiddled with her hair, her eyes darting back and forth as if sensing a trap. "Well, if you help someone break the law . . . I mean, if you help them do something illegal, like, *literally* illegal . . ." She trailed off.

"So, helping someone who has broken the law, helping a criminal, would be wrong. Is that what you're saying?"

Even Fiona could see where this was leading now and she blushed, glancing around for help. "I mean, I'm not talking about slavery, *obviously*! But illegal is illegal, right?"

"Yeah, you are, actually," K.K. said, her voice tense. "Because we are talking about when slavery was *literally legal*."

"Oh my gosh, Kay," Avery spoke up. "You don't have to take it so seriously. Fiona is not saying slavery was okay."

K.K. clenched her teeth, but before she could say anything else, Harry called out, "Just shut up, Ave! You don't know what you're talking about."

There were snorts of laughter and Miss Hill raised a hand. "Okay, let's keep our discussion civil."

Avery glared at Harry. "Don't call me Ave," she hissed at him as Miss Hill walked back up to the front.

"So maybe don't call me *Kay*," K.K. suggested pointedly, and Avery whirled back around with a *humph*. Fiona looked from Avery to K.K., her fingers still twisting the ends of her hair distractedly.

"*Sorry*," Fiona mouthed to K.K., and K.K. looked surprised.

"All right, class," Miss Hill said, switching the Smart board back on. "We do need to move on. But consider how you might incorporate some of this passion into our next project on social equity. K.K., one last question about your art. What was your favorite part and why?"

"Oh, the star," K.K. said. "See, the North Star guided people fleeing slavery to freedom."

Wendy couldn't remember having heard that before. It made sense, though. Polaris, the North Star, had always been important to navigation.

"And for my star," K.K. went on, pointing to Polaris in her collage, "I wrote quotes from people who I look to for guidance, like my mom and Simone Biles, on bits of yellow paper and foil."

Miss Hill clapped her hands, glowing with delight. "K.K., this entire piece is a stunning example of how art can tie history to our own lives. We all have our own North Stars, don't we? Guiding us on."

Wendy's mind lingered on that thought, wondering if she had her own North Star and which way it was pulling her.

TWENTY

ON FRIDAY BRETT brought in a huge box labeled "FRAG-ILE" and stored it in the office for safekeeping. Relieved as Wendy was that he had finally finished the telescope, she couldn't look at him without remembering what she'd heard in the hallway. He must just be a really good actor, smiling at her and complimenting her diagrams. Her stomach twisted at the thought of another week of working together, while he was probably telling people she smelled like tacos (which she 100 percent did not!). But the Science Fair was way too important. She had to make a good impression on the planetarium representative, even if that meant working with Brett a little longer.

Wendy hadn't been able to eat more than a few bites at lunch for days. Her insides just felt too tied up all the time. Today was no different, so she stashed her unfinished lunch in her locker. Ms. Park had told them to bring their project in to review with her today, and the extra time would help.

She wanted to explain how the base would fit with it, since Papá had been waiting for the finished telescope to build it. Would Brett remember to get the telescope before class? As she debated going to find him, she heard Brett's voice and turned toward it.

Tucked in the corner behind a row of lockers, P.J., Brett, and a couple of their friends were laughing at something. In the center of the circle of bodies she saw José, his dark eyes wide. P.J. was looming over him, an open lunch bag clutched in his hand.

"How are we supposed to celebrate your culture if all you bring is Lunchables?" P.J. asked, tossing the bag on the floor.

"There's always this," Brett said. He smiled and held up a bottle of Jarritos, the Mexican soda, in his hand. Wendy's numb brain registered it was pineapple. Her favorite kind.

Brett twisted off the cap and took a sip. "Not bad, Josie," he said, nodding appreciatively. "You are really contributing to our society. Too bad you didn't bring enough for all of us." Brett looked around at his friends and then his eyes fell on Wendy. She took a step back. Brett's smile widened and he lifted the bottle like he was about to give a toast. He winked at her and took another sip.

Wendy felt something shift, as if the axis of the world had tilted. She was looking at the same Brett with his shaggy, sun-streaked hair and his perfect teeth. But his crooked smile didn't look cute at all anymore. It was a smile that thought messing with José was funny. It was a smile that said she smelled like tacos, just because she was brown. It was a cruel smile, completely and totally cruel.

"Stop," she said quietly.

Surprise flashed across Brett's face. He looked at her, his eyes narrowing. "Stop what?" he said. "Celebrating Hispanic Heritage Month?"

José's black eyes darted from her to Brett. She swallowed and hugged her notebook.

"Ms. Park wants us to bring the telescope," she said quickly, trying to keep her voice steady. "Come on, Brett."

The boys, almost in unison, let out a drawn-out "oooOOOoo" and then snorted with laughter. P.J., sensing a change in the group's target, kicked José's lunch bag away and then stepped forward, his big shoulders towering behind Brett.

"What's your problem?" Brett asked Wendy. "I thought we were cool."

"I—I don't think we are," she whispered. Her body felt like it was sinking into the floor. What was she doing? Behind the boys she saw José backing slowly away down the hall.

Brett said softly, "You know I've always been nice to you."

He stepped closer, and it seemed almost as if they were the only two people in the hallway. Even now, after everything she had seen him do, Wendy felt it—the pull to follow his lead. He smiled at her, and it was the same confident smile she remembered from the beginning of school, when she had passed Yasmin the note from him that made her cry. The smile that said she was going to do what he wanted and they both knew it. The smile that said *he* was her North Star. *No*, she thought desperately.

Wendy licked her lips. "No, you haven't," she said. "I heard you."

Brett raised his eyebrows. "You heard me? What, thank Josie for his cultural contribution?"

"No, I—I mean, yes, but . . . I heard you talking about me. Before." Wendy's ears were burning, and she felt herself hunch down. "P.J. said I smell like tacos," she mumbled, her mouth nearly obscured by her notebook.

Brett laughed. "No one said anything about tacos." He squinted at her and tilted his head. "You know you sound crazy, right?"

For a moment, the thought flitted through her mind that maybe she *had* just imagined it. Or she wasn't remembering it right. But then, a tangle of memories crowded into her head—Yasmin's name written neatly across the folded note, her flashing crown at the skating rink, Brett's voice saying Wendy didn't belong in this school. She knew the truth. If anything was going to guide her, it was that.

"At least I'm not a racist bully," she said.

Everyone in the hallway seemed to hold their breath. Brett lifted one corner of his mouth and looked down at her. "You really are crazy." And he emptied the rest of the Jarritos bottle over her shoes. Wendy saw the yellow pineapple soda glug out of the bottle in slow motion, pouring onto the purple, silver, and white swirls of her galaxy Converse. There was a moment of suspended motion, then the air shattered as the boys erupted in guffaws.

A sharp voice cut through the noise. "What is happening here?" Immediately everyone was slinging backpacks and grabbing books. Wendy felt suddenly invisible. She looked up, miserably, to see Principal Whitman walking toward her.

"Principal Whitman!" Brett said. "I know we aren't supposed to have drinks in the hallway. She just walked right into me and it just . . . slipped! I really didn't mean to." Brett's voice sounded much younger, and he was looking up at the principal with such an earnest, forlorn face that Wendy could hardly believe he was the same person.

Principal Whitman peered down at them through her gold-rimmed glasses. "And this is precisely why we don't allow drinks in the hallway, young man."

"Oh, yes, I know!" Brett laid a hand on Wendy's arm. "You'd better go get cleaned up, Wendy. I'll take care of this."

Principal Whitman smiled fondly. "I'd hate for you to miss class, Brett." She held up her walkie-talkie and summoned the janitor in a buzz of crackling static. Then she turned back to them. "Young lady, what class do you have now?"

"We're in science together," Brett said helpfully. "I can talk to Ms. Park." He turned to Wendy and said, "Don't worry, I'll fill her in on our project, too." He took her notebook from her limp hands and walked away. Wendy stared after him, her breath coming in short, shallow gasps.

"Isn't he a gentleman?" Principal Whitman gushed. And she was gone, calling out to some kid not to run in the halls as she clicked away.

Wendy's shoes sucked at the tile floor with every step toward the bathroom, pulling her back down to earth with sticky little tugs. She wished they would keep pulling, dragging her down deep into the molten core where she could just melt away.

The bell rang loudly as Wendy pushed the bathroom door open with a shaking hand. It was unreasonable, she told herself firmly, to react like this. So her shoes were wet. Not a big deal. It wasn't as bad as Mamá's parents being killed or Tom fighting with Papá or ICE raids or everything else that was tumbling out of order in her life. A sob scrambled its way up out of her narrow windpipe, bursting out to echo off the tiled walls of the bathroom. Wendy pulled out her inhaler, squeezing her eyes shut as she sucked in the medicine. Once her chest was rising and falling steadily, she rubbed her face. There was no point in feeling sorry for herself. She wiggled her toes and felt the syrupy residue rubbing against her skin. Ew. Gingerly she untied the Converse, plopping them in the sink and watching the yellow water swirl down the drain.

"Wendy! There you are!" Etta rushed up behind her, the mirror reflecting her worried face. "What happened?" She looked intently at Wendy's shoes and then at her red eyes.

"Nothing." Wendy shrugged, turning quickly away. She

grabbed a giant handful of paper towels and shoved big wads into the shoes.

"Wendy, come on," Etta said, exasperated. "Brett Cobb comes waltzing into class with that telescope and tells Ms. Park he has no idea why you didn't show up to review the project. So I come looking for you and your favorite shoes are dripping wet, your eyes are all puffy, and your inhaler is on the sink, so don't say *nothing*!" Etta grabbed the shoes, her eyes drilling into Wendy's. "TELL ME!"

So Wendy told her everything. When she told her about José, Etta gasped and narrowed her eyes. For some reason the fury in her face made Wendy's breathing come easier and her muscles loosen. She was starting to feel a little less trapped and a little less crazy. Then, as she told her how Brett had taken her notebook to show Ms. Park, what Etta said earlier clicked in her brain.

"Wait, what did Brett tell Ms. Park?"

"He said he didn't know where you were. And he definitely made it sound like it was typical of you not to show up. That's why I came looking. It was real sketchy."

"But, I need to tell Ms. Park what happened!" She looked down at her socks, still a soggy mess on the floor. "I have to go see her!"

"Here." Etta slipped off her canvas flats and handed them to Wendy, taking the damp Converse in her small white hands. "They're probably too small, but they're pretty stretchy. Go! Class is almost over!"

TWENTY-ONE

THE BELL WAS ringing as Wendy rushed into the room in Etta's too-small shoes and looked toward the teacher's desk. Through the crowd of kids filing past she could see Ms. Park bent over something on a wooden stand by her desk. She was beaming and nodding at Brett, who looked pleased. When he saw Wendy his smug grin widened even more, then, in a flash, it dropped into a hurt look.

"Oh, hi, Wendy. It's okay, I showed her our project." He gave a dejected shrug and looked at Ms. Park knowingly. Her eyes frowned at Wendy from behind her glasses. "Miss Toledo, come here please," she called over the bustling classroom.

Wendy hurried over, then stopped in her tracks as she saw the telescope. It was painted a sleek black and mounted on a wooden frame, exactly like the one she had designed for Papá to build. It looked amazing. "Whoa," she couldn't help saying. "That—that looks really good."

Ms. Park lifted her chin and examined her. "You haven't seen it before?" she asked.

"Well, no, not like this. We got most of the basic part done at the library, and I was going to work on the stand . . ." She trailed off, feeling defensive but not sure how to explain why.

"Yes, Mr. Cobb told me you met him one time at the library. It seems he's been putting in quite a lot of time into this project."

Wendy stared at her, wondering what that meant. He had obviously painted it, and his parents must have helped drill the holes to attach the telescope pieces, just as she instructed him. And her designs for the stand had turned out great, but that was supposed to be for Papá to do. She'd just been waiting to get the completed telescope from Brett. He must have followed her notes to make it himself.

"I wonder, Miss Toledo, if you could share with me what your contributions have been?" Ms. Park was looking at her steadily, and Wendy suddenly realized what she was implying.

"Oh, I've been doing a lot!" She licked her lips and looked toward the door. Brett was standing there, watching her with a curious expression. "I designed it. I researched and sketched it out and everything."

Ms. Park tilted her head, considering Wendy. "Are you much of an artist, Miss Toledo?"

Wendy gulped and shook her head no.

"So, these"—Ms. Park took out several laminated pages

and laid them on the desk—"are not yours then?" Wendy stared at the beautiful ink drawings of the telescope design and the stand, the neat labels on the sides, and the close-up sketch of the lenses detailing how the magnification worked. "Well, they *kind of* are." She swallowed, the lump in her throat growing by the second. "I did sketch this originally, but Brett made these because mine were messy and . . . not as good? But they were accurate!" She could hear the desperation in her voice.

"Oh?" Ms. Park looked interested. "May I see your sketches?"

"They're—" She looked at Brett, whose face hadn't changed. "I gave them to Brett."

Ms. Park looked from her to Brett, but he just frowned and shook his head no.

"My notebook," Wendy urged, her eyes pleading with him. "Where is it?"

Ms. Park cleared her throat. "Mr. Cobb has written up a description of the process, complete with pictures of the work he did." She shuffled through the laminated pages so Wendy could see. All the pictures he had taken at the library were there with close-ups of each step. And of course, the one she had taken of a smiling Brett carefully holding up the lenses. None of the photos included even a sliver of Wendy's brown hands.

"Now, I haven't read his report yet, but this telescope is very impressive. It is obviously the result of a great deal of research and effort." Ms. Park continued. "But a group project is a group project, Miss Toledo. If you are unwilling to contribute to the process, you cannot receive credit for this project."

Wendy's heart was racing at a disbelieving, panicked speed. "No! It's—it's my project!" she sputtered. "It was my idea and I designed it! It's *my* telescope!"

"Look, Wendy, it's okay," Brett said earnestly. "You don't have to say that. I know you haven't really been into this. It's not a big deal." He smiled at her and shrugged sadly, as if he were bravely soldiering on in spite of hurt feelings. "You would probably rather work with someone else anyway. It's really okay."

Wendy's jaw dropped and she stopped breathing for a moment. Her ears were ringing. She couldn't even hear what Ms. Park was saying at first. Brett said something in response then he waved at Wendy, his eyes glittering with malice over his smile, and he left her standing speechless in front of the teacher's desk.

"Miss Toledo. Wendy!" Ms. Park's voice cut into her brain, and she turned weakly to look at her. "I'm reassigning you," Ms. Park said grimly. "If you still plan to enter the Science Fair, you will need to come up with a project this weekend. I expect to see a plan on Monday morning and a physical component completed by Wednesday. You may use class time all next week to prepare, but the bulk of your research will need to be done outside of school."

It was all Wendy could do to stay standing. Her legs felt wobbly, and she couldn't take her eyes off the telescope behind Ms. Park. Her telescope. All the lightness she had felt while talking to Etta had been stripped away.

"I don't need to tell you that this is your last opportunity, Miss Toledo," Ms. Park said quietly. "Do not waste this chance. Now run along to your next class."

The disappointment in her face was sharp as she turned back to her desk, and Wendy felt it like a final stab in the gaping wound that was her chest. She stumbled from the room.

TWENTY-TWO

"WHAT ABOUT ELEPHANT slime?" Etta said in a strained voice. "That fluffy stuff—you know, elephant toothpaste or whatever?"

"Too easy," Wendy answered without looking up from *100 Science Projects to Amaze and Impress.* Etta had climbed onto a beam in the attic ceiling and was hanging upside down. She insisted the rush of blood to her brain helped with creativity.

"How about"—Etta grunted as she shifted positions—"that thing where"—*grunt*—"you balance stuff with"—*ufff*—"magnets. That's always cool," she said, crossing her ankles around the beam and throwing her head backward so that her hair hung down like a blue-and-brown pom-pom.

"Nope." Wendy slammed the book shut and tossed it on the floor. "It has to be astronomy. It's for the planetarium rep to see. They're not gonna care about slime or magnets." She looked up at Etta. "What are you and K.K. doing?"

"Skittle milk. You know, where you put the Skittles on a plate and you pour milk and the colors all run." Etta's upside-down face was bright red. "Basically we just want to eat lots of Skittles."

Wendy flung herself onto her bed. "I'm doomed," she mumbled, her face smushed into her plush giant panda.

There was a shuffle, a thud, and an "*owww*," then she felt Etta plop down next to her on the bed. "Did I tell you that I found out about Óscar Romero?" Etta said. "The priest in the picture with your dad?"

"He's not my dad." Wendy lifted her head up an inch to protest. "He's just a random baby."

"Okay, sure," Etta conceded. "But Romero was this really cool dude. See, the government in El Salvador was totally about oppressing the people and they thought they could just use the church to do that, but Romero wouldn't."

Wendy buried her face in her stuffed panda again, but Etta's voice seeped through anyway.

"The military there was basically killing people all the time. Everyone was too scared to say anything, so he would preach on the radio about peace and the whole country would listen. They got so pissed that they bombed his radio station—twice! But he kept on saying violence was wrong, even when the government does it."

In spite of herself, Wendy was listening, picturing the gentle, bespectacled face from the clipping.

"So then he actually preached a sermon straight to the

169

soldiers saying they don't have to listen to orders that are wrong. He told them not to pull the trigger, because laws aren't always right."

"Laws aren't always right," Wendy repeated. *Laws like slavery*, she thought. *Or laws about where you belonged just because of where you were born.* She turned to Etta and asked, "How do you know all this?"

"My mom. She's a big fan. Remember how I said there's a quote by him on our wall? It's something about preaching the violence of love, not the violence of the sword. Whatever that means." Etta held up her arm, glaring at a fresh scrape. "So, they finally killed him."

Wendy looked at her. Etta seemed focused on her scraped arm, but her eyebrows were drawn together angrily as she continued. "Someone shot him right in front of everyone and escaped while they were all running to try and save him. No one could ever prove who did it, but everyone knows it was the government."

Wendy's mind flicked through the bits of paper and photos from the trunk, remembering the nuns bending over something on the floor. Then she remembered the picture of Celestina with the roses around the edge. "And . . . that stuff at his funeral? Remember how we thought those words meant—"

"Yeah, we were right," Etta sighed, and it was such a heavy, deep sound that Wendy felt the sadness from it wash over her. "There were bombs. And then soldiers started shooting into the crowd. They tried to blame it on another group later, but it was all real sketchy. Either way, a bunch of people died. Poor people who were there because they loved Romero. Just because they were at a funeral." Her voice sounded smaller than usual.

Wendy hugged the panda to her chest, the velvety fabric soft on her skin, and thought about Celestina, whose funeral was just a few days after the police shot into the crowd at the kind priest's funeral. Was it a coincidence that Wendy's middle name was Celestina? She shivered.

"So, that woman . . . the baby's mom . . ." Wendy couldn't finish the thought, so Etta did it for her.

"Was probably shot at his funeral. Yeah, I thought about that too." Etta sucked a scratch on her finger thoughtfully. "I wonder if the baby was there. And the dad. They must have survived."

Wendy shuddered. She didn't like this conversation. "Hey, I *seriously* need a science project! Like yesterday."

Etta's finger popped out of her mouth and, with her remarkable ability to switch gears, she exclaimed, "Wendy! If what you *really* want to do is the telescope, and what you already put *tons* of work into is the telescope, and the only thing that you want to show the rep is the telescope . . . then just do. The. Telescope!" Her voice crept into an excited squeal.

Wendy lifted her head up and looked at her. "It's *next week*, Etta. Brett took my notebook. I don't have any of the materials or the plans. I doubt Papá has time to make a base now either."

"But you designed it, right?" Etta leaned toward her, growing increasingly more animated, her hands flying through the air as she talked. "You came up with it all! It's in your head! What do you need for it?"

Wendy rolled over, staring up at the attic ceiling, thinking. It would be a lot of work, but maybe it was possible. Maybe she could pull it off and still have a chance. Maybe.

Ten minutes later, she had convinced Mamá to let her rush order the supplies.

"Your brother has the laptop. Go ask him," Mamá called after Wendy, who was already pulling Etta with her up the stairs. "And order what you need *only*!"

Wendy knocked and heard Tom mute the local news station that he was constantly streaming on his phone these days. He cracked open the door and his eyebrows shot up when he saw Etta.

"Oh, hey," he said at the same time that Etta said, "Hi, Tom!"

Wendy frowned in confusion.

"You—you know each other?" she asked.

"Just from the Alzando meetings," Etta said, grinning at him.

Wendy stared from Etta's delighted smile to Tom's sheepish expression.

"Okay," Wendy said, shoving past Tom. She pulled Etta into the bedroom with her and closed the door firmly behind them.

"Talk." She crossed her arms over her chest and looked up at Tom. "What meetings?"

"All right, geez." Tom held up his hands in surrender. He was holding a paintbrush, and there were several small containers of paint lined up next to a stack of thick, folded fabric.

"*Alzando,*" he said, setting down the paintbrush. "It means 'lifting up' in Spanish. Like rising above, improving, progressing, you know? It's a community organization that works with immigrants. I've been going to the meetings."

"With immigrants?" Wendy could almost feel the lightbulb click on above her head. "Oh! This is all about the illegal woman at the church, isn't it?" she asked.

"She's not illegal," Tom said sharply. "Human beings aren't illegal. Don't say that."

"He's right," Etta said, her eyes huge and earnest. "They want you to think about people like that, but it's not true."

Wendy looked from Etta to Tom. She couldn't help feeling as if they were ganging up on her. "I mean, she's here illegally, right? She *is* illegal."

"Wendy, you don't get it!"

Tom sounded angry now, and Wendy felt her whole body tense. Then Etta spoke up.

"But *she's* not illegal. Think about it, Wendy. If someone

speeds, they're doing something illegal, but that doesn't make them an illegal *person*." Etta's green eyes had that fierce light in them again. "Calling a person illegal is just another way to make them seem less human."

"Exactly," Tom said. "And a lot of immigrants have a legal right to cross a border if they are fleeing for their lives. So they haven't even done anything illegal. The whole system is just set up to make them fail." His voice was still angry, but Wendy realized now his anger wasn't directed at her. He shook his head. "Luz has been trying to get her papers. She's not a threat to anyone and she is for sure not a criminal."

"I'm sorry," Wendy said. "I just meant . . ." But then she stopped. She *had* meant that Luz was a criminal, different from them. Maybe, a tiny part of her whispered deep inside, maybe she had *wanted* to think of her as less human. Maybe then it would be easier to believe that Luz's deportation order was somehow okay. The thought disgusted her.

She focused on Etta instead. "So you knew my brother was going to these meetings? Why didn't you tell me?"

Etta shrugged. "I didn't know. You never told me your brother's name."

This was true, Wendy thought. She hadn't talked much about her family to Etta.

"I guess those friends of yours are part of this thing?" She frowned at Tom, thinking of the older teens outside the skating rink.

He shoved his hands in his pockets and nodded. "Yeah, Nadia is one of the organizers."

Etta's face lit up. "I LOVE Nadia. She's so *intense* and committed and she's also super smart when she talks to the reporters. Also, her hair." Etta put a hand over her heart and gazed off to the side with rapt, starry eyes.

"I know! Can you believe she just started college?" Tom added.

"Okaaayyy," Wendy said drily, "if you two can let your crushes go for a second." They both blinked, looking embarrassed. Wendy rolled her eyes. "Papá would *flip* if he knew you were involved with this, Tomás." She used the Spanish version of his name on purpose and Tom frowned at her.

"Yeah, well, while he's off hiding from everything that's happening right under his nose, Luz is out there giving news interviews. She's willing to stand up for something and he can't understand that." Tom turned his back. "But he can't stop me from doing what's right."

Wendy watched him unfold a bulky canvas and stretch it out across the floor. *What's right*, he had said. But wasn't telling her parents what was *right*? Should she be yelling for Mamá and stomping out of the room in righteous anger? Wendy squirmed. She hated the thought of more yelling matches.

Tom carefully painted letters onto the long fabric. He was making something for this whole Alzando thing, she was sure. Even if she told on him, he wasn't going to stop. She crossed over to the laptop and picked it up.

"We need to borrow this," she said, walking toward the door. "I'm going to pretend I don't know anything about what you're doing. But seriously, Tom, be careful."

She gave the thick canvas one last look. Her eyes skimmed over the neat seam down the middle, thinking how unwieldy it must be in a sewing machine. In fact, she was pretty sure it might even break a needle. Her brain whirred as Etta closed the door behind them and they headed off to order her telescope supplies. Wendy was 99 percent certain that Papá was the only one in this house who didn't know what Tom was up to, and Mamá obviously approved. Because Tom couldn't sew a seam like that to save his life.

TWENTY-THREE

IT TOOK WENDY most of the weekend to re-create her diagrams and order supplies. She sketched and researched for hours, fueled by sour gummies, chamomile tea, and energetic encouragement from Etta. By Monday morning her new telescope plans were ready to show Ms. Park. Wendy could think of little else. The whispers around school didn't catch up to her until after second period. She was in a bathroom stall when a group of chatty girls burst in and huddled near the mirror. Wendy wasn't trying to listen to their conversation, but their words rang out in the tiled bathroom.

"But was it more than that one time?"

"Who knows? I mean, if she lives around here, she could totally be following him around."

"Ew, stalker! That is so creepy!"

"I didn't know she lived in Rooville."

"She just moved here. And guess where she moved from? Mexiborn!"

The word "Mexiborn" was what finally made her pay attention. Of course she'd heard the word before. Last year at Tom's track meets, some of the kids from other schools had screamed *"Go back to Mexiborn!"* at the Melborn kids. It hadn't mattered too much, not with Tom blowing past all of them on the track. And he was always so popular that nothing seemed to stick to him. The *Mexiborn* chants had faded away in the dust, just like the disgruntled faces of the other runners.

But here they were again, and this time they weren't directed at Tom. She gulped and hurried from the stall. Avery, Morgan, and another girl fell silent as she pushed past them to the sink. Her ears burned as she washed her hands.

"So, Wendy," Morgan said, in a voice that was trying to sound casual. "You like Brett, right?"

Avery snorted, "Oh my god, Morgan, stop!"

Morgan gave her an injured look. "What? I was just asking."

The other girl giggled, not even trying to hide her laughter. Wendy shook her head no and turned to go. But Avery grabbed her arm, her sparkly fingernails digging in sharply.

"You know he likes Fiona, right?" Avery said, lowering her voice conspiratorially. She gave Wendy a pitying smile, and Wendy had to fight the urge to turn and run.

"I don't like him," Wendy muttered. She pulled her arm

away, feeling Avery's fingernails scrape against her skin, and walked quickly from the bathroom. The sound of their muffled laughter chased her into the hall. Wendy ducked around a corner, closed her eyes, and took a deep, fortifying breath. She barely even knew those girls. What was going on?

"Hey, girl."

Her eyes flew open to see K.K. and Mal both looking at her warily.

"Hi." She tried to smile.

"So . . . ," K.K. asked, "you don't have a phone, do you?"

"I mean, just a flip phone," Wendy said slowly. "Not with apps or anything. Why?"

Mal let out a breath. "Oh, okay, cool, just wondering," she said. She turned away, grabbing K.K.'s arm. "Come on! Lunch! Sooo hungry!"

K.K. didn't move. "Mal, it's not lunchtime yet."

"Oh, right." Mal looked around, avoiding Wendy's eyes.

"Plus, she's gonna hear it anyway," added K.K.

Mal gave a distressed moan. "Does she have to, though? Can't we please just ignore it?"

K.K. rolled her eyes. "Mallory, you can't just ignore bad things. We've talked about this."

Wendy swallowed. "Just tell me."

Mal's eyes roamed the hallway for any teachers while K.K. pulled out her phone and thumbed at the screen. She held it up to show Wendy. It was a post by Avery4Ever that showed a picture of Brett. He was on his bike, reflected in a store window, the sun glinting in one corner of the glass with an artsy burst of bright light. Wendy's throat tightened as she recognized the selfie she'd seen him take. Yep, there was her hand waving in the background, her face barely visible inside the window of the Walgreens. It was far enough away that no one would notice her, though. The post looked like a screenshot from someone's text chat and the picture was pretty small. Then K.K. swiped the screen and Wendy's stomach dropped. The next pic was a close-up, zoomed in on her hand and her fuzzy face. Still, it wasn't quite identifiable. Unless . . . She read the caption out loud, hearing her own voice as if from far away.

"OMG, my friend just found proof that this girl's been stalking him since before school!"

She stared at the words, then swiped back to the first pic. The screenshot showed a few lines from a group text under Brett's selfie.

BC: Look who's lurking in the back!

AA: OMG! She's creepin on you definitely.

PJ: She's thirsty 4 u dude!

The rest of the chat wasn't in the screenshot. But there were already comments on Avery's post. Wendy scanned over them, feeling her heart sink.

Ew she's so cringe

Hey, doesn't she go to our school?

Bild the waaallll

The last one made her suck in her breath, and Mal pushed the phone back to K.K.

"Hey, you don't need to look at the comments, Wendy," Mal said.

"Right," Wendy said to the floor.

But the rock-hard weight that had settled in her belly stayed there all through science, where she mumbled through her new telescope design with a skeptical Ms. Park. Even after Ms. Park approved her plan, the heaviness inside weighed her down until her whole body felt like it was 96 percent lead.

When she opened her locker at the end of the day, she found a note taped to the inside. Just one word was scrawled across it in black pen: *"Thirsty?"* Wendy pulled it down and stared at the letters, her brain processing it as if from a great distance. *This is all because I stood up to him,* Wendy thought numbly. *I never should have said anything.* Her breath came faster, and Wendy knew that if she started crying now, she wouldn't be able to stop.

Suddenly Etta's furious face popped out of the crowd right at her elbow.

"That's it!" she raged, tugging at her half-open backpack. "I heard about the post. He's gone waaaay too far. He's just— ugh!"

She hefted her backpack into her arms and zipped it shut violently.

"Principal Whitman *has* to hear what's going on, Wendy.

It's *not* okay. And about the Science Fair, too, because if that slimy little *weasel* gets credit for your work I'm going to—to *detonate!*"

A thread of panic wormed its way through Wendy's numbness. Standing up to Brett had already made things a million times worse. What would happen if Etta went to the principal?

"No, Etta!" Wendy grabbed her backpack to stop her from rushing away. "Seriously, please don't say anything!"

"Wendy, he is *bullying* you! And it's getting worse!"

"He didn't, though," Wendy insisted. "I mean, he sent that picture to his friends, but I don't think he meant for it to end up . . . online like that."

"Okay, fine, so Avery posted it. So we tell Ms. Whitman that Avery is cyberbullying—"

"Please don't!" Wendy felt her eyes filling with tears, even as her logical brain whispered that Etta was right. "It's just—I don't think I can take it. Not now."

Etta's jaw tensed, her nostrils flaring like tiny little vents. She covered her face with her hands and bent half-way over in the middle of the hall, letting out a muffled scream.

"Aaaarrggghhh!"

Wendy looked furtively around and caught a few curious glances. Etta lifted her pointy chin, took a deep breath, held it for a moment, and then blew it out.

"Okay," she said, in a surprisingly calm voice. She looked

at Wendy, her eyes searching. "I won't say anything. For now."

"Thanks," Wendy said, relieved. "I really don't want to make a big deal out of it. I bet it will all blow over anyway."

Etta's eyebrows scrunched together. "Um, sure . . ." She didn't sound even 20 percent convinced.

TWENTY-FOUR

THE TELESCOPE SUPPLIES had arrived while she was at school, and Wendy was grateful for something to take her mind off Brett. As she unpacked the boxes, Tom came clattering down the stairs carrying his guitar and the folded fabric.

"I'll be back later tonight, Mamá," he said.

"Tom," Mamá said uneasily, her accent leaning heavily on his name. "Please, you will be careful? Very careful?"

"Sí, Mamá." He grinned and leaned forward to smack a loud kiss on her cheek. Wendy watched Mamá as the front door closed behind him. Her eyes had always been laced with sadness, but now Wendy saw a shadow of fear there too.

As she measured the cardboard tubing, Wendy's brain flitted from one question to the next, wanting to ask Mamá so many things but not quite able to say the words. Before she could even jot down the measurement, Papá burst through the front door. From the look on his face Wendy knew immediately that something was very, very wrong.

"You entered a competition," he said to Wendy, his voice controlled. "At the library." It was not a question, and Wendy wasn't sure what to say.

"The fall reading thing?" she asked. "Yeah, I told you about that." She added uncertainly, "You didn't seem to care." Why did Papá seem so angry? Then she thought of something. "Wait, did I win? Is that how you know about it?" The thought was like a tiny bubble of joy in her chest. After this horrible, awful day, she might actually have won something! Even a small thing, like the magazine subscription, would be so great. She leaned toward him eagerly, the bubble expanding inside her, full of hope.

"You did, this 'Star Pack' thing, yes—" he began, and Wendy gasped, her hands flying to her mouth in surprise. She had won the Star Pack. The grand prize! She was going to the Astronomy Convention! She would get to hear from real astronomers. Maybe even meet them! She let out a squeal of excitement, but Papá's voice cut in over her, louder than before.

"Do you want to know how I heard?" He was glaring at her, but Wendy barely registered it. In the middle of all the mess that was her life, the universe had made this happen. *Well, not made it happen*, she reminded herself. *It was chance. But still. Thank you, Universe!*

"I heard it on the radio. The radio, Wendy! I'm on my way to a job site and I hear them say Dulce Ortiz Toledo can pick up her tickets at the library."

"They said I needed to put an adult's name down . . ."

"So you gave them your mother's full name to read out on the radio?"

The bubbling happiness inside Wendy suddenly fizzed to a cold, sinking feeling.

"Óscar!" Mamá held up her hands, palms out, and kept her voice low. "Please no yelling. It is okay—"

"It is not okay!" he yelled back at her, then turned to Wendy. "Your head was so stuck up in the sky that you didn't think about this? Three times, *three times* they repeated 'Dulce Ortiz Toledo.'"

Wendy's insides were breaking apart. She hadn't thought about that; he was right. Had the sign-up information mentioned that the raffle draw would be broadcast live? She should have read it more closely.

Papá was looking out the windows as if a SWAT team might pull up any minute. "This is silly, Óscar," Mamá murmured quietly. "It is nothing. They are not listening for names on the radio."

By "they," Wendy was sure she meant ICE. And even though Mamá said it was silly, Wendy saw the way her eyes flew to the window too.

"La migra comes at people over nothing," Papá said. "They think you look a certain way—they pull you over. They hear a certain name . . ." He threw up his hand in a gesture that looked both angry and helpless.

Wendy felt the coolness of the wall behind her and realized

she had backed as far away as she could. She was still trying to process what Papá had said, but she understood she had put Mamá in danger.

"So, let's just call them," she said, her voice cracking. "And they won't announce it again, right?"

Papá's eyes met hers. They were still blazing, but Wendy saw something else cowering behind the fear. Guilt.

"I did call. I said to take our name off the list. That we could not take them."

"What do you mean?" Wendy said slowly. She had spent so much of today wrestling to keep her feelings inside. She had clung to numbness because she was afraid she might explode if she felt anything at all. But as Papá's words sank in, anger flared inside her. He had given up her tickets. He had told them Wendy couldn't have them. Her chest clenched and she took a trembling breath. "Why?"

Papá started pacing again. "Because now they know. They heard about the tickets to that thing. If you go, they will know where you are—"

"Oscar, please, enough," Mamá said, her palms still facing out toward Papá, like useless stop signs. "What you say does not have sense."

Papá rubbed his face, as if he could push away the frightened look in his eyes. "I just—" he muttered. "I just didn't know what to do."

Wendy watched his strong shoulders slump and felt her anger surge hotter. Anger at his fear, his paranoia. His obsession with the whole family always sitting down to dinner together.

"Tom was right," she choked out, tears springing into her eyes. "You just want to live in some make-believe safe world!"

Papá looked like he had been slapped. But Wendy felt a supernova building inside her and couldn't stop it.

"You think we don't know?" she shouted, her fists clenched. "You are hiding in here, pretending everything is normal. Wanting us to be normal. Then you take away something normal, something I love, and you think we can just keep pretending!"

The tears were rolling down her cheeks. Mamá was coming toward her, reaching out her hands, and Wendy knew that if she let Mamá touch her, she would cry for hours, maybe days. She retreated, inching closer to the back door. She had to get out of this house.

With one last look at Papá, Wendy banged through the door. She kept going, through the gate and across the alley. She wasn't sure what her plan was, but when she saw the cars in the parking lot, she found herself walking toward the church. And there was Etta, taping a "Let Luz Stay" sign to the railing of the church steps. Luz, who loved the stars. Luz, who Papá didn't understand. Luz, who wasn't afraid to talk to reporters about the unjust laws trying to tear her family apart. There was nothing make-believe about Luz and her sanctuary.

Etta looked at her, her eyebrows diving down into a serious V shape. "What happened?"

Wendy wiped furiously at her cheeks. "Nothing. Everything." Then she lifted her chin and asked, "Can I meet Luz now?"

TWENTY-FIVE

WENDY'S FAMILY WASN'T religious, unless you counted Mamá's occasional exclamations of "¡Diosito lindo!" She wasn't sure what to expect from the people inside the church. A wrinkled woman with snow-white hair let them in the front door after Etta made a complicated hand signal through the glass.

"Wendy, this is Janice," Etta said brightly. "She's our Sanctuary Sentry. She won't let you in without the secret signal."

Janice held her cane straight at her side and gave Etta a sharp salute. But she winked at Wendy and mouthed *"Not true"* as they went by.

Etta giggled. "She really does have to keep people out, though. The sentries make sure only people they know come in, just in case of press or if ICE sends agents or something else."

Wendy wondered what "something else" meant. But, strangely, she wasn't afraid. In fact, just thinking about how much Papá wouldn't want her here, Sanctuary Sentry or not, made her hold her head up a bit higher. The room they entered was packed with people. Someone was playing guitar. A gentleman with the longest white beard she'd ever seen spoke halting Spanish with a short Latino man in a cowboy hat. Most people held signs with phrases like "Keep Families Together." Pinned to the back of a baby carrier was a sign with yellow letters that said "Never again" peeking out from under the baby's curly brown hair.

Suddenly the guitar strumming stopped, and she heard a familiar voice say, "Wendy?" And then Tom was there, pulling her into a hug.

"I didn't expect to see you here, Chiquitín! You're just in time!"

He pointed to the front, where a striking young woman held up a red bullhorn. She wore black leather boots and a deep-blue shirt with "justicia" scrawled across it in bold white letters. Dark curls fell in a glossy wave over one shoulder, but the other half of her head was shaved. The infamous Nadia.

"Welcome," she said, the bullhorn raised to her lips. "You who left work early or who skipped dinner or rushed here with your kids after school. You who couldn't sleep last night thinking about the injustice happening in our name."

She had a voice that was meant to be amplified, powerful even without the volume on the small megaphone. It had a tinge of an accent and a depth to it that surprised Wendy.

"You are here, instead of whatever else you could be doing,

because we cannot stand by and do nothing!" Clapping broke out around her. "You are here because our friend Luz matters!"

The cheers burst out in a loud roar as Nadia waved her arm toward a woman standing beside her. Wendy recognized Luz immediately. In spite of the smile she gave the crowd, there was nothing at ease about Luz. A golden rosary slid through her fingers and her round eyes flickered around the room like a stone skimming over water. The way she held herself, as if ready to scurry for cover, reminded Wendy of Mamá.

"La migra calls her a criminal," Nadia said, "for trying to keep her family together. And they make her check in at their office, surrounded by their hired guns, who could arrest her at any moment. But that wasn't enough for them. They also had to shackle her."

Nadia pointed down to Luz's ankle. Just above her right shoe a sock had been pulled up over a bulky shape. "Right now, this device they force her to wear is monitoring her—monitoring us! Just to have this meeting tonight, Luz had to put her cell phone in her sock, next to the monitor, with her music blasting. So that they can't hear what we say."

Exclamations of disgust peppered the crowd.

"This ankle monitor is inhumane. Every night, she plugs it into the wall, and tries not to move for hours while it charges. Last night it malfunctioned and sent shock waves up her leg while she was showering!"

Gasps of outrage rippled through the room. Luz was looking down, not at the ankle monitor but at the floor, her fingers clenched over her rosary. A sick feeling filled Wendy's belly. Mamá would be humiliated to stand, shackled with an ankle monitor, in front of a room full of people and tell them these things. Even if they were on her side.

"And what's more, she is being *charged* for this invasive surveillance device! Every. Single. Day. So tonight we say, 'No more!'"

Vigorous clapping filled the room.

"Tonight we say 'We are not animals to be leashed and shocked!'" A roar from the crowd swept even Wendy into applause. "Tonight Luz has decided that she is done with the shackles of oppression!"

Nadia held up a pair of heavy-duty scissors.

"Tonight Luz has decided to remove her ankle monitor. And we stand with her."

And with that, Nadia turned, kneeling on the floor in front of Luz. The tinny sound of mariachi music rang out, as Nadia removed Luz's cell phone from her sock and passed it up to her. Luz muted it, slipping the phone into her pocket. Her fingers found her rosary again. Nadia pulled the white sock down all the way, revealing a heavy black device on a thick strap. Looking down at her, Luz seemed to grow a bit, as if she suddenly took up more space than before. She nodded firmly, her fingers suddenly still over the gold chain.

There was an expectant pause as everyone in the room

waited, watching the metal blades cut through the strap. Then it fell away, and the crowd burst out in joyful cheering.

But Wendy found herself staring, mesmerized, at the bare inches of Luz's leg where the skin was rubbed red in a ring around her ankle. Nadia had seen it, too, and she reached forward as if to grab the leg for a better look. But Luz tugged her pant leg down, pulling away from her. Nadia said something urgently to Luz, gesturing toward the crowd. Somehow, Wendy knew that Nadia wanted Luz to put her injured skin on display and whip up more anger at what had been done to her. Luz's dark eyes flitted around the cheering faces, and Wendy saw exactly what would happen next. She saw how Luz would nod and Nadia would turn again to the crowd and stretch out that accusing finger to point at the cruelty of ICE etched into this woman's skin. And Luz's dark eyes would blink at the ground, and she would shrink again into a small, uncertain shadow. Wendy felt something pushing on her chest and she whispered, "No."

Before she knew she had decided to do it, she was moving toward them, calling out, "NO!" Her voice was mostly swallowed by the noise of the crowd, but Nadia and Luz turned to her in surprise. Wendy said, "She shouldn't have to prove her pain."

Nadia raised her eyebrows. "It's important for people to see exactly what they've done."

Wendy, stunned at her own daring, said, "But is that what she wants?"

Nadia turned to Luz, who was staring in confusion at the girl with the long dark braid who had just stepped up to them. Nadia said something in Spanish, and Luz, after a slight hesitation, shook her head no. "All right, then," Nadia said, looking at Wendy thoughtfully. Wendy sank back into the crowd, shaken. Had she really just stood up to Nadia, that powerhouse who had the whole room hanging on to her every word?

But then Luz met her eyes and gave her a nod. Just a small one, but Wendy felt a warmth spreading in her chest. She knew it was a thank-you.

A tall woman with a short brown bob took the megaphone. "Welcome, everyone," she said, in a rich, sure voice. "I am Alice Carpenter, the pastor here in Luz's temporary home." Wendy immediately saw the resemblance to Etta. Her strength of presence was a deeper, steadier version of Etta's unending energy.

"Thank you all for showing up to support Luz today. Luz has nothing to hide, but she is also in a very vulnerable situation. If she were to walk into the ICE office right now, she would be taken into custody and deported. We have a small group of volunteers who will drive downtown and hand in the ankle monitor at the ICE office for her. The rest of you will be here, standing with Luz, for the press conference."

Now, suddenly, it all clicked in Wendy's brain. This wasn't just a meeting at the church. This was a public protest. What had she gotten herself into?

The man with the long white beard was calling out instructions for everyone to make their way to the parking lot with their signs. Wendy searched the crowd for Tom. Maybe he would give her a wink, pull her away from the crowd, and make a joke out of it all while walking her back to the safety of the crooked house. But when she managed to find him, that hope fizzled out instantly. He was gathered in a corner with Nadia and several others, nodding seriously as Pastor Carpenter said, "Remember what we discussed last time. Do not interact with officers unless necessary. Anything you do could have repercussions for Luz."

Wendy had a sudden, sinking suspicion. "Tom," she hissed. "Please tell me you aren't going with the group to the ICE office!"

Tom looked down at her and his face blazed with determination. He shoved something into her hands, saying, "Hold it high, Chiquitín," and he followed Nadia out the door.

Wendy unfolded the long strip of fabric. "We Stand With Luz" was painted in bold black letters across the cloth banner. How much had Mamá known when she had sewn this? What would Papá do if he knew Tom was marching straight up to the ICE office? She gritted her teeth. Maybe if their parents hadn't shut them down every time they tried to find out anything, they wouldn't have ended up here. And maybe if Papá hadn't called the library and told them to give away her tickets to the Astronomy Convention . . . Tears sprang to her eyes and Wendy blinked them away.

"Come on, Wendy!" Etta called, grinning across the room, her hair sticking up in all directions like a spiky turquoise crown. And Wendy gathered up the banner and ran after her.

For most of the next two hours, Wendy's heart didn't stop racing. The people surrounding Luz on the church steps pulsed with upbeat energy, but it took Wendy some time before she could join the songs and chants. She kept looking suspiciously at every car that drove past, thinking of agents—or her parents. Etta had stretched Tom's banner out right in the front of the crowd and they stood together gripping one side with Janice at the other end. After a while Wendy relaxed a bit. She found herself chanting along with Etta, "Say it loud! Say it clear! Immigrants are welcome here!" It was strange to realize that these people she was pushed up against on the sidewalk were here because they cared about a Mexican illegal. *No, not an illegal*, Wendy thought, glancing back at Luz. A *woman*, a *person* who didn't have the right papers. A woman who reminded her of Mamá. Wendy's chest loosened and she breathed a long, shuddering breath. And when the news vans stopped by with their cameras, Wendy smiled and lifted the banner high.

TWENTY-SIX

THERE WAS A new camaraderie between Tom and Wendy when they got home that night. Papá, who looked immensely relieved to see Wendy, started asking her where she had been, but Tom saw her face and jumped in with a vague comment about sibling bonding. Surprisingly, Papá bought it. *And it's actually true,* Wendy thought, with a grateful smile to her brother. Later, working on her telescope and still feeling the high from the protest, Wendy heard Tom calling her name up the stairs.

"Something's up," he told her as she came down. "Mamá just yelled for me to get you."

"Really?" Wendy said. "Mamá yelled? Guess Papá is resting his voice or something?" She still hadn't forgiven him.

In the flickering light from the TV Wendy saw Papá's broad shoulders hunched in the armchair. Mamá was standing next to him, her hands clenched together. Without a word, Papá looked at them and clicked the remote.

It was a news report. Papá must have started recording it as soon as he realized what it was about, because the screen jumped straight to a close-up of Luz standing in the church doorway. Then the camera panned across the group, where Wendy stood at one end of the banner, clearly visible. The video cut to a reporter in front of the ICE office and a shot of Nadia speaking about Luz. And directly behind her was Tom.

In spite of how much she always tried to keep her head down and blend in, Wendy felt a thrill. Plain, boring, invisible Wendy was right there, on TV! She looked up at Tom to see a small smile on his face. They had done something big today. Something good. Something *newsworthy*. Then the image froze, and they both turned back to Papá. But Mamá was the one holding the remote now, looking stricken.

"This was . . ." She shook her head in disbelief. "Very bad, Tom. You said you were just going to the church. Not on a march to la migra." She motioned to the screen, the glass door of the ICE office clearly labeled behind Tom and his group.

Tom's voice edged into frustration. "We *had* to go to ICE! This is what Luz needed. We are fighting for her and she needs our protection."

"Your protection?" Papá sat forward now, his eyes blazing. "*You?* You are going to *protect*," he emphasized the word, "this illegal from ICE?"

He sounded so incredulous that Wendy felt her brain

stumbling. What had they been thinking? They couldn't really protect someone from the immigration police. Could they?

"Stop!" Tom shouted at Papá, and remarkably, Papá closed his mouth and stared up at his son.

"You don't get to call her that! She isn't illegal!" Tom shoved his hands into his pockets as he spoke, and Wendy noticed they were shaking. But his voice was strong.

"Asking for asylum isn't a crime. She is just a mother trying to live her life. Here with her kids. You know, *just like you*!"

Papá stood up now, slowly, carefully, his whole body wound tight like a spring.

"I belong here." One stubby finger jabbed down at the floor as Papá spoke. "I am not asking anyone to stand between me and ICE. Especially not some kids!" His voice rose.

"Really, Papá?" Tom said sarcastically. "What do you think we are, your all-American kids? Isn't that basically our job? Even our names! Tom? Wendy? You bent so far backward for American names that they're basically British!"

Papá stared at him, stunned. Her brother kept going. "Wendy might not remember, but I do. I remember life before you decided we had to be your American shields! You think I didn't notice when you shut down Spanish and started sending only PB&J in our lunches?"

Wendy furrowed her brow. What was he saying? That

Papá had just decided one day they couldn't be Salvadoran-Guatemalan anymore? It was true the enchiladas and tortillas from their family meals never ended up in their packed lunches. But she hadn't really thought about it.

"Our lunches are fine," she murmured.

Tom shot her a look, then went on, his voice hard. "You're just hiding behind us—"

"That is not true!" Papá shouted over him.

Wendy wished he would stop. She looked away from them, then blinked. She thought she saw something on the screen, behind the reporter's shoulder. Someone just inside the glass door of the ICE building . . .

"Tom," Wendy said shakily, and something in her voice made him turn. She pointed. The figure frozen on the screen was unmistakable. He hovered behind the door, watching the protestors, shoulders back. His cold eyes gazed at the group in front of the ICE building. Those eyes seemed to be fixed on Tom.

"It's him," Tom said quietly. He leaned toward the face on the screen, his eyebrows raised in surprise. "I thought I saw him by your school the other day too." He looked at Wendy. "Have you ever seen him there?" Wendy shook her head, bewildered.

"Who?" Mamá pushed forward, her hands fluttering nervously. "You, you know him? Does he know you, Tom? He is migra!" Her voice was rising in panic.

"It's okay, Mamá," Tom said, raising his hands. His voice

was soothing now, and Wendy felt a rush of hope that her brother, who always knew how to make people feel better, was here to calm things down. "We've seen him around a few times, but everything is fine."

"No!" Papá roared. "It is NOT fine! How could you do this, Tomás?"

And just like that, Tom's easy voice snapped. Wendy cringed as he turned on Papá.

"How could I what? Walk around outside in the daylight? I'm sick of your pretend world! What are you hiding?" He glared at Papá.

"I'm hiding nothing!" Papá shouted.

"Okay, then," Tom shouted back. "You were born in South Carolina, right? You have your papers, your ID, everything to prove it?"

He was breathing heavily, and Wendy wanted him to stop. But she looked at Papá. She couldn't help it. She wanted him to answer. Maybe even pull out his birth certificate. Then Tom would stop asking these questions. And she could stop thinking about the mysterious newspapers in the attic.

Papá opened his mouth, then closed it again. Wendy felt sick.

"Papi?" Her voice was small in the sudden quiet. Papá met her eyes, and Wendy swallowed. "You can tell us," she said, trying to sound brave.

Papá frowned. He looked surprised, as if just now realizing

her fear was for him. "I do have my papers," he said, his voice calmer now. "But . . . I was born in El Salvador." He saw their faces and hurried to explain. "I was adopted in South Carolina when I was a baby. So, I am American. By adoption. I—I am sorry I let you think I was born here. It was just easier."

Wendy felt relief loosening her chest even as her brain raced. That baby in the picture *was* Papá. And he *had* been born in El Salvador. But it didn't matter because he was American now. He was safe. She turned to Tom, expecting him to look relieved as well.

But Tom's face was still tense. "So you lied to us," he said.

Papá narrowed his eyes. "Oh, I am the one who lies?" His voice rose, the anger flooding back into it. "You go sneaking off—"

"Okay, then," Tom interrupted. "You are American, great." He pulled his shaking hand from his pocket and pointed a finger at Mamá. "But what about her?"

The last bit of air in the room disappeared as Mamá took a sharp breath. Tom turned his eyes to her, and Wendy saw a gleam in them. Was he crying?

"Mamá," he whispered. "We already know. You don't have to hide from us."

Mamá stared up at him, her eyes huge and dark and deep. In the middle of the room, Papá's shape seemed to shrink, as if the air were draining from him too.

"That is what you think?" Mamá whispered. "You think I

have been hiding behind you?" She took a step closer to Tom and reached out a hand as if she were about to touch his face. But her outstretched fingers froze in the middle of the room, looking lost.

"Mijo," she said softly, "you are so wrong."

TWENTY-SEVEN

"YOU THINK I am cobarde," Mamá said, her hand falling down to her side and grasping at the fabric of her skirt. "A . . ." She searched for the word. "A coward. You think your father has always been protecting me. And that I am this coward for hiding."

Tom shifted, his gaze falling to the ground. "I didn't mean—" he began, but Mamá interrupted him.

"Maybe I am. Maybe I am a coward for hiding the truth. But you are right. We cannot pretend."

"Dulce, no." Papá's voice was pleading now.

"We knew they would find out, Óscar," she told him gently. Then she looked from Wendy's worried eyes to Tom's expectant ones and sighed. "The war in Guatemala was very violent, very bad. And my family—" Her voice faltered. "I had to leave. I had to run away to save my life, and when I came here, I got a green card."

Wendy heard the words like a beacon in the darkness.

Tom's face lit up. But Mamá held up a hand to stop them from speaking.

"The man told me to do the document, to put in our names and to pay the money. It was all the money I had. And they gave us our papers."

Wendy furrowed her brow. "You and Papá?" she asked.

Mamá shook her head no. "Your father is American. He has his American papers. I thought I did too. But I was wrong."

"What do you mean?" Wendy's voice was hoarse, and she swallowed hard. "You just said you got papers."

"I didn't know for a long time about those papers," Mamá said, looking down. Her hands were clenched at her sides, the fabric of her skirt bunched in her fists. "We thought that after ten years with a green card I could get citizen papers. Because we are married. But . . ." Mamá's voice lowered. "When we tried, they say it is a false green card."

Wendy hung on to every word, trying to sort it out. Mamá's papers were fake?

"They say I cannot get citizen papers because my green card is no good. They say . . ." She took a deep breath before continuing. "They say I will be deported."

Wendy had imagined words like this, many times. She'd known that there was a shadow hanging over Mamá. But hearing her say it out loud, in the middle of their living room, with the images of the ICE office frozen on their TV, was a whole new brand of awful.

"And that's when we moved to Ohio?" Wendy asked, her brain trying to piece things together. "We left South Carolina six years ago. Because they were going to deport you?"

"Wait," Tom said. His words were quiet and slow, as if he were working things out as he said them. "You said . . . you said *we*. You said 'they gave *us* our papers. But . . . Papá already had papers."

The room shuddered, as if the air were gathering itself up for something wild and destructive. Mamá lifted her dark, sad eyes and looked straight at Tom. "Yes," she whispered. "You and me, mijo." She stared at him and the trembling tears finally spilled down her cheeks. Papá groaned softly. Tom had gone pale and very, very still. Mamá, her face wet, reached out her brown hand and laid it gently on Tom's cheek. "I was never only hiding for *me*," she told him quietly. "I was hiding for *you*."

Wendy leaned closer to the little round attic window and adjusted her binoculars. The stars in Cassiopeia's constellation came into focus slowly, as if they were drifting up toward her from the deep sea. They weren't, she knew. Scientists had big arguments about how fast the universe was spreading out, but everyone knew it was. It had started as this tiny, dense ball of all the building blocks of everything that would ever exist, atoms and water and planets and elephants and bubble gum all smooshed together, then—*boom*! And ever since then all of it had been expanding, each piece drifting farther away from the rest.

Like her family.

Even though Mamá was downstairs, frantically cleaning or cooking or somehow keeping her hands busy, Wendy felt light-years away from her. And Papá was driving around somewhere looking for Tom, who was moving away from them the fastest of all.

Tom. Her charming brother with the perfect face that made strangers want to smile when they saw him. Her illegal brother who had been using fake documents his whole life without knowing it.

Not illegal. No human being is illegal, she reminded herself.

Mamá came up the attic steps cautiously, placing each foot with care. She crossed to Wendy and held a piece of paper out to her, cradling it in both hands.

"Here," she said, lowering it reverently toward her. "For you to see."

Wendy took it, her eyes scanning over the embossed seal of South Carolina and the official signature below. And right there in the middle was her name, *Wendy Celestina Toledo*, and her birth date.

"You see." Mamá smiled faintly in the moonlight shining through the round window. "You are American. I want you to know this is true."

Wendy stared at her hopeful face. Did Mamá think all she wanted was an American birth certificate? Proof that she was untouchable, when her mom and her brother could still be sent away at any time? She looked down at the document in her hands.

"Mamá," she said slowly. "I don't get it. I mean, Tom and you and even Papá! I don't get any of it! Is Papá actually American? Where was Tom born, then?" She laid the paper down to the side and looked at her mom. "What is going on?"

Mamá sighed heavily. "Yes, it is . . . complicated." She settled back against the chest and closed her eyes, as if gathering herself in. "Your papá became American when he was a baby. He grew up here, with his aunt and uncle. Because he spoke English and Spanish, he got a job on the border with a group that helped immigrants. That is where I met him. The men who brought us across and gave me papers . . . they were very bad people." She shuddered. "And Tom was very little, he was just born. I was so, so scared. But Óscar rescued us from them and took us to the migrant center. He is very brave, your papá."

"But . . ." Wendy licked her lips, hoping Mamá would tell her she had misunderstood. "Tom was a newborn when you met Papá? You mean . . ."

Mamá squeezed her eyes shut and nodded.

Papá wasn't Tom's father. It seemed like everything kept getting worse. Wendy pictured Tom's face when Mamá had told him he was undocumented. There had been something feral, like a trapped animal, in his bright eyes. When he grabbed his coat and left, Mamá had followed him outside, speaking quiet words that Wendy didn't hear. "Does Tom know?" she asked.

"Now he knows, yes."

"Why didn't you tell us?"

Mamá's answer was slow, as if it hurt to say. "It was better, we thought. Because we thought our papers were okay. And when they said they were false papers, we thought maybe Tom was okay. Because of DACA, the program for DREAMers to get papers. You know the DREAMers?"

"Doesn't that mean if you grew up here you can stay?" Wendy asked.

Mamá nodded. "If your parents brought you here when you were little, you could get papers when you turned sixteen." She wiped her eyes. "Then in 2017 they stopped it."

Wendy thought back to last year and Tom's sixteenth birthday. That was the same time the president ended DACA. Everyone in Melborn wanted to talk about it, worrying over what it would mean. She hadn't paid too much attention. At the time, the raids were starting and that seemed like a bigger deal. But she hadn't thought DACA had anything to do with Tom.

"And then we hoped that it would maybe change," Mamá said tiredly. "There are people trying to get DACA back."

"So, what happened to the other . . . to Tom's . . ." But Wendy couldn't finish the thought. Calling anyone other than Papá his father didn't seem right.

"His name was Daniel," Mamá whispered. "He was a

mechanic. Daniel could fix anything—buses, tractors, motorcycles. He played guitar too." Her gaze slid past Wendy, as if seeing into another world. "But then they came for him. The gangs. They wanted him to drive deliveries. To cross the border. He told them no, he would not touch their drugs. Many times he told them. Finally they said they would kill him if he did not join. So he ran from Guatemala, thinking I would be safer if he was gone. He wanted to protect me. And our baby."

There was so much pain in Mamá's voice, Wendy didn't know if she could bear to hear it. She could sense something deep and dark pulling Mamá back to that place as she talked.

"But they caught him in Mexico. They put him in a cage. Like a dog. They said to bring money. I brought everything I had to Mexico, but I was too late. Daniel was dead. And I was so . . . broken. And that's when the baby came. I used the money to cross over, to escape. But the men who took us over were bad too. Without your papá and the migrant center . . . I don't know. I had nobody, no home, everyone was gone."

Wendy bit her lip and then said, "Your brother too?"

Mamá tilted her head, her black braid hanging to one side. "You know about Felix?"

Wendy pulled her hand from Mamá's and reached behind her for the clasp on the trunk. She opened it and carefully held out the folded fabric. Mamá made a small sound of recognition as she unwrapped the family photo. Mamá cradled the picture with the same kind of reverence she had shown Wendy's birth certificate. She touched the tip of one round finger to the face of the little boy.

"Our mamita had to give him a big bath this day because he was building a mud palace for the worms."

"Like, an ant farm?" Wendy asked.

"Oh, no, not a farm. A *palace*! With two floors and a swimming pool." Mamá let out a whisper of a laugh. "He had mud all over him. And the man with the camera was coming so Mamita made him clean himself. But he didn't want his worms to escape. So he put them in his pockets!"

Wendy leaned closer to the photograph. The boy's hands were not actually in his pockets; they were cupped protectively over the openings. Next to him the little girl smiled at him adoringly.

"This is you," she said quietly. Then she asked, "Was he older?"

"Only a few minutes older."

"You were twins!" Wendy leaned closer. "What happened to him?"

But Mamá looked away and her eyes were deep like the endless blackness of space. She had drifted away again.

"I . . . I am finished talking about this now."

Wendy's throat clenched as Mamá carefully put the photo back in the fabric. As Mamá got to her feet and gently closed the lid of the trunk, Wendy thought of all the different theories about how quickly the universe was expanding. She wondered which was right. And if any of them included a way to stop it.

TWENTY-EIGHT

"ARE YOU OKAY?" Etta asked, leaning against her locker. "You look . . . foggy."

Wendy started to answer, but stopped as a gigantic yawn made her eyes water. "Didn't sleep much," she told Etta.

At one a.m. Tom had finally responded to Papá's messages with a single text. *At a friend's.* Even after she eventually fell asleep, Wendy's dreams were strange and she woke up again and again. First she was sinking into an underwater volcano past floating stars. But it wasn't a volcano. It was a Jarritos bottle, and she was wearing a round pineapple slice as a life preserver. Only it didn't float because it was full of holes that a unicorn kitty had poked into it. She wished Papá had let her stay home from school.

Wendy opened and closed her heavy eyelids again, peering at Etta. "You don't look so good yourself. You have actual blue circles under your eyes."

"Oh," Etta said. "Yeah. I didn't sleep much either. My mom

stayed at the church overnight to be with Luz, and I just kept thinking about them. Did you see the paper yesterday? Luz was on the front page."

Wendy shook her head. She didn't read the newspaper. What middle schooler did? Well, Etta, apparently.

"Anyway, there are some scumbags that want to get her deported. They've been standing out on the sidewalk with signs . . ." Etta trailed off, looking distracted. Wendy eyed her curiously. She really didn't seem like herself today.

"Etta!"

They turned to see K.K. and Yasmin hurrying toward them. "It's happened again," K.K. said, her face serious.

Etta seemed bewildered at first, then her eyes flashed with that familiar Etta spark. "The posters?" she asked. Yasmin nodded, and Etta let out a huff. "Show me," she demanded.

"*What* happened again?" Wendy asked, hurrying after them.

"You know how it's Hispanic Heritage Month?" Yasmin said. "The student council and the GSA United have been putting up those posters about different Latinx people?"

"Um, yeah?" Wendy had honestly not paid too much attention to Hispanic Heritage Month. Her own personal Hispanic heritage had been taking up too much mental energy.

"Well, our posters are being targeted!" Etta called back over her shoulder as she hurried after K.K. "Two of them have been torn down and someone drew a mustache on my poster of Sonia Sotomayor yesterday."

"And now this," K.K. said grimly, leading them to the wall next to the art room and pointing up at a poster of Cesar Chavez.

Someone had drawn a pizza over his face with black marker and a speech bubble over his head that read: "I invented Little Caesar's pizza. Hooray for yummies!" The handwriting was neat, written in thin, sharp lines that angled a bit to the left.

"Unbelievable!" Etta said, her voice rising. "Cesar Chavez was a hero for workers' rights and some jerk writes this crap." She smacked a hand on the poster. "Did you tell Ms. Whitman?"

K.K. snorted and mimicked a soothing, adult voice. "Now, K.K., this is a minor graffiti incident. There's no reason to get upset." K.K. rolled her eyes. "Then she said we shouldn't put up any more posters. Because," K.K. continued, adding air quotes, "'highlighting our differences is causing division.'"

"What?!" Etta said indignantly. "Our differences don't cause division. Whoever is out there graffitiing our posters is causing division!"

"Maybe it's just some kids messing around?" Wendy asked.

"Except it's not just this one time," Etta insisted. "Someone scribbled Sharpie on K.K.'s campaign poster, too, remember?"

"And remember how the Unity Club sign-up sheet went missing?" K.K. added.

Yasmin bit her lip and said hesitantly, "And I've gotten more notes."

They all stared at her. "Like that one at the beginning of school?" Etta asked. "The one you wouldn't tell me about?"

Yasmin nodded. "It was about my hijab." She blushed. "I actually just started wearing hijab this year and I was a little nervous at first. So I thought I was being too sensitive. I tried to ignore it, but . . ." She reached in her pocket and pulled out a folded piece of paper. "There have been more. This one was in my locker today. I think it's the same person who did that." She pointed at the poster.

Etta snatched the note and read it aloud. "*What are you hiding under there? Are you bald?*" She made a disgusted noise.

Yasmin shrugged. "I mean, it's not a big deal. It doesn't really mean anything."

"Does it make you uncomfortable?" K.K. asked. Yasmin looked down and nodded. "Then it *is* a big deal," K.K. said firmly.

"Definitely," Etta agreed. "Whoever is sending you these notes is trying to mess with you. And it does look like the same handwriting." Etta stared at each of them, her green eyes blazing. "If Ms. Whitman's not going to do anything, we'll figure it out on our own. Who do you think it is?"

"Um . . ." Wendy felt her exhaustion pulling her down even more. She did not want to get sucked into this.

"It could be P.J.," K.K. said, looking at the pizza drawing.

"P.J. writes like a toddler hippopotamus," Etta said,

waving the note in the air. "This handwriting is practically a design font. No way it's him."

Wendy felt a chill run down her spine. She knew this handwriting. She remembered how Brett's ink pen rolled over the paper, labeling the telescope picture with narrow, slightly slanted letters that looked almost printed. But when she opened her mouth to speak, she felt her throat constrict. What would be the point of telling? Even if her friends believed her, would Ms. Whitman? She'd already seen that her word against Brett's wasn't enough.

The bell rang before Wendy could bring herself to speak up. As they all hurried to class, Etta reminded them to keep an eye out for the graffiti bandit.

"His handwriting at least. Or hers. Or theirs," Etta called over her shoulder.

Wendy ducked her head guiltily and focused on relaxing her breathing. Ms. Park had made it clear that if her telescope wasn't done by Wednesday she wouldn't be able to enter it in the fair. This was her last day to finish it. She just had to keep her head down, make it through school today, and get home. And joining Etta's quest was not going to help with any of that, she told herself grimly.

"This is too heavy, mija," Mamá said as she helped Wendy shift the blocky wooden frame Papá had built for her across the pavement of the church parking lot.

"It has to be heavy," Wendy insisted, grunting from the

effort. "If the base isn't stable, the whole thing will be super wobbly and it'll be impossible to get a good picture."

Wendy had been working frantically to put her telescope together all evening. She still couldn't believe she'd gotten it done and she wanted to make sure it worked before showing it to Ms. Park tomorrow. Papá had mostly finished the base she had designed, although it didn't have the phone mount she wanted. But she'd managed to rig Mamá's smartphone to the eyepiece with rubber bands, and she was hoping to get a few nighttime pictures before the Science Fair on Saturday. Even more important, she needed something to take her mind off her brother. It had only been one day since she'd seen him, but so much had shifted in their world. She just wanted him to be okay.

Now she let all that slide away as she turned to the sky. In spite of the noise that spilled down from the bars and restaurants on Main Street, Wendy felt a familiar quiet filling her as she angled her telescope toward the North Star. She turned the focus ring and Polaris came slowly into view. Wendy tapped the phone, snapping a pic of the tiny pinprick of light.

Mamá came over to see and Wendy showed her the picture, sighing in disappointment. "It's not great magnification," she explained. "I knew it wouldn't be, not with a DIY telescope. But . . . it's just *so* small."

Just then the side door to the church banged softly shut, and Wendy looked up to see Luz peering at them under the dim streetlights. Mamá hurried over, greeting her warmly, and Wendy waved. Luz walked up to her and gestured toward the telescope, saying something in Spanish.

"I—I don't understand," Wendy stammered. Luz's eyes settled on her curiously.

"I'm sorry," Wendy said. "I know some Spanish, I just . . ."

"Is okay," Luz said, her voice soft and heavy with an accent even stronger than Mamá's. "You and me," she said, placing her hand on her chest. She said something in Spanish again, then said slowly and carefully, "We speak *here*. The language of the heart."

Wendy smiled back at her gratefully, then Luz asked, "You will see la luna?"

Wendy knew that word, since it was like the word "*lunar.*"

"No, not the moon. The stars. Estrellas. I was going to study their movement," Wendy explained. "The moon's not as interesting. It's always the same."

Mamá translated for her, and Luz looked thoughtfully at the sky. "Sí, exacto," Luz said. "Stars move. La luna, she looks same here as everywhere. She is ours."

Wendy looked up at the rising moon. It was nearly full. She knew it didn't actually change as it went through its phases. The moon always faced toward them as it orbited the planet. Half of it was always lit by the sun; it was just their perspective from Earth that made it look different. *Parallax.*

"You see?" Luz whispered.

It was the same moon that Alicia would be looking at,

wherever she was. The same moon Jesús and Celestina would have seen, fighting for justice in El Salvador. And in Guatemala, and in Mexico, and in the US—no matter where her family was from, they all shared the same moon. Luz was right. Wendy smiled and turned the telescope toward la luna.

As she tapped Mamá's phone screen to focus it, a sudden spasm of laughter from down the street startled her. Three dark figures walked down the sidewalk. Wendy heard a man swear as one of them stumbled. She edged closer to Mamá. *They're just some randos out with friends*, she told herself. One of them turned to flick his cigarette and looked straight toward them. Wendy felt an eerie chill. His hair was a shaggy brown and the brim of a red cap hid his eyes. His gaze lingered a little too long. Why was he staring at them like that?

After a moment, the men walked out of sight past the church, one of them swaying unsteadily. Wendy felt her shoulders relax and was sure she heard a sigh of relief from Luz.

"Does that thing work?" a familiar voice called out.

"Tom!" Wendy raced to her brother. She threw her arms around him and pressed her face into the fake leather jacket he always wore. It smelled like him, like spearmint gum and soap and a little sweat. There was so much she wanted to talk to him about. Deportation, ICE agents, his birth dad. Did he think of her any differently now that he knew they weren't full siblings?

"Hey, Chiquitín, breathe," Tom teased, squeezing her back. "There's no way you missed me that much."

She pulled away, leaving damp spots on his jacket, and smacked his arm.

"I was *worried*!"

Then he was bending down to hug Mamá and she was wiping tears from her face too. She whispered something in his ear, and he kissed her on the cheek, murmuring a response. Then he stood and looked at the telescope.

"So you finally did it, Chiquitín? You actually built one!" He walked around the telescope and let out a low whistle. "It works?" he asked, and she rolled her eyes.

"Obviously!"

"Sorry, genius. Of course it works."

But as he stepped forward to look more closely, someone behind them slurred, "Izz her, right?"

The three men were back. The unsteady one scratched his belly through his coat. He pointed toward Luz. "Dinna I say so? Izz her."

TWENTY-NINE

TOM INHALED QUICKLY and the sound of it was like a shot of adrenaline to Wendy's brain. *Tom is afraid,* she thought, and everything around them seemed to come into focus. Luz stood frozen, staring at the men who stood between her and the church door. Wendy's eyes flashed to the man's red hat, and she thought of Etta's words earlier that day. Luz's face had been on the front page of the newspaper that morning, in an article about how she was living in sanctuary at the church. Etta, excessively optimistic Etta, had been so worried about the "scumbags" trying to get Luz deported that she hadn't slept well. Wendy felt a jolt of panic. They had to get away from here. It wasn't safe.

Then Mamá took a small step in front of Luz. It was a nearly imperceptible movement, but Wendy felt it like the shifting of a planet. Mamá was choosing her own orbit, just like Wendy had done when she'd stood up to Brett. Wendy swallowed her fear, her brain racing. She reached toward her

telescope, switched the phone to selfie mode, and tapped record. Her eyes flew back to the men. Red Hat's shadowed
face turned from Luz to the rest of them as he blew smoke
into the night air.

"Yeah, I think we found her, Stev-o. Looks like she's got
friends too."

His teeth made Wendy think of an animal, sharp and
predatory. He jerked his cigarette toward Luz. "You got some
more illegals to come hole up here with you, huh?" he snarled.

For some reason Stev-o found this very funny. "Hidey-
holes!" he chanted. "They're in their little hidey-holes!" The
third man slumped against the wall laughing quietly.

Red Hat sniffed and flicked his cigarette. He didn't seem
nearly as drunk as the other two men, but his movements
were twitchy. Watching him made Wendy's breath come
faster. Tom took a step forward, trying to move closer to Luz
and Mamá.

"Don't you come at me!" Red Hat said, his muscles tight
under his denim jacket. "Don't you even *breathe!*"

Tom raised his hands very slowly, palms out. "Hey, hey,"
he said soothingly. "We were just leaving."

"Great, so get out. Cuz this ain't your country."

Luz and Mamá exchanged a glance, and Wendy knew
they were thinking about the church door, so far away and
unreachable behind these shadowy figures.

"But she's not leaving," whined Stev-o. "She's the one in
the church, remember?"

223

"Maybe she just needs a little help leaving." Red Hat tossed his cigarette to the ground and held up his phone. "I'm a nice guy. I like to be helpful. Why don't we make a little phone call?"

Luz reached toward her pocket.

"Whoa!" Red Hat threw up a hand to stop her. "You armed?" He shifted his weight, almost bouncing on his feet.

"I'm so *sick* of all you drug mules and criminals," he spat at them. "Well, you're not the only one who knows how to protect himself."

He hiked up his denim jacket. The butt of a pistol stuck out from his waistband.

"Ay, Diosito lindo," Mamá whispered softly.

"Look, we don't want any trouble," Tom said. He edged closer to Mamá but then glanced back toward Wendy.

Red Hat saw him hesitate. He lurched at Luz, grabbing her arm in one quick motion, raising his phone with the other. Stev-o cheered and Mamá screamed. Tom leaped toward the man. He pulled Luz from Red Hat's grip, and the phone clattered to the pavement.

"You little—" The man threw himself at Tom, his fist connecting with the neat angle of Tom's chin. The sound was sickening.

Wendy saw her brother's stunned expression as he let go of Luz to catch his balance. The man snatched a handful of Tom's jacket and threw a punch at his stomach. Tom doubled over as Red Hat clobbered him again, his movements rapid and angry. Wendy gasped. It felt as if her own lungs were being pummeled.

Tom fell to one knee, wheezing and clutching his side. Red Hat kicked him, hard. Then he reached for his waistband and Wendy's brain flashed to the gun. She hurtled forward and collided with muscle and fabric, blindly lashing out at his hands. Red Hat gave an angry yelp as something hit the ground and he scrambled to regain his footing.

Wendy stared down at the gun he had dropped. She aimed her galaxy Converse at the gun and kicked with all her might. A hand slapped her face and she gasped. The air was thick with the smell of cigarettes. It mixed with the taste of blood in her mouth. Red Hat swore. Wendy felt hard hands grip her arms from behind. Her throat clenched and her head spun from lack of oxygen.

"Dude," a voice said, and she felt the fingers digging into her arm shift. Someone was tugging at Red Hat's sleeve, but he didn't let go. She forced air into her lungs.

"Dude, sheeeze just a kid. Come on," said the man called Stev-o. Red Hat ignored him.

"Looks like I caught one," he said in a singsong voice.

Even through her jacket, Wendy could feel his fingernails stabbing into her skin.

"Leave her go." The words were trembling and heavily accented, but Luz's voice was loud and clear.

Wendy blinked. Luz was holding the gun. She wasn't

pointing it at the man. It seemed as if she just wanted him to know that she had it.

Everyone froze. Then the man yanked Wendy backward toward him. His breath was loud and fast behind her. Wendy's heart raced. Tom's crumpled body coughed on the ground. Mamá's mouth hung open in a silent scream, and Luz's dark eyes looked back at her over the barrel of the gun.

"Ohhh, you gonna shoot me?" Red Hat said with a mocking tremble in his voice.

He wasn't scared. He had no reason to be, not with Wendy as his shield. He gave her a shake, holding her in front of him. She tried to pull away again, but he swore and kicked the back of her leg so hard she cried out in pain.

Mamá's eyes widened and in the lights of the parking lot the fear on her face suddenly hardened into rage. She let out a sound Wendy could hardly believe came from her, it was so wild and furious. And she launched herself toward them.

But Tom was closer. The man must have been watching Mamá, bracing himself for a frontal attack, because when Tom's weight hit him from the side, he toppled like a bowling pin. Wendy, free at last, scrambled away.

This was their chance, while Red Hat was on the ground. They had to make it to their backyard and latch the gate behind them, she thought frantically.

But the man rolled over and swung at Tom again, who was clutching his chest and couldn't seem to stand up all the way. Mamá screamed something in Spanish and brought her fist down hard on the man's shoulder. He lunged to his feet and reached for her but jerked to a stop. Tom had grabbed a handful of his denim jacket and he wrenched the man backward with a loud grunt.

"Keep your filthy hands off me!" Red Hat screamed, turning on Tom again.

Glaring beams of light flooded over them. For a second, everyone was still as a car pulled in and braked to a stop in front of them. Wendy's eyes flew to the phone the man had dropped. *He couldn't have called immigration, right?* she wondered frantically. And then she saw the third man holding his phone in his hand. Her heart sank.

THIRTY

RED HAT TURNED to Tom with his animal grin.

"You ready to meet my buddies from ICE?" And he landed another punch on Tom's face.

"Hey!" A man leaped out of the still-running car and ran toward them, both hands raised. "Step back!" he shouted.

Red Hat looked up, confused. The man kept his hands up, as if quieting a crowd of noisy children, and stepped between Red Hat and Tom. Wendy looked at the man's long white beard with a flash of recognition. She'd seen him before, at the protest for Luz.

"Who are *you*?" Red Hat asked, then, deciding it didn't matter, added angrily, "Back off, grandpa!"

"You are on private property, young man," the bearded man said calmly. "The police are on their way."

Red Hat's clenched fist looked ready to swing again when another voice broke in, wavering just like the woman whose cane was tapping toward them.

"Oh, honey, you don't want to do that," the old woman said.

Red Hat squinted at her as she hobbled closer. It was Janice, the woman Etta had called the "Sanctuary Sentry." She stepped carefully up to Red Hat, who was now looking wary.

A gagging sound came from behind and everyone turned. Stev-o was staggering over a wet puddle of vomit, groaning.

"Goodness, I think your friend might not be feeling well," Janice said, her feeble voice concerned. She reached into her pocket and stepped up to Red Hat.

"Here, honey." Janice pressed something into his hand. "Give him a peppermint."

Red Hat twitched his hand back and stared from the old woman to the wrapped candy in his palm.

"Dude, come on." His other friend threw his arm around Stev-o and looked toward the main road. From somewhere far away the sound of police sirens drifted toward them. "They called the cops."

Red Hat turned to look at Luz, who was still holding the gun loosely in her hand. He took a step toward her but the man with the white beard blocked his path.

"I think we should hang on to that until the officers arrive, don't you?" he said grimly. "They'll want to check the registration."

Red Hat looked at the two wrinkled faces in front of him,

his jaw working. The sirens were getting closer, and Wendy could see the red-and-blue glow of the lights over the buildings a few blocks away.

"Dude!" his friend called one more time.

Red Hat cursed again, scooped his phone up from the pavement, and ran after his friends. He spun around and hurled the peppermint at Janice before disappearing.

"Thank goodness," Janice said, tapping her cane on the ground. "I was hoping I wouldn't have to use this."

"You sure you don't want one?" Etta licked the last red drops off her Popsicle stick. "Your lip is all swollen, and they said to just ask."

Etta hadn't left Wendy's side since the moment she'd jumped out of her mom's car at the church. She had insisted on coming to the hospital with them, even though her mom had to stay to talk with the police and Luz.

"I don't think I can handle anything cold," Wendy said, poking at her split lip with her tongue. A Popsicle would probably help the swelling, but she shuddered at the thought. Even after the paramedics wrapped her in blankets and the nice hospital nurse checked her over, she still felt chilled deep inside her bones. "My mouth still tastes like blood, though." She grimaced.

Etta dug into the front pocket of her hoodie and handed her a peppermint. When Wendy looked at her in surprise, she just said, "Janice."

Wendy smiled and unwrapped the candy. "I still don't get how they knew what was happening," she said thoughtfully, popping it into her mouth. "We didn't have time to call anyone." The peppermint stung a bit, but she was grateful for the taste.

"That was Nadia," Etta said. "Luz's team has this check-in thing. They take turns to call her every night at the same time and she has to answer. If they can't get ahold of her, they put out an emergency call. The closest person goes to check. Janice and Artie were the closest when Nadia called." She shrugged matter-of-factly. "It was mostly in case ICE tried to get into the church, but good thing they had that plan."

Wendy nodded, impressed by Luz's team and their organization.

"Coretta! Wendy!"

Etta's mom was walking down the hospital corridor toward them, her face tight but smiling. The tall woman pulled her daughter in close and kissed her forehead.

Then she looked at Wendy and, before she knew it, Wendy was pressed into a hug as well. "I'm so, *so* glad you are all right, my dear," Pastor Carpenter whispered. She wiped at her eyes with the tip of one finger and took a deep breath.

"How is Tom?" she asked.

"He's in a lot of pain. Broken ribs." Wendy looked anxiously down the hall. "They said at least two, probably. He's getting a scan now to see how bad it is."

Pastor Carpenter nodded and said quietly, "The police found the men."

"Really?" Etta said, clutching Wendy's arm.

Wendy's eyes squeezed shut for a second as her brain conjured up the three shadows from the parking lot. *The police found the men*, she repeated in her head. *They are in jail. They can't hurt you.* But the relief was slow and her bones still felt cold.

Etta's mom continued, her face serious. "They are holding the main perpetrator for questioning, based on Luz's statement of the events. But," she added, and for the first time Wendy saw a trace of real anger on her face. She looked so much like Etta. "But his friends have completely backed him up. And their stories are quite different from what we know really happened."

The cold chill spread inside Wendy. "What do you mean?" she asked slowly.

"Their story is that they were attacked. That they were held up at gunpoint, in fact." She shook her head in disgust. "It's an unregistered gun, too, so they are trying to say it belongs to Luz. Or possibly Tom."

"But—that's ridiculous!" Wendy stammered. "It's not his gun; he never even touched it!"

Pastor Carpenter nodded. "And the fingerprints should confirm that. Also, your mom and brother are both witnesses. And that could be useful."

They wanted Mamá, and probably Tom, to talk to the

police, Wendy realized, shivering. All that her parents had done to lay low, for so many years, would be pointless. Their move to Ohio, the false papers they had let Tom believe were real, Mamá quitting her cleaning jobs and staying home— none of that would matter if the police took down all their information. They'd be in the system, easy to find. Just a step away from ICE. Wendy's heart ached.

"What about me?" Wendy said suddenly. "I was there; I could talk to the police."

Pastor Carpenter's eyebrows lifted. "That is a brave offer, Wendy." She squeezed Wendy's shoulder. "I think, with three adults as witnesses, your testimony would not be necessary. And your parents may prefer you not go through that."

But Wendy knew exactly what Papá would prefer. No matter what Pastor Carpenter said to him, there was no way he would want any of them talking to the police.

THIRTY-ONE

THE MOOD WAS subdued inside the crooked house the next day. Everyone was preoccupied and unsure what to say to each other. Tom was still at the hospital. One of his broken ribs had punctured a lung, and they were trying to inflate it again. He'd be in the hospital until his lung could function on its own, which could take a week. Wendy had slept for most of the morning, since even Papá agreed school that day would be pointless. Now she sipped broth around her sore lip, trying to ignore the worry that filled the air and settled into the cracked floorboards around her. Everyone was still here, still safe, still *alive*.

Her parents were discussing when would be the best time to go see Tom again, when Nadia paid them a surprise visit. She stepped inside and introduced herself in Spanish. But she didn't spend any extra time with smiles and handshakes. Instead she looked seriously at them and held out her phone.

"I think you need to see this."

The video was shaky, and the lighting kept shifting under the lights of the parking lot. But suddenly the recording focused, and Luz jumped into clarity on the screen, the gun in her hands.

"Ohhh, you gonna shoot me?" a voice asked. The shot stayed on Luz, her hands wrapped around the handgun. Next to her Mamá raced forward and on the side something moved. Wendy knew it was Tom, injured and on the ground, scrambling up to help her. But on the screen there was just a blur in the corner. Then the picture swung and steadied to show Tom grappling with Red Hat and Mamá's fists flying. The last thing the video showed was Tom, grabbing the man's jacket and hauling him backward.

They stood, their heads in a tight circle around the phone, and stared. Wendy remembered the third man and the phone she had seen in his hand. He hadn't been calling ICE. He had been filming. Wendy read the title under the link aloud. "'Illegals attack citizen at gunpoint by sanctuary church.'"

Mamá gasped. Papá grabbed Nadia's phone and tapped the replay arrow.

"Someone posted it to Luz's Facebook page," Nadia said. "It's disgusting! It makes you all look like the perpetrators." She looked grim. "We can't let them twist this."

"They already have," Papá said flatly, handing back her phone. He was right, Wendy realized. All they'd had to do was cut out some of it and it looked exactly how they wanted.

"I'm sorry you have to see this, especially now. I'm sure you are all so worried." Nadia's black-lined eyes softened. "How is Tom?"

"Getting better, we think," Papá said. "They had to insert a chest tube. It's supposed to help the lung expand." Emotion rippled over his face. "It could take several days."

Nadia nodded her head. "We are all rooting for him." Papá didn't seem to know how to respond to this statement. Wendy, however, thought of the crowd of people standing around Luz on the church steps. She knew who Nadia meant when she said "we" and it warmed her to think of those same people on her family's side.

"If you are able to get any documentation from the hospital, that would be a great help," Nadia added briskly. "Oh, and any pictures of the injuries. Bruising or broken skin."

"Pictures?" Papá asked.

"Yes," Nadia said. "It's important to corroborate the stories."

"Stories," Papá said. He lifted his chin, eyes narrowing.

"Their statements," Nadia explained, tapping something into her phone. "Luz and Tom. And you, señora." She gave Mamá a respectful nod.

"This video has given the perps some credibility, especially with the public." She shook her head at the screen. "We need to get the truth out there ASAP."

Wendy took half a step forward, remembering the moment

when things had shifted in the church parking lot. Her brain had raced ahead of her, the way it did sometimes, and she had hit the record button on Mamá's phone almost without thinking.

"We *can* get our story out," she said slowly. "I think I have—" But Papá raised a hand to stop her.

"*We*," Papá said tightly, "are going to stay out of sight and wait for this to blow over. They caught the attacker, the police will deal with him, and people will soon forget all about it."

Nadia's head snapped up and she locked her gaze on him. Her eyes with their dark eyeliner narrowed slightly, and Wendy saw Papá lean back a fraction. "Unfortunately it's not quite that simple." Her voice was almost apologetic. "The cops released him this morning."

The news sank in slowly and there was a moment of total silence as a shadow seemed to drift over them all. Mamá stepped closer to Papá, clutching his arm. Wendy wrapped her arms around her body, feeling a slight pain as she squeezed the bruises the man's hard fingers had left on her skin. The shivering was starting again.

"But, why?" Mamá asked.

"He posted bail," Nadia explained. "But we can still move forward once we get everyone's statements. Luz is working with the cops, and we are doing what we can to—"

"We are done with trouble," Papá interrupted, stepping in front of Mamá. "So you can take your phone and your plans for us and leave now." He gestured stiffly toward the door.

But Mamá's soft brown hand landed gently on top, lowering his arm. She looked up at Papá's face. "We cannot hide from this trouble, Óscar. They have us on the video."

Nadia cleared her throat and said gently, "She is right, señor. It is too late." Nadia looked down at her phone again. "This video posted around four hours ago. Want to see what's happened since?"

Papá's lips tightened uncomfortably. He didn't respond.

"It's been shared heavily by alt-right groups on social media. But it's getting traction on local networks too. Two news stations have just posted the video on their page, with bare bones info. But there've been three articles basically telling the attackers' side. They hint, not subtly either, that you are all connected to gangs. And"—she frowned—"Tom seems to be the one they are really pointing fingers at."

"What?" Mamá asked, her voice choked.

"That is ridiculous!" Papá burst out. "He was obviously defending himself! He defended his sister!"

"That's not what they see," Nadia said. "He's a brown teenager. In a fight. With an unregistered gun involved." Her even voice carried an undercurrent of bitterness. "It doesn't take much to spin that against us."

"But what if we had a video that showed the whole thing?" Wendy began.

Papá shook his head and raised a hand to cut her off again. "Mija, no," he said. "We have to ignore this and let it go away. If we bring more attention, it will only get worse." He came over to her and laid his rough hands gently on her shoulders. "The only good thing about any of this so far is that you at least are not on the video. Please, mi estrella, stay out of this."

It was the fear in his eyes that made Wendy swallow her words. She nodded at him, understanding what he meant. She was to keep her head down, just like always. But the thought of staying in her own safe orbit didn't carry its usual comfort.

THIRTY-TWO

IT WAS AS if they were all on a collision course with an asteroid and Papá was trying to steer them around it. Nadia wrote down her number for them in case they changed their minds, but he shoved it into his coat pocket without looking at it. He warned them not to say anything to Tom about the video when they visited the hospital later. Wendy wasn't sure what she would say if he asked about the attackers, but she needn't have worried. Tom was still groggy enough from the pain medication to keep the conversation at a minimum. Wendy did her homework curled in a hospital chair while *The Empire Strikes Back* played on the TV in the background and Tom dozed. She tried not to look at the tubes running under his nose and out from under his blankets. The nurse told them he should be more awake tomorrow. Wendy fell asleep that night hoping her brother would be more like himself when they came back the next day.

But Thursday morning Papá, still pushing for "normalcy,"

insisted that Wendy go to school. She grumbled and dawdled until finally he yelled that she'd need to take her bike to get there on time. As she wheeled her bike out the door, Wendy felt as though a cloud followed her—a cloud made up of oxygen tubes and red hats and thin, slanted handwriting.

Wendy had been thinking so completely about Tom in the hospital that she didn't notice the group on the corner with their signs until she rode closer and heard the chanting.

"Build the wall! Deport them all!"

Her stomach churned and her bike skidded as she swerved to avoid them. Then she saw the signs.

CITIZENS FIRST.
BUILD THE WALL. DEPORT THEM ALL!

It was a small group, but the anger of their chants loomed over the road and made her hands shake. She tried desperately to keep her eyes straight ahead and not to stare at the people behind the signs. She had almost passed them when a figure stepped out from the crowd and looked up. Brett Cobb locked eyes with Wendy, his face a blur under his golden hair as she sped past.

Wendy's fingers cramped from clenching the handlebars so tightly. Had Brett actually been standing with those people? The ones with signs saying people like Luz should leave? The thought of sitting in class next to him that day after seeing him there made her long for the safety of the crooked house. But she was almost to school, and she definitely didn't want to turn around and ride home again past those hate-filled faces. Instead she focused on pedaling faster. And trying not to cry.

When Mal called down the hall to ask where she'd been yesterday, Wendy shrugged her off and hurried straight to the bathroom. How did you tell someone that half your family was hiding from immigration agents and had just been attacked at gunpoint? It wasn't the kind of thing you could just casually mention in between classes. Besides, her brain felt sloppy and scattered. It would take too much energy just to open her mouth. Wendy took a deep breath and envisioned her insides hardening, like iron. She just had to make it through the day. She pushed into the stream of students in the hall.

"Hey!" Etta, as usual, popped up at her elbow out of nowhere. "I wasn't sure you'd be here at all today. You okay? How's Tom?"

"Okay," Wendy croaked.

Etta squinted at her. "You could have stayed home, you know. I mean, you were legitimately assaulted, and your brother is in the hospital."

"You didn't tell anyone that, did you?" Wendy asked, her pulse speeding up. She had gotten by with just saying "family emergency" at the office and was grateful no one asked for details.

"No way!" Etta linked her arm through hers and steered her to their next class. "Oh, and I forgot to tell you. My mom picked up your telescope that night."

Wendy had almost completely forgotten about her telescope during all that had happened. When she had finally thought of it, she hadn't wanted to go back to the scene of the attack, even for her telescope.

"I brought it in yesterday," Etta continued, "but since you weren't here I showed it to Ms. Park for you. I told her how hard you worked on it and that you would be there yourself if it weren't for forces beyond your control."

It took Wendy a moment to register what Etta meant. The Science Fair didn't seem nearly as important anymore. But did she still have a chance?

Etta grinned. "She gave it a thumbs-up!"

Wendy let out a long breath. "Really? Etta, you are THE best!"

"Obviously." Etta nodded. "Oh—" She reached into her bag and pulled out a cell phone. "This was rubber banded to the telescope. I think the battery's dead."

It was Mamá's phone. Wendy blinked down at the screen. Everything had happened so fast after she hit record. Had it even worked? Did it show the attack? She remembered Nadia's words, about how people only saw her brother as a brown teenager with a gun. A dim flicker of hope stirred in her mind. Her video might show people the truth. Everyone would know what had really happened. They would see how

Tom had been attacked. They would see what the man in the red hat had done to Wendy. For a second, the smell of the man's cigarette flooded her memory. Wendy could almost feel his fingers digging into her arms. The thought of watching it happen again made her want to throw up right there in the hallway. She pressed the phone's power button, feeling a guilty relief when nothing happened. The video probably didn't show anything, she told herself. If there even was a video. And Papá did not want her to get any more involved anyway. He was probably right. This would all blow over soon.

Just get through today, Wendy told herself. *Don't think about what happened.* She slipped the phone into her binder and followed Etta into the classroom, telling herself that everything would be okay. Her telescope was safe, and Ms. Park had approved it. Tom was getting excellent care at the hospital, and she would get to visit him again after school. But no matter how much she tried she could not erase the image of Brett Cobb's face in the crowd on the corner and she spent most of the day avoiding him.

Wendy kept a lookout the whole way home, but the protestors from that morning were gone. The relief she felt was short-lived, however. As Wendy lifted her bike up the steps and opened her front door, she stopped in surprise.

The crooked house was full of the smell of coffee and murmuring voices. Several people she didn't know looked up as she entered. Bewildered, Wendy pushed down her kick-stand and parked her bike. She stepped into the living room and saw Mamá on the couch, her hands clutching her skirt into knots at her sides. Dread settled over Wendy like a cloak when she saw her mom's face.

"Mamá," Wendy said, her throat dry, "what . . ."

Mamá's mouth quivered as she said, "Oh, mija. It's Tom."

"What happened?" Wendy gasped. "His—his lung?"

"No," Mamá said. "His lung is getting better. He is still in the hospital. But la migra is there too."

THIRTY-THREE

ALL THE AIR left the room. Wendy felt like she'd been sucked out of her body, as if she were spinning away into space.

"ICE?" she said numbly. "In the hospital?"

A cane tapped against the floor, and someone laid a hand on Wendy's arm. Distantly, Wendy realized it was Janice, her skin papery and soft as she guided Wendy to the couch. The room swirled around her as Wendy sank down next to Mamá. She tried to breathe slow and deep as Mamá, tears streaking her cheeks, gave her the bare bones of what had happened.

Tom had felt stronger that morning and asked for his phone. He'd seen the video that was going around. He had called the police to give his statement to support Luz's story. By the time Mamá and Papá had arrived to visit him, a man was standing guard outside the hospital room and Tom was handcuffed to his bed. Out of desperation, Papá had pulled Nadia's number out of his pocket and asked her to bring Mamá straight home while he tried to talk to ICE.

Knowing the facts should have helped it all make sense, but Wendy's brain was struggling. It didn't seem real. How could Tom be under ICE custody at the hospital?

Then Papá marched through the front door, and everything began to happen very fast. He moved through space with new purpose, bringing a small army of people with him. Nadia hurried in, words pouring from her mouth into her cell phone like sparks from a bonfire. A curly-haired redhead who had been at the protest went straight to the table and pulled a laptop from his shoulder bag. Older folks from the church arrived with baskets of muffins and a casserole. Someone enveloped Mamá in a hug and a soothing stream of Spanish. The crooked house seemed to swell at the seams with people. To Wendy, everything seemed distorted and fuzzy, like a lens out of alignment.

Luz's lawyer, Mr. Richards, was showing her parents documents and information on the redhead's laptop. Mamá's face was hard and free of tears now and Papá asked occasional questions. The phrase "U visa" kept coming up, and Wendy pushed her sluggish brain to tune in. A U visa, Mr. Richards explained, gave victims of crimes permission to stay in the country if they helped the police catch the criminals. If Tom had given the police information that would help prove the men attacked them, he might be able to stay. Mamá would be eligible for the U visa as well if she gave information to the police.

"They could both get visas?" Papá asked. He sounded breathless, as if he'd been underwater for too long.

"Theoretically, yes," Mr. Richards said. He went on, talking about the difficulty of getting the U visa, but Papá had looked at Mamá with a desperate light in his eyes that Wendy felt deep inside her. She wanted so much to feel hope. But Tom was still handcuffed to his hospital bed.

Papá seemed to be thinking the same thing. "ICE can't take him before he is discharged, can they?" he asked, glancing from Nadia to the lawyer.

"I wouldn't put it past them," Nadia said grimly. "They've pushed the boundaries of human rights often enough."

"It's doubtful," the lawyer countered. "From what you say he will have the chest tube in his lung for several more days. That buys us some time."

"We need to mobilize as many people as possible," Nadia said. "If we put our bodies on the line we can block them from leaving the hospital."

Heads nodded and someone suggested contacting local politicians. Wendy watched as people gathered to discuss crafting social media posts and a press release. Mr. Richards and her parents pored over U visa information. Wendy felt helpless and disconnected, like a leaf drifting in the current of the universe. She had felt like this before, and it had always been easier to let herself get pulled along. But now, with her stomach churning at the thought of Tom's wrist cuffed to his hospital bed, she didn't want to just sit back. She wanted to choose the current.

"The biggest issue," Mr. Richards was saying, "is that the police do not seem inclined to believe your version of events. If they discredit Luz's story, then any information you or Tom provide isn't going to matter." He looked seriously at Mamá and Papá. "We can of course build public pressure but it is still their word against yours."

Suddenly Wendy's brain lit up like a supernova in a blaze of light and hope. She jumped to her feet, looking frantically for her backpack. She raced into the other room, past Nadia, who was speaking to the social media group.

"—the more pressure the better," Nadia insisted. "Our story has to build traction."

"But right now everyone sees them as violent attackers," a serious-looking young man with a ponytail argued. "It's a tough image to shift."

Wendy scooped up her backpack and fumbled to unzip it. Mamá's charger was already plugged into the wall in the corner of the dining room, and Wendy connected the dead phone, her heart racing.

Nadia kept talking. "We need to tell their stories. Paint a picture of Tom as the track star and hero who tried to save his sister."

"Yeah, but they have that video," someone else said gloomily.

"Wait!" Wendy's voice was so loud it surprised her. The murmurs died down and it felt as if every eye in the room was on her. Wendy licked her lips and looked at Mr. Richards. "So, this visa . . . it all hangs on proving what really happened, right?"

"Well, yes, but not simply that—"

Wendy didn't wait for him to finish. She whirled back to the phone, jabbing eagerly at the power button until it flickered to life.

Wendy's fingers flew over the screen. Then she took a deep breath as she found what she was looking for and tapped play.

Red Hat's harsh voice rang out from the phone. Mamá made a strangled sound and rushed to look over her shoulder as Wendy fumbled to turn up the volume. On the screen, Red Hat lunged out, grabbing Luz's arm. The room around Wendy shifted as everyone moved closer to see the video. It was strange to watch the struggle now, safe at home. Wendy felt her stomach twist as she watched Red Hat reach for his weapon, and suddenly she saw herself, a blur colliding into the man with the gun. Someone in the room behind her gasped in horror as they watched Red Hat slap Wendy's face. Suddenly the phone in her hand felt strangely heavy. She tried to hold it still, even though part of her wanted to throw the phone across the room, as if she could throw away the memory. Wendy's chest rose and fell too fast and the screen wobbled. Then Mamá's hands fluttered out and cupped around hers, holding it steady. Papá put an arm around Wendy, his presence behind her warm and solid. Nadia and Mr. Richards leaned their heads close to see the Luz on the phone hold up the gun in trembling hands.

The rest of the scene was the same as the video everyone had seen online. But this time the *whole* scene was clear. The man kicking harshly at Wendy's leg, Mamá's angry cry as she charged him, and Tom barreling into him from the side to save Wendy—it was all there.

Wendy felt a twinge of guilt as Papá pulled her close. "I know you said to ignore it," she started to say, but Papá shook his head.

"No, mi estrella," he said. "You were right. This is not something we can ignore any longer." He sighed. "Perhaps we never should have."

Mamá's phone was passed around the room. Everyone wanted to watch it, and everyone wanted to congratulate Wendy on her quick thinking. She tried to smile and thank them, but she felt uncomfortable. She barely remembered hitting record that night and the images of the attack hung over her like a cloud.

"You okay?"

Wendy looked up to see Nadia's intense gaze on her.

"It will help, right?" Wendy asked. "That video?"

"Definitely. You showed everyone the truth." Nadia bent down a bit to look Wendy right in the eye. "It sucks that people have to see this, doesn't it?"

Wendy looked at her in surprise. Nadia smiled. "Someone very wise once told me that no one should have to prove their pain." She squeezed Wendy's shoulder. "You shouldn't have to do this. None of you."

Wendy nodded slowly. "Yeah, we shouldn't. But it's the truth." She looked at Nadia, matching the fire in her eyes. "And people need to see it."

THIRTY-FOUR

THE TEAM DECIDED to hit social media with the video first, then share it with the police while it was spreading. They worked furiously, posting and contacting the press while Mr. Richards helped prepare the documents for the U visa. When Mamá finally insisted that Wendy go to bed, she didn't even argue. She was exhausted. As she waved good night to the few people still working, Nadia looked up and met her eyes. She gave Wendy a respectful nod and a half smile that warmed her inside, like hot chocolate. Almost as soon as she stretched out on her bed, she fell asleep, the gently creaking house wrapping her in a kind of lullaby.

Friday morning felt eerily quiet after all the bustle from the day before. And the empty seat at the table gaped like an open wound. Wendy's throat was tight as she swallowed her oatmeal. What was Tom having for breakfast? Would they uncuff him to let him to eat?

Papá cleared his throat. "Listen, both of you," he said. His voice sounded slightly hoarse, like he hadn't gotten enough sleep. Mamá and Wendy stared at him over their bowls.

"The people from that church . . . Nadia, Mr. Richards, all of them . . ." He took a breath. "They are very good people. I had no idea how much they were doing for that wom— for Luz." He shook his head. "And to see them yesterday—the way they jumped in to fight for us—for Tom . . ." He trailed off and lifted one rough hand to cover his eyes.

"I've been a fool," he muttered.

Mamá stood and walked around the table to him. She put a hand on his shoulder and said, with a hint of a smile. "Not always."

Papá lowered his hand and raised his eyebrows at her. "Oh, not always?"

She laughed quietly, then said more seriously, "You made a choice once, Óscar—we made a choice. To hide. Maybe it is a better choice to fight."

Papá didn't say anything, and Wendy looked back and forth between them, watching for the flickers underneath the words that hinted at more.

"You were one time a luchador," Mamá said, looking steadily at Papá. "A person who fights. I think that is who you are still."

"You know where that got us," he said in a low voice. "And where it got my parents."

Wendy sat up, her back tensing. She stared at Papá.

"My abuelos?" she whispered.

Mamá looked at her, then back at Papá.

"Óscar," Mamá said softly. "There is no reason to hide anything now."

Papá nodded and swallowed, his Adam's apple moving up and down under his stubble. Wendy hadn't noticed earlier how shabby he was looking.

"Wendy, mi estrella," he said. "You remember your abuelos, but . . . they were actually . . . not." He spoke hesitantly, as if piecing the words together took great effort. Wendy tried to breathe as quietly as possible so as not to interrupt. She had already figured this part out after he told them he was adopted. She'd thought about it again and again—the abuelos she remembered couldn't be his real parents. But she wanted him to explain it.

"They were my tíos, my aunt and uncle. I was smuggled out of El Salvador when I was a baby and they adopted me." He sighed again. "It is so much," he muttered. "So much that we have kept from you kids. I almost forget how much." He looked at her and she saw tears in his eyes. "I am sorry. It was just to protect you."

"So, your parents are . . . dead?" she asked slowly.

"Yes." His voice hardened. "They were fighters, luchadores, right, Dulce?"

"You cannot blame them for what was done *to* them, Óscar," Mamá said firmly.

Papá's jaw worked back and forth. "My mother was killed by a bomb when I was just a baby in El Salvador." Wendy saw the newspaper clipping again in her mind, the story about the explosions at the priest's funeral. And the card with the roses around the edge of the woman's picture.

"My papá was a journalist. He wrote about things that were happening there, and the government didn't like it. He knew his life was in danger, even before Mamá died. A Mexican reporter he knew had arranged to get his own family out of Mexico, and he agreed to take me with them. My tíos in South Carolina were supposed to watch me until my papá made it out. But . . . he never did."

Mamá reached across Wendy to put a hand on Papá's knee. "He was one of the many desaparecidos of El Salvador—the disappeared," she explained. "The ones the government got rid of. He was a brave man."

"He could have come with me," Papá said, his voice softer than Wendy had ever heard it before. "He could have come and just been my father." He nodded, his jaw tight. "But he was brave, like you say. So he stayed."

"And he wrote," Mamá said boldly. "He reported on all of it. He told what was happening—"

"And it made no difference," Papá said bitterly. "They read it and they did nothing. The world did nothing."

"No, Óscar, it *did* matter," Mamá said firmly. "People know about what happened in El Salvador. They would never know without your papá's words."

"Like who?" Papá muttered. "Who knows any of it anymore?"

"I do," Wendy said.

They both stared at her.

"He wrote about Óscar Romero, didn't he? The priest. He reported his words to the papers. That's why they named you Óscar."

Papá looked stunned and Wendy said quickly, "That trunk, in the attic." She glanced at Mamá. "There are newspapers and stuff." Papá started to say something to Mamá, but Wendy hurried on.

"He told everyone what really happened to Romero, how he was killed during the Mass. And then his funeral and the explosions. Your papá wrote about that too. I read it. I mean, sort of. It's in Spanish, so . . ."

"What else did you put in that trunk?" Papá asked Mamá. She looked down sheepishly.

"I couldn't throw away the past, Óscar." Mamá looked up at him, smiling her sad smile. "It matters."

"Yeah," Wendy agreed, standing up and turning to face them. "And it's my past too. I get that you want to protect us, Papá. You don't want us to lose someone the way you did, even if it's for a good cause or whatever. I get it. Really."

She stepped closer to where her father sat, her eyes nearly level with his. "But I think we have a right to know our history. And maybe . . . Maybe we have a right to choose our future too."

Papá's eyes looked back at her, crinkled around the edges and dark brown, just like hers. "I just want you to be safe," he whispered.

"I know," Wendy said. "But honestly, staying safe hasn't worked out so well for us."

Mamá gave a little laugh, and Papá pulled Wendy into his strong arms, reaching out for Mamá to join them in a hug.

"You, mi estrella," Papá murmured against Wendy's hair, "you are a light for us all."

In spite of the sick feeling in her stomach whenever she thought about Tom, Wendy felt a bit steadier on her way to school that day. Part of her, the part with a growing headache, had wanted to stay home. But another part of her wanted to face whatever the day held. *Maybe that's my luchador part*, she thought. *After all, my abuelos were fighters. There's a whole team of people fighting for my brother. Why shouldn't I be a fighter too?*

But as she stepped into the hall at school, she caught a glimpse of Brett and Fiona, and the luchador inside her fizzled out. Wendy waited for Brett and Fiona to turn a corner so she could get to class without being seen, but suddenly Fiona whirled away from Brett. Her lips were pursed in an angry frown, and she was heading straight toward Wendy. Without thinking, Wendy veered in the opposite direction. She just needed to be alone for a little bit to clear her mind.

The bell rang as she turned the corner and stopped

suddenly. The art room door, covered in colorful pop art portraits, was halfway down the hall. Across from it stood Etta, furiously scrubbing at the wall. Wendy walked slowly closer. Etta didn't see her; she was glaring at the surface in front of her with singular focus. She ran a stiff-bristled brush back and forth so fast that Wendy's arm ached in sympathy. Wendy stopped a few steps away and took in the graffiti Etta was frantically trying to remove. The words had been painted straight onto the wall with artsy letters and outlined with thick Sharpie. Wendy felt something rising in her throat and she clapped a hand over her mouth. Etta's scrubbing had scraped off most of the paint, but the black outline was still visible. "Deport them all."

THIRTY-FIVE

WENDY SHUFFLED BACKWARD from the horrible words on the wall. Her feet felt disconnected from her reeling mind. They were the same words the people on the corner had chanted. The same words on the signs they had held over their angry faces in the crowd. The crowd she'd seen Brett step out of as she rode past.

Her back bumped against the opposite wall and she stood there, not knowing what to do. The dull pain from that morning was throbbing now, just behind her eyes. She wondered if she really was going to hurl.

A murmur of voices came from the art room beside her. Wendy turned, dazed, and peered through the door. Principal Whitman's back was to her, and she was speaking urgently to Miss Hill. "—and all art supplies in a locked closet from now on. Even in between classes."

"Joyce," Miss Hill said in a tense voice, "we have to do more than hide the art supplies. Our students are hearing this kind of rhetoric all around them. On the news, on the streets, even from their own parents—"

"Well, it has no place here," Ms. Whitman said sharply. She sighed. "I'll send out another letter."

"A letter?" Miss Hill barked out a laugh. She did not sound amused. "What we need is a focused, intentional approach to understanding and celebrating our differences, not a slap-on-the-wrist letter. As I've said before, if you are serious about wanting this to stop—"

Ms. Whitman's hard voice cut her off. "Don't question my sincerity, Nikki. I have a very good idea who is responsible, and I've already called his parents in for a conference."

"You can't honestly believe Preston did this?" Miss Hill said, incredulous.

Wendy furrowed her brow. *Preston?*

"He doesn't have an artistic bone in his body! You know why he goes by P.J.? Because he's too lazy to write his whole name! And those are *his* words, not mine." Miss Hill pointed toward the hallway. "Those words were painted by someone who has artistic ability. And I've told you who fits the bill. You have to at least consider—"

"Thank you, Nikki," Ms. Whitman interrupted loudly.

I'll bet Miss Hill suspects Brett, Wendy thought. *But what does it matter if Principal Whitman doesn't believe her?* Her breath was coming in quick, shallow bursts. Ms. Whitman had dropped her voice, but Wendy could still hear her clearly.

"My job is to protect our scholars. I won't allow you to

slander a family that has been one of this institution's strongest supporters." Wendy heard the principal's heels clicking toward the door and she jumped back against the wall, hoping she wouldn't be noticed. The sound paused and Ms. Whitman added, "And keep an eye on your supplies!"

Ms. Whitman pushed the door a little too hard as she left and it blocked Wendy from the principal's view as it swung open. She clicked off down the hall. Wendy bit her lip, listening to the rough sound of the bristles against the wall and staring at the words. *"Deport them all." Them* meant people like Wendy. Those protestors on the corner wanted her gone. And Luz and Mamá and Tom. And Yasmin and José. Did Brett want them gone too? Anyone who didn't look or speak like him? She closed her eyes, trying to block out the glare of fluorescent lights that buzzed overhead. Fuzzy blotches of light moved uneasily across the darkness inside her eyelids. Wendy imagined they were galaxies—clouds of planets and dust spreading slowly yet steadily out into the liquid of the universe. This paint on the wall was nothing, she told herself. Not while actual stars were being born and dying. None of these insignificant things down here in this hallway mattered. All she wanted was to leave all of this far behind. She wondered how hard it would be to hold her breath until she passed out.

Suddenly Etta let out a strangled yelp of frustration and threw down the brush. "Just—get—off!" She slammed her palm into the wall with a thud. Then she hit the wall again and again. Wendy gulped and watched her friend's shoulders tremble as she hammered at the awful words. Wendy wanted to go to her, but her feet were solid blocks of lead. Miss Hill hurried out of the classroom and rushed to Etta's side.

"Oh, honey," she said, catching Etta's small white hands in her dark brown ones. "Don't you worry about it. The paint will cover it all up."

"I know," Etta said, wiping at her cheek with her sleeve. "I just—I didn't want—" She gulped and, for the first time ever, Wendy heard Etta's strong, clear voice break. "Wendy might see it."

Something inside Wendy shifted. She felt a slow burn flicker somewhere deep and seep up into her chest. The parts of her she had tried so desperately to turn to iron were slowly turning hot and liquid. And it made her want to blast this whole wall to pieces. Her feet moved now, stepping toward her friend. Miss Hill had wrapped her arms around Etta and was gently patting her back. Etta's sniffling was the only noise in the hallway, but inside Wendy's head there was a growing roar. She'd never seen Etta break down like this. Etta, the luchador, who was always *on*, ready to tackle the world for her friends. Wendy was done. The molten fire inside her made her feel more alive, more real, more present than someone who just let things happen to them. She looked at the black words and gritted her teeth.

"Enough," she said. She held her head up straight and tall, glaring at the graffiti.

Etta's head jerked up in surprise, and Miss Hill turned, staring at her.

"He's done enough," Wendy said, this time looking at Etta. "You were right." She narrowed her eyes. "We have to stop him."

Etta opened her mouth, but before she could say anything Wendy turned to Miss Hill.

"I know who did this. And I think you do too."

Miss Hill's kind, round face sharpened. "Talk to me," she said grimly.

Wendy didn't make it to even one class that day. Instead, for nearly an hour, Wendy talked to Miss Hill and Mr. Evans, the counselor. Etta went to get Yasmin, who had kept all the notes. None of them seemed like that big a deal on their own. But when Yasmin laid them all out on the table, a weight settled over the room. Wendy told them about Brett giving her Yasmin's crown at the skating rink and how the girls had called Wendy's friends exotic. Miss Hill shook her long braids in disgust.

"This is why we need an actively inclusive curriculum," she said to Mr. Evans. "Some of these kids only ever hear one side. They are taught a very biased view of people who aren't like them."

Wendy thought about Mal's mom arguing with other parents at the PTO meeting. Parents like Brett's dad, who thought kids like Wendy only got into this school because of their ethnicity. If Brett heard stuff like that all the time, no wonder he thought they didn't belong. Maybe Brett's parents had even been out there on the corner holding signs. Wendy shivered at the thought.

"Ms. Whitman says it's better not to draw attention to our differences," Yasmin said quietly. The adults looked at her and she blushed. "I asked her at the beginning of the year if I could put up something inviting other Muslim kids to pray in the library with me during lunch. But she said I shouldn't advertise it. For my own protection."

Miss Hill made another sound of annoyance and looked meaningfully at Mr. Evans. He nodded at her and jotted down more notes. He kept writing, asking questions calmly about when and where and who exactly was involved. Wendy added her "thirsty" note to the table and explained about Brett's screenshot calling her a stalker. Then Yasmin pulled up a picture of the Cesar Chavez poster and set her phone on the table. They all stared down at the notes and the poster. It was obvious to everyone that the handwriting was a match.

"I believe we have enough here to move forward," Miss Hill said quietly to Mr. Evans. "I can bring you some samples from his schoolwork as well." Mr. Evans nodded and seemed ready to wrap things up.

"Wait," Wendy said, her heart pounding. "There's more."

She explained how Brett had poured the Jarritos on her shoes when she had stood up for José. And then she described the telescope, *her* telescope, and how Brett had taken the pictures and copied her notes. When tears stung her eyes, she realized they were more from anger than anything else. There had been so much, for so long. How had she let him do all this to her? The angry, burning feeling pushed her through until she had nothing left to say. It was as if poison had been drawn out of her, leaving a hollow ache behind.

Yasmin and Etta stayed with Wendy while Mr. Evans called her parents. Wendy stared at a plaque on the counselor's desk, feeling dazed. Under an engraving of the school crest was the motto *Non ducor, duco* with the English words underneath. *I am not led, I lead.* The phrase felt important, but her brain couldn't seem to process why, exactly. She shivered violently, even though the room felt hot. She wondered if the heat was on.

"You okay?" Etta asked.

"I don't know. I feel sort of hot and cold at the same time," she said. "And like a deflated balloon."

"Well, yeah," Yasmin said solemnly. "You just talked longer than I've ever heard you."

"Maybe longer than I've ever heard *me* actually," Etta added. "Which is impressive."

Wendy looked at Etta skeptically.

"You were impressive," Yasmin agreed. "Most of the time at school you just kind of go along with whatever, but today you were so . . . solid about everything. Like, so sure and calm."

Wendy smiled weakly. "I guess I'm finally my own force," she said. "You need to have mass to pull other objects. Or else you just get pulled along." She wanted to explain more about orbits and gravitational pulls, but the words in her brain felt mushy. "Non ducor, duco," she murmured.

Mr. Evans came back in then, with Papá right behind him. Papá's face was a mixture of emotions. Wendy couldn't tell if he was angry or scared.

"Ay, mi estrella," he said, bending over her. "Mr. Evans told me everything." He looked at her closely and now she could see that his eyes were all concern and love. She leaned her head forward onto his arm, her eyelids closing in relief. It was so bright in this classroom. Papá's rough hand landed on her forehead, the pressure pushing against the slow throbbing that Wendy had felt building all morning behind her eyes.

"I think you have a fever, mi estrella," he said. "Let's get you home."

He shepherded her out of the room. The smell of fresh paint zapped through her mental fog as they walked past the art room. The school custodian hadn't gotten the right shade of paint. The patch glistening wetly on the wall was lighter than the rest of the hallway. Wendy squeezed her eyes shut for a second to keep the tears from leaking out, then forced herself to look straight at the patch shining like a scar on the wall. *Deport them all* echoed in her brain. She shivered again and leaned into Papá's arm as they left the building.

Wendy slept for most of the day, waking now and then to sip the broth or tea Mamá brought. Her fever was the mild kind that made everything feel surreal. She didn't dream, but in her waking moments she thought she heard Nadia's voice flowing in a steady current from floors below and it comforted her.

THIRTY-SIX

WHEN WENDY CAME downstairs Saturday morning, Mamá immediately rushed over to feel her forehead with the back of her hand. Her skin was warm from the heat of the stove, and the smell of tortillas filled the house. Wendy's stomach rumbled.

"Any better today, mija?" she asked.

Wendy nodded, sliding into a chair and reaching for a plate. Papá sat down next to her, a line of worry between his eyebrows, and watched her spoon eggs onto her tortilla.

"What?" she asked. "I wasn't *that* sick."

"No, not that," he said heavily. "The bullying at school. I am so sorry, mi estrella." He looked so serious that Wendy set down the spoon.

"It's okay, Papá," she said. "It's not that big a deal."

He shook his head back and forth, rubbing his forehead with a rough hand. "I should have known," he muttered.

Wendy felt a rush of guilt. Mamá and Papá had been so

busy trying to figure out how to help Tom. Now she had added her whole school drama on top of it.

"No, really—" she tried to assure them, but Mamá put a hand on her arm.

"But we *should* have known," Mamá said. "All of this you have been carrying. Alone." She shook her head. "It is too heavy alone."

Papá nodded. "I am glad we know now. But I think it might be good for you to talk to someone else about all of this too."

Wendy frowned. "What do you mean? I talked already. A lot."

"That Mr. Evans at your school told us about a therapist at the Children's Hospital," Mamá said. "We are thinking you could talk to her."

"Talk to a therapist? About the stuff at school?"

"And about what happened in the parking lot," Papá added. "What do you think?"

Wendy opened her mouth to say that she didn't want to talk about that ever again. But then she thought about sitting in Mr. Evans's office with Etta and Yasmin and telling him and Miss Hill everything. She thought about how she felt after, like she'd been wearing around a backpack full of science textbooks and had finally taken it off. She was tired, sure. But mostly, she felt relieved.

"Okay," she said. "I'll talk to a therapist."

Mamá smiled at her and Papá nodded. But he still had

worried creases around his eyes. He rubbed the back of his neck, then looked down at his hands.

"I am sorry," he said softly. "About all of this."

"Papá, it's not your fault," Wendy said quickly, but he was shaking his head.

"We thought it would be better here," he said. "We thought getting away from Melborn would be safer. This seemed like such a good school."

"It is!" Wendy insisted. "It's just a few kids, that's all." But even as she said it, she couldn't help wondering how many of the other students thought like Brett.

"I like LPA," Wendy said, "I really do!" She started to bite her sore lip and stopped herself. "Please don't take me out."

Her parents looked at each other skeptically.

"We will see," Papá said. "I know the academics are good, but . . ." He sighed. "I really thought, maybe if we just laid low, this kind of thing would go away."

"Papá," Wendy said. "That kind of thing doesn't go away. People like Brett will always be around." She swallowed hard. "And ICE. And laws that aren't fair. But—it's not like gravity, you know."

They both stared at her blankly, and Wendy looked at her plate, fiddling with her spoon as she tried to talk through what she meant.

"I mean, there are all these forces out there, trying to pull us around. Trying to make us do what they want and be who they want us to be. Telling us we don't belong. Or that we're too sensitive when we stand up for ourselves." Wendy looked up. "But it's not like gravity. We don't *have* to get pulled in. We can set our own orbit." Then Wendy slammed her spoon down and said firmly, "You aren't illegal, Mamá! You're amazing! And we're all going to fight for you and Tom and Luz!"

Mamá wiped at her eyes and walked over to kiss the top of Wendy's head. Papá cleared his throat and put a hand over Wendy's.

"I think our daughter might be more like Abuela Celestina than I thought," he murmured.

Wendy thought of the spirited face surrounded by roses. Celestina looked like someone who would choose her own path. "I think I'd like to be like her," she said, squeezing Papá's hand.

Papá smiled, then suddenly pulled away. "We'd better hurry, mi estrella!" He slid his cell phone from his pocket to check the time and clicked his tongue. "Ay, no!"

"Hurry for what?" Wendy asked.

"The fair is at ten, yes? At least it is close. You have your report or whatever else you need?" Papá was rushing into the living room, stashing his phone as he called back to her.

Wendy still didn't understand. "The fair? The Science Fair? But . . . Papá, I figured . . . I mean with Tom—"

Papá stepped back out of the living room, his arms wrapped around the heavy wooden base for the telescope.

"Wait, how did you even get that?" Wendy asked in surprise.

"Yesterday. Your friend brought it over. Come, we have to go!" He was halfway to the door.

"Papá, wait!" She stood and hurried after him. "Look, the Science Fair"—she swallowed—"it's not that big a deal. I mean, we have to get Tom home!"

Papá ignored her, calling back to Mamá, "Dulce, the telescope is in the living room. You bring that so Wendy can grab her papers!"

"Papá!" Wendy said again, grabbing hold of the wooden base to make him stop. "Listen, I know I acted like this mattered more than anything—"

"But it does matter," Papá interrupted. "You have worked so hard on this, mi estrella. I had no idea how hard." He looked away and blinked rapidly to clear his eyes. "I didn't know what you went through to build this telescope until yesterday." He shook his head and swallowed.

Wendy felt a shiver run down her arms. Could they really still make it to the fair? Was it even okay to want that right now? ICE was hovering over her brother's hospital bed. The planetarium's junior internship was a speck of nothing compared to that asteroid hurtling toward them.

Papá leaned forward and met her eyes. "The doctor said Tom won't be discharged for a couple more days. And while we wait, we *are* working on getting him free from ICE. But missing your fair won't help with that." He smiled. "The time is ticking! Go!"

The rush to school had Wendy feeling a bit giddy as she hurried into the gym with her parents. They raced through the rows of tables, looking for her spot. Each table had a trifold display board covered with photos and information about their project. Some kids had brought tablecloths, a few had special lighting, and Wendy saw one display completely draped in a tented sheet with an opening in the front for the judges to look through. She felt her heart sink a bit. She knew she had all the information she needed, but it didn't look nearly as cool as some of these.

"Wendy, over here!" Etta's voice called over the crowds. Etta and K.K. had gone with a rainbow polka-dot theme for their Skittle milk project and the empty table next to them looked impossibly gray next to the riot of color.

"I asked them to put you next to us," Etta said in a rush, pulling her over. "Hurry, hurry! They've already started judging at the front! Hola, Señora Toledo, Señor Toledo."

Mamá greeted her warmly and Papá shook her hand, pleased to meet Pastor Carpenter's daughter. Wendy introduced them to K.K., and then turned to set up her table, her brain buzzing with energy. The printed papers glued to the board might not look colorful or fun but they were precise and clear. The only creative thing she had managed was the string of battery-operated twinkle lights she had pulled from a Christmas bin in the attic.

"Nice touch," K.K. said. Etta gave her a double thumbs-up, then offered her some Skittles from the giant bag at their table. Papá chatted with Etta's mom and K.K.'s parents. Mamá stared at the section of the board that explained Wendy's hypothesis about parallax and measuring the distance to the moon, her lips moving silently as she read over the words.

Just then Wendy heard a confident voice in the row next to them and she felt her throat tighten. K.K. and Etta exchanged a look. Together they all edged over to the display in the next row and peeked around it.

THIRTY-SEVEN

BRETT'S SCIENCE FAIR display was draped in a black velvet tablecloth, and tiny lightbulbs shone through holes in the cloth. Wendy noticed with satisfaction that they didn't resemble the actual position of the stars at all, but it looked good enough that she doubted anyone would care.

"I can't believe they let him compete!" Etta hissed. "After everything you told Mr. Evans?"

"He must have convinced Ms. Whitman," Wendy said. She bit down hard as she recognized her own diagrams redrawn and attached to the black fabric.

"What did you find most difficult about this project?" asked a man in a paisley tie.

"Making the telescope was a challenge," Brett answered swiftly. "But I don't mind a challenge. And it works!" He waved a hand toward the telescope.

Ms. Park leaned in to read the information on the board. "Your hypothesis had to do with using the telescope to show

how the brightness of heavenly bodies can affect distance measurements. How did that go for you?"

Wendy smiled. Brett had copied her old hypothesis exactly. She had detailed the experiment she was going to try in her stolen notebook. But she'd bet a five-pound bag of Skittles he hadn't actually done any of it. In front of her, Brett hesitated.

"Really well," he said, fidgeting slightly and pushing his hands into his pockets. "Yeah, it, uh, it worked great."

Ms. Park nodded and jotted something on her clipboard, but another judge asked, "And how *does* brightness affect distance measurements?"

Brett shuffled his feet slightly. "Um . . . it's just, you know, brighter when it's . . . closer."

The judge who had asked the question stepped forward. She had shoulder-length brown hair and wore a blue silk scarf over her black turtleneck. "And how did you demonstrate that?" she asked.

This time Brett didn't answer at all, and Wendy clamped her lips together to keep from calling out.

The woman in the blue scarf tried again. "What measurement did you use to quantify the brightness of the different light sources?"

Brett gave a smooth laugh and said, "All that info is in the report. Honestly, I really spent most of my time making the telescope. Isn't it great?"

"You totally know how to answer all those questions, don't you?" K.K. whispered fiercely.

Wendy nodded, her eyes on Brett. How could he look so completely confident when he didn't even know what he was doing? It made zero sense to stand up there with all that info he didn't understand and smile at these judges like it was his work.

"Why did you choose this type of telescope?" the woman asked again. She seemed to be trying to give Brett a chance to answer *something*.

"Oh, it seemed like the coolest, you know?" he said, shooting her a charming smile. "I love telescopes!"

Wendy rolled her eyes and let out a huff of disgust. Brett's head jerked in her direction and his eyes narrowed. He moved his body as if to block Wendy and her friends from the judges' view, but Wendy was feeling reckless. The rush of actually making it to the Science Fair, the feeling that she had done something that might be helping Tom with that video, and this new closeness she had with her parents all seemed to merge into one strong push. Besides, if Brett could speak up without even knowing anything, then she definitely could. She stepped forward.

"It was going to be a Galilean telescope, originally," she said clearly to the judges. The woman turned to her and cocked her head. "But I decided that a Kepler telescope would offer greater field of vision. Which I needed in order to properly capture the brightness of different objects."

There was a moment of silence, then the judge in the blue scarf said, "Oh, is this your project as well?"

"No!" Brett stepped in front of her. "She got kicked out. It's mine."

"She has her own project, in fact," Ms. Park said, her hands shooing Wendy away from the table.

Wendy lifted her chin higher and said to the blue scarf woman, "Yes, I made another telescope *after* making this one."

"*I* made this telescope," Brett snapped. The likable charm he usually wore had peeled away completely, and Ms. Park looked startled.

The judge had been watching all this quietly. "Excuse me," she said. "May I ask one more question about your telescope?"

Brett nodded sullenly.

"What does *Celestina* mean?"

The look of complete confusion on Brett's face almost made Wendy laugh out loud.

He swallowed and said, "W-what?"

The woman pointed at a diagram of the telescope and all the judges leaned toward the display board to read it. Written in tiny letters along the side was the word *Celestina*.

"It—um, that's just part of the telescope," Brett said.

Wendy grinned. All she had said when she handed Brett the torn notebook paper was to make sure it looked right. He had meticulously followed Wendy's notes without understanding what any of it meant.

"It means heavenly," Wendy said, loud enough for all the adults to hear. "It's a name."

"I think my son knows more about his own project than this girl," said a cold voice.

Wendy felt all the warm confidence freeze up inside her. The man with blue marble eyes walked up to the table and laid a heavy hand on Brett's shoulder. He was dressed in normal clothes, jeans and a blazer over a plain shirt, but she would have recognized him anywhere. He was the ICE agent from outside the library and the skating rink. The one on TV staring out at Tom from the ICE office.

And then another thought zapped through her like an electric shock. *Maybe he was the officer who handcuffed Tom in the hospital.* Wendy let out a slow, angry breath through her clenched teeth and then she turned deliberately away from the man. In a voice that didn't tremble one iota, she said, "Celestina was my grandmother's name. And it's mine too."

The woman smiled fully now, a wide, genuine smile that made her look younger than her slightly graying hair. "That seems a perfect name for a budding astronomer," she said.

"Well, it's my middle name," Wendy clarified. "My first name is Wendy."

The woman gave a quick, delighted laugh. "I see we have more in common than our love of the stars." She shifted her clipboard under her arm and reached out a hand. "Wendy Celestina, I'm Dr. Wendy Freedman. It's nice to meet you."

Wendy's jaw dropped. "W-Wendy Freedman?" she choked out. She shook the woman's hand in a daze. "The astrophysicist?"

Dr. Freedman's eyebrows shot up. "It's not often I'm recognized by the middle school demographic. But yes." She smiled. "I look forward to seeing your second telescope."

As Dr. Freedman walked away, Wendy turned and mouthed *"The astrophysicist!"* at Etta, who nodded excitedly. Before going back to her table, Wendy glanced at Brett. His dad's hand was on his shoulder, but Wendy didn't think it looked very comforting. His dad's knuckles were white from clenching so hard. In fact, Brett looked so miserable that she felt a flash of pity for him. She was sure she saw fear in his face.

Then his dad's icy stare landed on Wendy, and she felt some of that fear trickle down her neck. She gulped, but before she could worry about what came next, Papá stepped up beside her, wrapping his arm around her shoulders. When he saw who she was looking at, Papá's body stiffened slightly. He stared steadily back at the agent and Wendy leaned into him. His arm across her shoulders felt strong, as if it were protecting her from the world. *Like a sanctuary,* she thought. "Come, mi estrella," he said gently. Wendy felt the power of the cold eyes diminish as Papá turned her away.

"Miss Toledo, one moment," a voice called out. Ms. Park walked up to her, adjusting her glasses and looking uncomfortable. "I owe you an apology. It has become clear that I underestimated you and treated you unfairly." Her lips pressed together firmly. "I am willing to admit it. I hope you are willing to forgive me."

Wendy wasn't sure a teacher had ever asked her forgiveness before. She felt her ears going hot.

"Yeah—yes, of course," she stammered.

Ms. Park glanced toward Wendy's table, at the detailed printouts on her display and the telescope. She gave a quick nod. "Well done, Wendy."

As she left, Etta gave a squeal and bounced up and down on her toes. "That was SUPER satisfying! When you decide you're not going to be pulled along, Wendy Toledo, you don't mess around."

It was hard not to hold her breath as Dr. Freedman examined her telescope. Wendy hadn't been too nervous when she set it up, but that was before she knew a world-famous astrophysicist would be judging it.

"The original hypothesis had to do with measuring brightness," Dr. Freedman said. "Did you stick with that focus on this one?"

"Oh, no," Wendy said. "You know how you asked about measuring the brightness of different sources? I couldn't really find a way to do that precisely. So I decided to focus on parallax."

"Parallax." Dr. Freedman nodded. "So you chose to measure using different perspectives instead. Interesting." She jotted something down on her clipboard.

Wendy added, "I'm really interested in orbits and gravity." She shrugged. "I know a DIY telescope isn't really strong enough for that. But I thought I could start by studying the moon."

Dr. Freedman nodded thoughtfully. "The moon can teach us quite a bit about gravitational pull," she agreed. "That sounds like the right place to start." Before following the other judges down the row to the next display, Dr. Freedman paused.

"There is a project at the Slettebak Planetarium that I'll be doing some work on this coming year. I've been told they are also developing a junior internship for eighth graders next fall. Make sure you apply, Wendy Celestina."

THIRTY-EIGHT

WHEN THEY GOT home later, Wendy was spent and happy. There was a lightness bubbling inside her, and it felt strange because the dark worry about Tom was still solidly there underneath. In spite of the sincere praise from her parents, she knew they were thinking of him too.

She suggested they check in with Nadia, and Papá put his phone on speaker so they could all hear. Nadia cautiously admitted that the news was good. Public opinion had completely shifted. Wendy's video of the attack had been liked and reposted too many times to keep track of and five different news stations had shown it. There was no question anymore who was telling the truth. The social media team had found a couple videos from Tom's track wins, his body soaring over the finish line like some kind of Greek god. An old teammate had tagged him and then other school friends started posting their own videos. Tom, celebrating with his team. Tom, good-naturedly posing for a picture with a group of cheering girls. Tom leading a group of friends in the baby shark dance down the school hallway. Her handsome, likable brother was developing quite a fan base. Nadia's petition for ICE to release him had over two thousand signatures.

Wendy felt little bubbles of hope rising up inside. But just as quickly they sank back down. Because it was all up to ICE. They didn't have to let him go. Yes, he could file that special U visa that the lawyer said was for victims of a crime who helped the police. But that would take time. And ICE had him in custody right now.

"Pressure like this makes a big difference. They hate all the bad press," Nadia said. "I think our next step is a press conference in front of the ICE office. We can invite the politicians who have—" but just then another call came in on Papá's cell.

"We need to take this," Papá said quickly, scooping up the phone. "It's Mr. Richards."

As the lawyer spoke, Wendy saw Papá's face drain of color and the last of the happy bubbles inside her fizzled away. Papá hit the speaker button and Mr. Richards's voice rang out.

"—absolutely furious. She says even with his lung functioning without the chest tube he was supposed to be observed for another day or two before discharge. But she wasn't attending today. The officers must have bullied the weekend shift doctor into it." Mr. Richards's voice, always brisk and in control, was shaking.

Mamá had a hand to her mouth and her eyes were wide and glistening with tears. "No," she whispered. Papá's chest rose and fell as if he'd been running. "Where—where is he?" he asked.

"They took him to the office downtown for processing. But they can't hold him there. They don't have the space for it and he's a minor. They'll have to transfer him."

Wendy focused on her breathing. In, hold, out. In, hold, out.

"But he only has sixteen years," Mamá said, her accent heavier than usual. "They—they cannot dep—" She broke off, a sob choking out of her mouth. The word Mamá couldn't say rang in Wendy's mind and all the air whooshed from her lungs. *Deport.*

"No, I don't think they can deport a minor," Mr. Richards said. "But once he is transferred to the detention center, it will be significantly more difficult to get him out." Wendy stared at her parents, her heart thudding. Papá's face was gray and Mamá's eyes flooded with tears.

Then Mamá wiped her cheeks angrily. "Not my boy," she said, taking out her phone. "Óscar, maybe the doctor can talk with the reporters." Papá gave one quick nod, then picked up his phone and began speaking to Mr. Richards. Mamá punched a number into her own phone, her jaw clenched. She looked like there was a fire inside her. Like she was ready to break out of orbit.

"Nadia, you have a plan for a press conference at ICE,

yes?" Mamá said into the phone. "We are going to need a lot more people. And we need them today."

The crowd outside the ICE office was already big and still growing as Wendy and her parents arrived. She stared at all the people filling the street around the parking lot. "Qué cachimbazo de gente," Papá murmured, his eyes roaming the crowd. "Who are all these people?"

"Wendy!" Etta screamed, hurtling into her. She gave Wendy a crushing hug. "That video! Why didn't you tell me about it this morning?"

"I kinda forgot," Wendy said truthfully.

"Mom showed me after the fair and I just—" Etta shook her head. "I can't believe that *actually* happened! You were a frickin' Wonder Woman! I can't even—I mean, you *disarmed the bad guy!*"

A few curious faces turned toward them, and Wendy saw people pointing. She wished Etta would keep her voice down. But the strangers were all smiling warmly. Then Wendy realized they weren't all strangers to her. There was Janice, her eyes crinkling into a smile as she leaned on her cane and nodded their way. Nadia, talking to Etta's mom, raised her bullhorn in a wave when she saw them. And the curly-haired redhead spotted Wendy, raised a fist, and shouted, "We're with you, Toledos!"

"Stay strong!" shouted someone else and the people around them started clapping.

Wendy's parents stared, bewildered, at the crowd of people. "Look," Wendy said, pointing to Artie, who spun the "Keep Families Together" sign he held to reveal "Bring Tom Home!" on the other side. Papá took Mamá's hand and squeezed. He looked from her to Wendy, his eyes filling with tears.

"We are not alone," he said simply.

THIRTY-NINE

THEY HELD THE press conference right next to the ICE entrance. The reporters were especially interested in hearing from Tom's doctor, whose eyes flashed angrily as she spoke.

"He should have remained under observation. By detaining him, they have endangered this young man's life," she said, looking directly into the cameras. "And if the immigration authorities attempt to transport him by plane with a recently collapsed lung, the change in air pressure could have fatal repercussions."

Mamá gasped, whispering frantically to Papá. Wendy trembled. She hadn't even thought about flying being dangerous for Tom. There weren't any detention centers for minors nearby. What if they tried to fly him somewhere else? What if his lung collapsed from the air pressure change? Wendy could feel a spiral of panic pulling at her brain and she gritted her teeth, trying to hold it off. She forced her attention back to the front, but the doctor had stopped speaking. The people nearest the parking garage were waving and calling out. The crowd swarmed in that direction. Wendy craned her neck to see over the people around her. What was going on?

Nadia's voice rang out on the bullhorn. "A van is headed down the ramps to the parking lot exit. Tom might be in there. Remember: Stand strong!"

Wendy started to surge forward with the crowd, but Papá grabbed her hand and guided them to the side. They watched as the white van drove down the ramp toward the street. But when it reached the gate, bodies packed the parking lot exit. The van slowed and edged forward, but the protestors linked arms and the driver had to stop completely. Wendy saw Artie's long white beard just inches from the van's front bumper. The moment lengthened and Wendy gripped Papá's hand. Her insides felt like a rubber band stretched past its limit. She strained her eyes, hoping to catch a glimpse of Tom through the tinted windows. They were all too black to see through, except the front windshield where the driver was speaking into a walkie-talkie.

Along the sidewalk, people waved their signs and TV camera operators angled for the best shots of the standoff. A few people were live streaming, talking excitedly and holding up their phones to show the solid wall of protestors blocking the ICE van. Then Nadia was on the bullhorn again and everyone turned toward her as she introduced their state representative in Congress. Wendy could tell this woman was important, just from the way she held her head. The politician spoke about the power and importance of community and keeping families together. She looked straight at Wendy's parents and said clearly, "I am here to accompany you into the detention center to speak to the officer in charge of your son's case. We will do everything possible to get your family back together." As Papá, the congresswoman, and Pastor Carpenter entered the building, the cheering was wild and contagious. It tugged Wendy's heart a bit closer to hope.

They waited for over an hour. Mamá and Wendy clung to each other, their minds on Papá and the officers inside. And Tom. But the crowd around them held them up with fierce smiles and words of encouragement. The people in front of the van eventually sat down right there in the road and Artie led them in a round of old protest songs. It was like a magic spell. The music kept everyone relaxed and smiling in spite of the uniformed ICE officers who had stationed themselves around the van. Wendy saw their shoulder holsters and her skin prickled at the memory of the gun in the parking lot. But at that exact moment, the song about overcoming that the crowd was singing launched into a new verse and the words wrapped around Wendy like armor. "We are not afraid. We are not afraid," the voices all around her sang out, warm and certain, and she looked at the officers, opened her mouth, and sang.

Suddenly, without any explanation, the white van backed up, turned, and drove back up the parking garage ramp. The singing morphed into frantic cheering, and everyone leaped to their feet in a wave of excitement.

After what felt like a millennium, the front door opened. The congresswoman stepped out, followed by a beaming Pastor Carpenter. Then Papá stood in the doorway, and next to him, looking rather dazed as the happy roar of the protestors enveloped him, was Tom. Shouts of "Torpedo Tom!" burst through the cheers. News reporters rushed forward, but Tom didn't seem to see them. He scanned the faces in the crowd. Papá put an arm around him, pointing toward Wendy and Mamá, but the waving signs blocked their view. Suddenly Nadia's voice called out, "Make way! Let's get this family back together!"

Immediately the bodies in front of Wendy shuffled aside and a path opened. Tom's bruised face lit up. He started to rush toward them, but his steps faltered and Papá hurried to his side. Around them cameras rolled and phones lifted high as Tom, leaning on Papá and holding his side, moved their way drawn by a force stronger than pain. Mamá and Wendy ran forward, and they wrapped their arms around each other in the middle of the crowded sidewalk. Wendy took a shaky breath and let herself feel the realness of her family. Tom, with his new push to make a difference in the universe. Mamá, who carried the weight of a past that would always haunt her. Papá, always alert to the forces trying to break them apart. And Wendy, who was solid and strong enough not to be pulled anywhere she didn't want to go. This was her center of gravity.

Wendy didn't really feel safe until they saw the lights of home shining out at them from behind the curtains. Just a month ago everything about the house had creeped her out. But walking through the door now would feel like curling up under a fluffy blanket. Tom and Mamá headed up the steps, but Papá stopped, looking toward the church.

"What is it, Óscar?" Mamá asked, her hand on Tom's arm.

"You go on in," Papá said, motioning them toward the house. "I'll be there in a moment."

Wendy hesitated, watching him walk away. As far as she knew, he had never even met Luz. So why would he go to the church? Her curiosity piqued, she hurried after him. The door was closed, but it opened from inside as they approached. Luz stood there, clutching her rosary. Her worried eyes darted from Papá to Wendy and the empty sidewalk behind them.

"It's okay," Wendy spoke up quickly. "Tom is home."

Luz closed her eyes in relief, the tight lines on her face relaxing. In contrast, Papá had distress written across his. He stepped toward Luz and swallowed hard. "I didn't understand what you were doing here. With this sanctuary. Maybe I just didn't want to. But you supported our family anyway. Thank you."

Luz stared back at him, her eyes bright. "Juntos," she said. "Luchamos juntos."

"We fight together," Papá repeated slowly. "I had forgotten what that was like. To fight with others." He looked down, his fingers rubbing over his calloused hands. "I'm sorry."

Luz looked from him to Wendy and said something in Spanish. Papá lifted his head and looked at Wendy. He patted her shoulder and gave Luz a nod. They said a few more things that Wendy didn't quite grasp. Then Papá wished Luz a buenas noches and turned back toward home. Wendy looked up at him as they walked, but his eyes seemed to be looking past the stars in the sky to something she couldn't see.

"What did she say?" Wendy asked.

"She said I must still have some luchador in me since I raised kids who are luchadores." He was silent for a moment, wrapped in his thoughts. "Have I ever told you about the work I did on the border?" he asked Wendy.

Wendy stared up at him. "No," she said.

Papá smiled thoughtfully. "Remind me to tell you and Tom about it sometime. I think you have earned the right to hear about it. My luchadores."

FORTY

WENDY FOUND HERSELF wishing for a normal, boring, extravagantly ordinary day at school on Monday. But as she passed Principal Whitman's office, the door banged open. A blond woman stalked out, clutching a tissue to her face and pulling Brett along by his slumped shoulder. Wendy drew back against the wall. Neither of them saw her. They were looking back into the office where a man's voice was raised in anger. The principal's response cut off abruptly as Brett's dad shoved his way into the hall and slammed the door shut behind him.

Brett pulled back, turning to watch his dad pass by him, and that's when he noticed Wendy. The nervousness on Brett's face twisted into something hateful. His hands twitched and Wendy leaned away reflexively, her back hitting the wall. Brett's dad glanced back, and his eyes locked on Wendy's, pinning her with an icy glare. The pull to look away was so strong Wendy's breath caught in her throat. Her fingers pressed against the smooth, familiar wall. Wendy gritted her teeth. She had been retreating for too long, hiding along the edges of things. She was done letting others choose her path. She stepped away from the wall, planted her feet firmly in the middle of the hallway, and looked straight back at him, narrowing her eyes. Miraculously, Mr. Cobb blinked. Then his glare moved to Brett. He jerked his head toward the door and after a split second of hesitation, Brett followed his parents out of the building.

Wendy forced her lungs to fill slowly and evenly, counting each breath. Brett was gone. The ICE agent had looked away from *her*. As she rummaged in her locker Wendy felt lighter than she had in a long time. Everything was going to be fine.

"So. Happy now?" Avery Adams's chilly voice startled her.

Morgan stood there, too, fiddling with the zipper on her pencil case and looking uncomfortable. Avery leaned closer to Wendy, lowering her voice.

"Brett's suspended just because you're an ugly loser who can't take a few jokes," Avery hissed. "If anyone should be in trouble, it's you."

"Avery, come on," Morgan said, tugging at her friend's sleeve.

Wendy glanced over her shoulder. There were no teachers within earshot. She slammed her locker door and turned toward Avery. She could feel her ears burning, but she wasn't embarrassed by it. In fact, the fire felt good. She imagined all the anger and hurt as a beam of energy shooting straight at Avery.

"Except that I'm the one still here, not him," Wendy said.

Avery twisted her mouth in annoyance. "Well, we know why that is. The school can't kick you people out." She wrinkled her nose and looked Wendy up and down. "It might make them look bad."

"You people?" said a mild voice. Avery whirled around to see K.K. and Yasmin walking up to them. K.K. had a curious expression on her face. She smiled innocently at Avery. "Who are 'you people,' exactly?"

Avery sniffed. "You know what I'm talking about."

She tried to turn away, flinging her perfect waves over her shoulder dismissively. But Yasmin stepped in to block her path and K.K. shifted slightly closer.

"Um, helll*oooo*, personal space?" Avery said, trying to squeeze past.

"I'd just like to know exactly who we're talking about," K.K. said, her eyes wide. She looked at Wendy. "Is 'you people' girls who braid their hair? Or maybe, girls who are super good at science?"

Yasmin leaned in and said in a loud whisper, "Do you think Avery means kids who have cool shoes?" Wendy laughed. The fire inside her was cooling to a warm glow.

Avery's fingers tightened around her notebook. "You know the school has to keep people like you," she hissed.

K.K. tilted her head to one side. "Like who?"

Avery looked from K.K. to Wendy and Yasmin. Her face was turning an angry red. "You know," she said. Avery lowered her voice and her eyes flicked away from them. "People who aren't white."

"And there it is," K.K. said in a voice like steel. "Thanks for the clarification. That really explains a lot about how you think."

Morgan had been standing at the edge, looking horrified. "Not me," she said quickly. "I didn't say anything."

Yasmin put a hand on Morgan's arm. "You didn't say anything, that's true," she said gently. "And maybe that's the problem."

Morgan stared at her in confusion. K.K. smiled at her. "It's okay, Morgan. I know you don't get it, but that's going to change. As the new vice president of the student council, I've put together a proposal to start a schoolwide conversation about race and microaggressions."

Avery snorted, but Wendy grinned at K.K. "New VP?" she asked.

K.K. nodded. "Brett is no longer permitted on student council this year, even after his suspension is over. And I had the next highest number of votes." She looked back at Avery and Morgan. "Microaggressions are little things people do or say to others about their identity that alone don't seem like a big deal, but together can be really damaging."

"Oh my god, how did I get stuck in this lecture?" Avery said, pushing her way past Yasmin. "Come on, Morgan."

"Wouldn't you like a preview of some of the examples?" K.K. said, pulling out her phone and opening her Notes app. "I've been keeping track of some things."

Avery stopped, looking suspiciously at K.K.'s phone.

"First day of school," K.K. read from her notes. "Avery calls three different Black girls Tameeka, even though no one by that name goes here."

"Oh, please—" Avery scoffed, but K.K. continued, louder. "September eleventh: anti-Muslim cyberbullying."

"That's not—you can't—" Avery stuttered, her eyes shifting to Yasmin.

"Some of these are totally uncreative too," K.K. muttered. "It's like you swallowed *How to Be a Racist for Dummies* and then threw this up." She held up the screen with a picture that showed where an extra K had been written next to K.K.'s signature on homework assignments. "Multiple dates listed," she said in a quiet, deadly voice.

Avery stared, her face whiter than ever, then she grabbed for the phone. K.K. snatched it back out of her reach, and Avery's lip began to tremble.

K.K. sighed dramatically, raising her eyes to the ceiling. "Oh, please, spare us the waterfall!"

Avery's eyes welled, and she gasped in short, rapid breaths, "You. Are. Such. A. Bully!"

"Really? You're going to play the victim now?" K.K. gave her a skeptical look and leaned closer. "Well, you better figure out your story. Because it looks like Ms. Whitman's finished reading the copy I sent her." She nodded pointedly down the hall. Principal Whitman was headed their way, her lips drawn tight. It was the face of someone who was having a very difficult morning.

"Avery Adams, I'd like to see you in my office."

Avery's mouth moved up and down soundlessly. Then she said, pointing at Morgan, "Okay, but she's coming too!"

"Yes, Morgan, you may as well come along," Ms. Whitman said curtly. "It will save time."

Morgan looked like she wanted to disappear as they followed the principal down the hall. Wendy watched them go, stifling a sudden urge to laugh.

"Nice one," she said to K.K. Then her eyes fell on the phone and her smile melted away as she thought of that extra *K*. "I . . . I didn't realize," Wendy started to say.

K.K. shrugged. "I know you didn't. I didn't tell you. And *I* didn't know about the mess *you* were dealing with."

Yasmin nodded. "And I didn't want to overreact or anything, so at first I didn't tell anyone about the notes I was getting."

"Well, I'm glad we're finally talking about it," K.K. said. She smiled at Wendy. "You were sort of my inspiration. I mean, I've been tracking the hate, obvi." She waved her phone. "But after you took on Brett it seemed like time to pull it all together."

"Oh . . ." Wendy had no idea what to say as they headed to class. Could it be true that her actions had pulled at other orbital paths, nudging them in a different direction? She shook her head to break the thought. Right now, her orbit had better be taking her to language arts or she would be super late.

"Wendy!" Mal threw her arms around her, catching her off guard. "I'm so glad you are okay and you are also awesome and super-duper brave," she babbled.

"What?" Wendy asked.

"You disarmed an actual Nazi!" Mal said, her shaggy black ponytail bouncing in excitement. "I saw the video! But right now, come with me! You need to see this!"

Wendy let Mal pull her down the hall. They were definitely going to be late.

"Where are you . . ." Wendy trailed off as the smell of fresh paint hit her nose. For a second she felt that sick feeling again as she remembered the graffiti. But something was different in the hallway. There were more kids outside the art room than usual, and she stumbled through the bodies as Mal pulled her along. "Mal, wait!"

Mal stopped and urged Wendy forward gently, pointing at the wall.

FORTY-ONE

WENDY'S BREATH SLOWED. The ugly patch of white paint was gone. Instead a giant rectangle of deep sapphire blue shone on the wall, scattered with painted stars of various shapes and sizes. A few kids stood on step stools, busily adding more stars to the sky. Along the bottom edge someone had painted a crowd of heads in silhouette—heads with afros and pixie cuts and braids and headscarves—all of them looking up at the stars. Stretching across the black paint of the kids' shadows, large white bubble letters spelled out YOU BELON. And crouching on the floor, carefully painting on the letter G, her clothes paint-splattered and her face glowing and focused, was Etta.

"I did that one!" Mal whispered, pointing to a star and dragging Wendy closer. Wendy leaned in and saw that there were words on the white painted star, written in black Sharpie.

Love recognizes no barriers.

"It's from Maya Angelou." Mal grinned at her. "See, I don't just watch TV shows."

Wendy beamed at Mal and threw her arms around her in a hug. "It's perfect!"

Etta heard them and glanced up. "Wendy!" She scrambled to her feet. "I know these stars are horrifyingly inaccurate, but they all came from the heart." She pointed at one that looked like a spiky scribble. The words written inside read, *You make us great*. "That was Derek from math class." She pointed to a pastel blue-and-pink star that read, *Trans rights are human rights*. "Kit, they're in the GSA with me. And, oh! Look at how cool this one is!" She showed them a star with elegant script inside. "It's the Arabic word for love," she explained. "Yasmin helped me look that up."

Wendy let her eyes travel over the stars and all the kids still adding more. She felt a jolt of surprise when she saw Fiona's blond hair, carefully pulled back in a sleek ponytail. Her pretty face was a bit red and her eyes looked puffy. But she gave Wendy a small smile before she went back to the swirly orange star she was painting. The whole wall would soon be a constellation of stars—each one completely different. There wasn't any way to erase the memory of the graffiti. But Wendy knew that if she thought about this wall again, it would be different.

"Scholars!" A voice rang out behind them and the kids holding paintbrushes froze. Ms. Whitman stood there, staring at the wall and the collection of paint cans, Sharpies,

303

and brushes spread out over the drop cloth. "This—this is unacceptable," she spluttered. "Nikki!"

"Right here, ma'am," came a cool voice. Miss Hill was leaning casually in her doorway, watching the activity with a very Zen look on her face.

"I gave you *strict* instructions," Principal Whitman hissed, "that the art supplies be kept locked up *at all times*!"

"Oh, yes, you did indeed, didn't you?" Miss Hill smiled slowly. "I can't imagine how I let that slide."

Ms. Whitman's face turned several shades of grayish red, but before she could respond another voice called out.

"Why, Principal Whitman, this is absolutely brilliant!"

Etta's mom was walking toward them with another adult. Etta gripped Wendy's arm and jumped up and down with excitement. Wendy looked at Mal, but she just shrugged.

"Pastor Carpenter," Principal Whitman said, her face shifting into a strained smile. "What brings you in?"

"I was hoping you might have some time to meet with us," Etta's mom said in her rich, commanding way. "Allow me to introduce Diedre Martínez. She's working on an article about combating the culture of intolerance in middle schools."

Principal Whitman's smile slipped a bit. "An . . . article?" she repeated, glancing down at the notepad and phone in the woman's hand.

"Yes. I'm sure you are aware of the increased reports of discrimination in schools across the country," Miss Martínez said. She stepped closer to the wall and examined the mural in progress. "I'm interested in how schools can take an active approach to combat hate."

She smiled up at the kids with paintbrushes. They looked relieved and went back to painting, darting glances at their principal.

"Principal Whitman, I'm impressed," Miss Martínez said. "Bringing the students together to share messages of inclusion and welcome? And in the very spot where the hateful graffiti was found?" She gave a nod. "Well, it's a start, anyway."

"Y-yes. It's been . . ." Ms. Whitman trailed off. Then suddenly she said, "Well, it was all"— she waved her hand vaguely toward the art room—"Miss Hill . . . "

Miss Hill smiled graciously but shook her head. "Oh, no, ma'am. I'm not taking the credit for this one. This was all the students. First, Miss Braun came to me with a proposal for educating students about microaggressions. I'm sure you'd be interested in her plan, Miss Martínez; it is very proactive. And then first thing this morning, Miss Carpenter had this art project idea." She pointed at Etta, whose freckled face grinned up at them madly, specks of paint on her nose.

"Not really," Etta said. "I just did a blue background and a few stars at first. For Wendy. Then someone else wanted to do a star, and then someone else." She shrugged. "Kids just kept getting pulled in. It was like—"

"Like gravity," Wendy said. She looked at the stars and warmth filled her body.

"Exactly," Etta said excitedly. "Like some force pulling us all in! And it started with the stars I put up for you, Wen—OH!" Etta's eyes widened. "It's Wendy's Law!" She jumped up from the floor and did a happy dance, her paintbrush waving through the air wildly. "I figured out Wendy's Law!"

Wendy stared blankly at Etta.

"It's like what you said about having mass. You know, being solid enough so you don't just get pulled along. Hang on." Etta tapped the paintbrush on her chin thoughtfully. "I need to make it sound science-y." She cleared her throat as if preparing to recite something and said dramatically, "When one person chooses to set their own orbit, the force of their movement can affect the orbits of everyone around them. Wendy's Law!"

Wendy looked at Etta's fierce grin and her pointy chin smeared with white paint. She felt alive and real, and for once, all the eyes that looked curiously her way didn't make her want to blend into the background. She knew they were on her side. None of these kids had added to the racist graffiti when it was on the wall. They hadn't let themselves get pulled in, even though they could have. Wendy gave Etta a glowing smile, stepped forward, and picked up a paintbrush. "Let's set our orbit then," she said, and she examined the mural, looking for the perfect spot to add her North Star.

EPILOGUE

Wendy and Tom stood on the sidewalk and stared up at the crooked house. The uneven corners were round and soft, all imperfections smoothed over with a layer of snow. It frosted the pointed gable over the attic window, and Wendy thought longingly of her warm room inside. Now that Papá had finished the insulation and drywall, it was the perfect place to curl up and watch the winter settle over their neighborhood.

"After this, I'm not leaving the house all break," she said, her words a puff in the chilly air.

Tom, his voice muffled in his scarf, said, "Why? Are you scared of a little . . . snow?"

Wendy turned to him suspiciously and a snowball hit her in the chest. Letting out a yelp, she scooped her mittened hands into the bank and flung one back. They hurled missiles of cold fluff until Mamá, her hands waving protectively in front of her, joined them outside. "Ay, Óscar," she called. "Hurry, please, so that they stop!"

Wendy and Tom, breathless and laughing, turned to look up. On the porch Papá grinned proudly at them and held up an extension cord. He bent to plug it in, and the crooked house immediately transformed. The strings of Christmas lights dripped gold from each windowsill and trailed along the porch roof, spilling their buttery glow into the snow. They all gasped appreciatively at the sight as Papá jogged down the steps to join them. Wendy leaned against Papá as he pulled her close and they all huddled together a moment longer, enjoying the lights in the dark chill of the night.

"Can you make your hot chocolate?" Wendy pleaded, gazing up at Mamá.

"Dímelo en español," Mamá said, her eyes twinkling.

Wendy smiled and said carefully, "¿Puedes hacer chocolate caliente?" Then she added in English, "The Guatemalteco kind, with melted chocolate and a cinnamon stick?"

"That is the only kind," Mamá said with a smile. "But then you have homework, yes?"

"Just my application for the internship," Wendy said as they made their way up the steps. "I've just been thinking about what to write." Papá opened the door and Wendy looked out at the fluffy snowflakes dancing through the air, gravity slowly pulling them downward. She smiled. "I have a pretty good idea, though," she said, and followed her family into their sanctuary.

What is your personal motivation for pursuing this internship?

For as long as I can remember, I have loved looking into the universe. There are so many life lessons out there in the stars. For example, gravity. The way it can actually move giant objects through space is amazing. It reminds me of the forces that control us in society. There are all kinds of forces on Earth pulling us around, and not all of them are good. I've found that when I stand up to those forces, for myself or for people I love, I don't have to get pushed around by them. So I guess I have a power inside myself that's kind of like gravity.

Astronomy can also change how we see things. Stars look different depending on where you are in the universe. That's called parallax. And in life, things can look different too. You might think someone is doing something wrong or illegal, but some people face unjust laws and hard choices. And you might never understand unless you choose to break away from the orbit you are on and look at it from another angle. I may not know what the universe will throw at me next. But I do know that whatever happens, there is more than one way of looking at things. And I have the power to choose my own orbit.

ACKNOWLEDGMENTS

EDITH ESPINAL TOOK sanctuary in the Columbus Mennonite Church in 2017, just after my eight-year-old was diagnosed with soft tissue sarcoma. With the world around me full of unpredictable, uncontrollable dangers, I sat in my son's hospital room and started to write.

Without the wide galaxy of people that lifted my family up during that time, this book would not exist. Thank you to the team at Nationwide Children's Hospital and Cincinnati Children's Hospital for getting my boy through cancer. Thank you to every person who supported us financially and brought us meals and did house repairs and watched the kids. Thank you to friends who let us break.

Without Edith, the Solidarity with Edith Espinal team, the Colectivo Santuario, and the Columbus Mennonite Church, the hope that I wrote into Wendy's story would feel like a fictional thing. Thank you for making that hope something real and tangible. Thank you for standing outside the ICE office for Edith, for taking her story to the media, for lobbying congress, for selling food and T-shirts and post-cards. Thank you for centering her voice and for not giving up for three long years, until she was able to go home. Thank you, Edith, for being a guiding star to so many.

To my agent, Brent Taylor, who is stellar at what he does in ways that leave me winded and wondering at my good fortune. Thank you for being my fairy godagent.

Thank you to the constellation of talent at Quill Tree/HarperCollins who surrounded my story and made it shine. To my remarkable editor, Jennifer Ung, who challenged me to go deeper by quoting my own characters back at me, thank you. You are truly a guiding force. To Celina Sun, whose passion for meaningful stories is as bright as her name, thank you. Thank you to Rosemary Brosnan, David DeWitt, Jon Howard, Monique Vescia, Annabelle Sinoff, Suzanne Murphy, Jean McGinley, Robby Imfeld, Patty Rosati, Andrea Pappenheimer and the Harper sales team, Tara Feehan, and Laura Raps.

Thank you to Johanie Martinez-Cools. I am glad the stars aligned for you to be my authenticity reader.

To Laura Bontje, freelance editor extraordinaire. Thank you for your insight and expertise in crafting those early versions of this story and cheering me along in my writing journey.

To Dr. Wendy Freedman, whose name I found by googling "Wendy" and "astrophysics." Thank you for your inspiring work exploring the mysteries of our universe.

To all my friends who received my enormous first draft, thank you for not reading it. I don't blame you. This version is better anyway.

Thank you to my family. To Matthew, who frequently loses me to my imaginary worlds and is always here when I return. To Graciela, who was the first one to meet Wendy and has been rooting for her ever since. To Mateo, whose chaotic good antics have brought joy to so many. To Rosali, my littlest critique partner, who is always up for a deep dive into character and plot.

Thank you to the immigrant community in Columbus, Ohio, whose stories are messy, hopeful, painful, and inspiring. To the kids who are growing up here, finding their own identities and guiding forces, and their parents who did remarkable things to give their children a future. Melissa, Clelia, Gisella, Rae, Rosibel, Ruby, Ramiro, Veronica, Oscar, Dariel, Beatriz, Ostin, Marely, Lidia, Amilcar, Audrey, Liam, Steven, Christopher, Fatima, and Wilmer, thank you.